Caitlin Davies was born in London in 1964. For the past five years she has lived in Botswana. She currently works as editor for a local newspaper, the *Okavango Observer*.

DATE DUE

D1313391

CAITLIN DAVIES

Jamestown Blues

PENGUIN BOOKS

PENGUIN BOOKS

Published by the Penguin Group
Penguin Books Ltd, 27 Wrights Lane, London w8 5tz, England
Penguin Books USA Inc., 375 Hudson Street, New York, New York 10014, USA
Penguin Books Australia Ltd, Ringwood, Victoria, Australia
Penguin Books Canada Ltd, 10 Alcorn Avenue, Toronto, Ontario, Canada m4v 3b2
Penguin Books (NZ) Ltd, 182–190 Wairau Road, Auckland 10, New Zealand

Penguin Books Ltd, Registered Offices: Harmondsworth, Middlesex, England

First published 1996
1 3 5 7 9 10 8 6 4 2

Typeset by Datix International Limited, Bungay, Suffolk
Printed in England by Clays Ltd, St Ives plc

To Mozambia

BOOK ONE

Chapter One

God knows why, exactly, my mother decided to come to this country, but of course that was some time ago now and despite all that has happened in the past you could say she has settled down nicely. I hear that at one point she almost went home, but in the end she decided to stay. The people of Poloko where my mother now stays have all sorts of names for her and most are quite complimentary. Others back home in England, however, think she has Let Herself Go. This is my grandmother's expression, my grand-mother who after twenty-odd years has finally admitted that I exist. Personally I think that if my parents had stayed in my father's home village of Lephane and not moved to the terrible township of Jamestown none of what happened would have happened, if you see what I mean.

I would sum my mother up in those days, the mid 1970s when she first arrived, as ignorant but well meaning. She wanted to DO something, she tells me, and teaching English seemed like a good idea. 'Thank god for colonization,' my father used to say. 'Now your mother can get a job anywhere in the world.'

Of course these days, even more than when my mother arrived in Botswana, it is quite possible for some people to say, 'I am going to the other side of the world to live now.' Only I have never heard anyone on this side say, 'Oh, I think I'll go and live in England.' People might say, 'I would like to go and see England,' but I have never heard anyone say they want to go and *live* there. And we never went to Europe to teach people about *our* ancestors, did we?

My mother actually stays some way outside the village of Poloko on the banks of a river. There used to be many rivers but now there's only one. There is a constant pool of water where my parents have chosen to settle. Sometimes, but not often, a hippo turns up, having moved across from Zimbabwe or perhaps down from the north in search of water. 'I heard those hippos dancing here last night,' my mother told me recently, she has always been a fanciful sort of person.

My mother has set up a chicken farm while she waits for my father to join her. He is still down in the capital wrapping up his affairs in preparation for his next business venture, whereas my mother stopped teaching some time ago and is therefore freer to move around.

Poloko is a dusty sort of village and it stands at the crossroads between the north–south road and a road heading east. You know you have reached a settlement because suddenly out of the bush there are palm trees and you don't see many of them until you are really in the north. Considering our mania for *development*, Poloko has remained a traditional sort of village. There is still a functioning Kgotla for example, where the people elect development committees and listen to politicians' speeches, where the chief and the elders try criminal cases, administer justice, iron out disputes and delegate responsibility.

The old ways of decisions made by the people, however, are fast disappearing. At the last Kgotla meeting I attended in Poloko the chief's police stood all around the edge of the gathering because of a rumour there was going to be 'trouble'. People couldn't believe that sitting around talking constituted trouble, but there you are, our government is a bit nervous these days. And yet we are lauded as being an island in a troubled region, a shining example of democracy and so forth.

Somehow or other my mother has managed to set up the chicken farm, which was my father's idea. Our relative Kennedy does most of the managing though, and to me it's unsettling seeing an old man scrabbling around in the dirt after chickens. Kennedy is

4

a relative from my father's home village, and my father ordered him to Poloko to help my mother. Since Kennedy gave up the drinking, he seems to like living a low-profile life, and there's something to be said for always being provided for. We Batswana believe you must provide for your relatives, even if the god of development has shattered our families like an axe on a soft piece of wood. And if you don't provide for your family, then, as my father says, you'll have Bad Luck.

My mother tells me she has yuppy flu, but not to worry, she's dealing with it. Where the hell she got yuppy flu from I have no idea. The house where my mother stays is still not finished, which I find sad but she shrugs this off. I suppose when my father finally moves up to Poloko they will complete it together. I remember the burst of enthusiasm with which my mother first started building while my father stayed down in Gaborone. But the house is still just four brick walls on a type of wooden stage, a half-thatched roof and a screen of sorts which does seem to keep off most of the snakes. The last time I saw my mother she seemed to take great pleasure in filling me in on snake stories.

There are no doors or windows in the house; instead the bedroom, my mother's everything room, is open to the yard. If you go looking for her in the mornings, you will find yourself at the foot of her bed without realizing you have crossed and entered the territory of a room.

I recently asked her old friends back in England if they thought she was weird, because they seemed to be suggesting she was. They said they never would have imagined she of all people would be living in Africa. But then what do they know about Africa?

My mother had always liked what she called her Creature Comforts and Poloko has few of these. She liked her own bed in her own house with hot water and a bath within easy reach. She liked reaching up to put on electricity and loved to watch TV. She liked new ironed clothes and make-up and mirrors. She has none of these things now. She used to like to dress to go out, to the cinema or parties or restaurants. Now when she wants something to eat or drink she calls Kennedy, who in turn calls whichever young boy is around and he comes and builds the fire and puts the kettle on. Coffee and sugar and powdered milk are lined up in her outside-cooking area in old jam jars. There's usually a food-encrusted plate balancing near by. And her awful mangy dogs, the grand puppies of the dog we owned when we lived all those years ago in Jamestown.

While my mother has become sloppier as she's grown older, I have become neater. My mother, who used to clean away a person's plate before they had quite finished eating, who used to rant at my father and me for leaving sand on the floors, now doesn't seem to let such things bother her at all. Whereas I, who used to be a bit of a slob, now have a paranoia for cleaning up and putting away. My father, who has always been a self-contained sort of person and never a mess-maker, used to endure her rages quietly and that's one of the ways they got on so well, he simply walked outside when she started one of her tirades about domesticity. But then if my parents hadn't moved to Jamestown, she wouldn't have found herself doing the things she didn't want to do. She was more vulnerable then and her sense of isolation meant she was easily taken advantage of. Age seems to have increased her confidence.

Her hair these days is uncombed, which some people comment on, though personally it doesn't bother me. She wears shorts with a T-shirt in the summer, which is most of the year, and shorts and a jumper in winter, which doesn't last long in these parts. Her legs are so skinny these days, and her skin has cracked with the dryness of the sun. I last saw her in July, mid-winter, and the heels of her feet had cracks as dark as a thunder cloud.

My mother has a couple of friends in or around the village, and it's amazing how other white people have managed to home in on her. Perhaps, she says, she caught this yuppy flu off one of them. I think my father used to worry that he had separated my mother from her 'own kind', but he doesn't have to worry about that any more. Nowadays she is more responsible for herself and quite content with her status in life.

Of course when my mother first arrived in my father's birthplace of Lephane she was just about the only white person. At that time, we didn't have so many visitors as we do today, and the white people who did come came to kill the animals or preach God to the people. I want to know about those days, about what happened when she first arrived in Botswana, but my mother is very closed-mouthed about it all. Yet I go on searching for some sort of ridiculous clue.

And then there is the question of why did we go to Jamestown, why did my parents allow themselves to become caught up in the scandal of the pre-school, why did they let Christine and Frank take over their lives? I was just a child at the time, so what do I know? But I was the sort of child who watches and listens and stores it all away. And after all it was only fifteen years ago. My grandmother − my father's mother − can quite happily list off events and people from four generations past. No doubt when she tells me her stories she embellishes them a bit, but then how else can a story be told? It is always necessary to use your imagination.

My mother was what they call an 'only' child and didn't get on particularly well with her 'only' parents. She was born, she went to school, she dropped out of university and she came to southern Africa. First she travelled with two of her friends and then she ended up in Lephane and got a job as a teacher. When I asked her recently why she did come to Botswana, she said, 'Does there *have* to be a reason?', which is fair enough really. She had great respect for Botswana then, the way you do when you come from a totally fucked-up country like England and the idea of living in the bush seems a good and proper thing to do.

As for my father, getting information out of a Motswana is like getting blood from a stone, as my mother used to say. To him, life is divided into stages with appropriate behaviour for each stage, and questioning people is not appropriate behaviour at any of those stages.

Thus when I was a child I was to be quiet and obedient and run errands and do what I was told. 'Child,' as an adult said in those days, 'fetch me water,' and the child would do so. Then when I became older my father frequently asked me when I was going to act like an adult. Acting like an adult means being responsible and, I suppose, caring for others. He has never, but never, understood why I don't want children myself. Both he and my mother say I will change my mind, but as my mind hasn't changed in the last twenty years why should it now?

Sometimes I wonder how on earth my parents met. I am sure when I was a child my mother told me, but then of course I wasn't interested. So when I look back, I reconstruct the past, but I find it impossible really to describe somebody, for the moment I say, 'This person was a peaceful person,' an image immediately springs to mind of that person angry and in a rage. And yet Botswana has changed, has *developed* so rapidly, that my parents' life in Jamestown seems a story worth telling. A new town was built and the old ways were destroyed. Having been abroad myself, I am razor-sharp when it comes to looking at our past. 'You are so sharp you'll cut yourself one day,' my mother used to say. I suppose I remember her expressions so well because she was the only person saying them, they belonged to another culture, another place. Or perhaps it's just because, like it or not, you remember what your mother says.

Chapter Two

My mother arrived in Lephane sometime in the mid-1970s. In England she had spent a year or two as a secondary-school teacher though she had dropped out of university. Then she worked, saved money and set off with her two friends to 'do' Africa. They eventually found themselves in Lephane. The friends returned to England and my mother stayed on. The village of Lephane was all sand at that time and to outsiders it seemed quite remote. People in the south joked about how the people of Lephane danced: being as everything was sand, they said they did a shuffle.

In fact people in the south still make quite a lot of jokes about Lephane. But it's no longer remote: you can drive there on a tar road all the way from South Africa and send a fax back to where you came from with very little bother at all, considering five years ago there were no public phones. If you have the money, you can even watch South African TV in one of Lephane's three hotels.

Of course we in the tourist industry work hard to convince people that places like Lephane still *are* remote, because tourists like to think they are coming to a frontier, that they are being daring coming to a place where a lot of people go on living quite mundanely every day. The business section of Lephane has been carved up by the expatriates, which is a code word for white people most of the time, but where my grandmother lives it is crowded and still sandy. People like my grandmother are not exactly driving cars, so the sand doesn't bother them too much. However, these developments mean now they have to travel much further into the bush and the swamps in search of good palm wine and leaves to make baskets from and reeds to build with.

My mother isn't one to bare her heart and nowadays she talks in riddles, which all begin with, 'Well, to tell you a fact ...' This is even more confusing because she is something of a liar, so I am rather sceptical when she begins her, 'Well, to tell you a fact ...' But my mother did write letters to her mother back in England on a regular basis and I recently discovered my grandmother had kept them all. Having finally admitted that I exist, my grandmother expects me to accept strange family ties and to act as if I have always had a grandmother on that side.

Whatever it was that my mother said in all those letters home, it was never enough to make my grandmother come and visit us, though I think she could have afforded the fare. My grandmother seems to have simply stopped her mind at the point where her daughter left England and now, some twenty years later, she's just fast-forwarded things a bit. This neatly allows her to forget about the existence of my father. She did once comment that my English is rather good and that I seem to have been well fed, which suggests what her image of Africa is.

My mother was in her mid-twenties when she left England. When she and her friends decided to 'do' southern Africa, she didn't know the first thing about Botswana – how could she? Even today I would guess many people on that side couldn't even pinpoint us on a map, though they may know we have many wild animals. So it seems quite a giant step that she left everything she knew and came over to us. My grandmother, so I hear, was furious although my mother promised she was going only for a year or so. I guess she was glad to leave home, to leave her father with whom she did not get on and to leave England. If things aren't working out, well, go and live on the other side of the world for a while. Once she had left, I have a feeling that she felt there was no turning back. I never met my grandfather on that side but my mother used to call him a Right Bastard, and that was after he was already dead. Perhaps my mother also wanted to escape the responsibility, as an only child, for caring for her parents. Or perhaps it was just basically a sense of *adventure* that brought her here.

To begin with, my mother was incredibly isolated in Lephane. It was, and still is, a sprawling sort of settlement, huge in comparison with the small villages that surrounded it. There was one short strip of tar road cutting through the flat, sandy centre on which were built concrete shops and government buildings. There was a huge mix of people living pretty much side by side. The village was busy and active and growing every day.

My mother got a job at a secondary school, Kagiso, which had been set up by the missionaries. In those days we had primary schools and junior schools known as 'private schools' which were run by the community. At the secondary school my mother was teaching English to children who didn't know that much English and she knew not a word of Setswana. She did make an effort at first, but when we later moved to Jamestown she let it slide. You could say she's bilingual now, but her pronunciation is embarrassing. People seem to understand her though, and she acts like she has mastered things.

I think my mother rather likes being surrounded by people who can't talk to her so well in her own language. But I've seen her at breaking point sometimes, and then she lets rip, yelling and abusing whoever's at hand in English. She has always been a bit of a swearer, although my father tried hard to wean her of this habit.

If things are going badly, there comes a time when an expatriate turns on the people whose country it is and abuses them with a venom that is breath-taking. Or so it seems to me. I am thinking now of the white people who work in Lephane, mostly in the tourist industry. They behave as if we *invited* them over here, which I can assure you we never did. Our government might have though, as there was, and still is, a general belief that white people are pretty clever and if you need an expert it's best to get one of them to come over and sort things out for you.

But, to be honest, my mother did have some skills in that she had taught before and knew English. And she was only too willing to be taken advantage of. Having a total inability to say no, she was roped into all sorts of things at Kagiso school until she had very little time for herself. We Batswana do love to 'volunteer' people and my mother was forever being volunteered to be on school committees, or to run the netball team, or to serve at the tuck shop.

'Miss Paul . . .' they would say – she was always known by her surname – 'Miss Paul, you have been volunteered to help slaughter the goat for parents' day.' She would protest weakly that she didn't know how to slaughter a goat and then offer to do something else, which was exactly the motive behind assigning her to slaughter the goat.

Because she was English – or perhaps just because she was who she was – she couldn't say no directly. If the headmaster volunteered her, with a laugh, to go on a school trip somewhere, she would say she was busy that weekend, but she considered it rude to give an outright no. It's a complicated strain in my mother's character and it got her into a lot of trouble later on.

Kagiso secondary school was near the old cemetery, set on a sandy road heading east. There was a central area of about four classrooms, the administration block and a kitchen. Then outdoors there was a concrete assembly ground, a big school garden and several teaching spaces where my mother sometimes taught under a tree. The students easily distracted her during these lessons, all they had to do was scream 'Snake!' for her to drop everything and run around in alarm.

The pathways around the school were lined with stones slapped with white paint, and along the path to the main buildings were old car tyres painted in the colours of our flag, black, white and blue. The students were proud of their surroundings, which was lucky as a big portion of their day was devoted to keeping the place clean.

By the time my mother started at Kagiso most of the missionaries had gone. She was the only white teacher to work there any length of time, though not the only expatriate. Several white teachers came and went, however, mainly Christians, and I wonder how they had found their way to Lephane in the first place. Lephane was then known as a frontier town, so I presume it must have been an exciting place for them.

My mother was assigned a small concrete house near the school buildings. The system was you began in one of these small houses and then you were promoted to a bigger one set further back in the school grounds. Only my mother was never promoted. For the first three months in Lephane hardly anyone talked to her. Now, my mother is not exactly the friendliest sort of person, but still this must have been hard. She also took it quite hard living in a tiny square concrete house with no bath or hot water, though I'm sure she was better off than most of the people in the village, and she had probably been expecting – perhaps even hoping – to live in a mud hut. But she got on well with her pupils, who were stunningly well behaved, though nowadays when school kids pass her yard in Poloko she says, 'To tell you a fact, I can't stand school children.'

She spent her days, then, teaching in the mornings and sometimes supervising afternoon study. Then when school was over for the day, she meticulously did her marking and preparation before heading off to the shops some three kilometres away. She says people were constantly offering her lifts as she trudged along the sand pathways, being under the impression that a white woman couldn't possibly manage in our heat. It wasn't that people were unfriendly then, but that they just weren't much interested in her. Hunters, missionaries, teachers came and went, so what was the point in getting involved? And it's hard to talk to someone when you feel you don't have a handle on their language, so the ones who did talk to her felt they knew English and this made them braver.

It must have been after those first few months that she met my father. He was working in one of the first government offices in what is today called the Mall, near the District Commissioner's office. His office was next to a small music shop where my mother often went. She says our music is a bit frantic for her, but she liked to pause outside the shop to listen before heading off on the hot sandy road back to school. She made friends with one of the women working there and sometimes they chatted together as best they could. And as we Batswana like to be outside as much as possible, she must have met my father when he took his breaks on the porch next door.

Perhaps two outsiders were drawn together. My father had been studying in the United States and knew English and so on, and was a bit of an anomaly in the village to which he had just returned. At that time not nearly so many children went to school, let alone university. But like a true Motswana my father felt very strongly about where he came from and about serving the community to which he belonged. I don't think he ever recovered from the years he spent studying in the States. He hadn't had the faintest idea of how black people were treated there. He found out the hard way, as they say, and one of his favourite conversation pieces after he returned was why, in detail, no one should ever go to the United States. 'Let me tell you about the US of A...' he would begin, stroking his chin.

But this had the opposite effect on people such as me. You can't very well tell someone not to go somewhere so many times without raising their interest in the place. And ridiculously enough (when you consider people over there don't even know we exist), America was part of my growing-up. When we lived in Jamestown the few times I saw a video it was Americans I saw. You could already buy T-shirts with the names of American places on them and the music we heard was American music, mainly Country and Western.

My father had returned home to Lephane to find Botswana had undergone great changes. When we got independence in 1966, we were, as our politicians are always telling us, one of the poorest countries in Africa, if not the world. We had a grand total of twelve kilometres of tar road and our cattle were dying because of the drought. Then diamonds were discovered and it turned out we had the second largest diamond pipeline in the world. Perhaps it is because of this that one of our favourite English expressions is 'in the pipeline'. The government is forever telling us things are 'in the pipeline' and people are forever asking how long exactly this pipeline is.

After returning to Lephane from his studies in the States, my father turned a blind eye to some things. For a long time he refused to see corruption for what it was, saying instead that corruption didn't exist until the British came, and now the American hunters and missionaries. Which is a strange thing, for if he hated the British and Americans so much, at least the white ones, why did he marry my mother?

I found out recently that people in the States and in the UK seem rather obsessed with 'mixed' couples and are forever making movies and writing books about black men who want a white woman as a prize and white women bitches who want black men for some sexually related reason. Myths are all a matter of history, I suppose.

I don't think my father chose to go out with my mother because she was white, the way some men might do, and it was extremely unusual for someone to marry a white woman, partly because there weren't many of them around. It was unusual then and it still is now. But we had not been occupied the way other colonized countries had been, and so perhaps our attitude to white people was slightly different from that of our neighbours. And of course look at our first President, Sir Seretse Khama, he brought a white woman back with him from England, didn't he, and still we loved him.

Anyway, my parents began meeting regularly on the porch of the building where my father worked. They began 'going out' with each other as they say in English, though I wonder where it was exactly they went.

It began by my father giving my mother a lift back to the school one day. She was trudging along using her hand to shield off the sun when he drove by and offered her a lift. My mother says that in England you shouldn't accept lifts from strangers, but it was hot, she had some heavy shopping and because she'd talked to my father a few times he wasn't officially a stranger. I suppose it was nice for her to have a companion, someone who wasn't in the claustrophobic atmosphere of the school and to whom she could talk. My father felt a bit of an outsider, having gone from the bush to university to America and back again. I think he rather liked showing someone around, while my mother says that when you don't know anyone you have to grab the chances that come your way.

I have always seen my parents as loners. By this I mean they were largely contented with their own company. They didn't go to people, people came to them. My father has always seemed to be somebody who knows himself, and for this reason his relatives always turned to him for help and advice – even when he was still so young himself.

About that time tourism was just beginning and makeshift camps were being set up in the Okavango Delta just east of the village of Lephane. The tourists came for adventure, the untouched wilderness and all that, but because it was mainly in the north other people in Botswana didn't really notice what was going on. My father invited my mother to go to one of these lodges and it became a regular outing. 'Oh, God, we used to laugh in those days,' my mother says now. 'At what?' I ask. 'To tell you a fact, I can't remember,' she replies.

My father had a small pick-up truck that was on its last legs, and they would drive along the deep sandy roads out of Lephane, through the bush and to the lodge. This lodge was on the banks of a huge river and the workers had to cross by canoe to reach it, shouting out as hippo ears peaked out of the water and caused warning ripples. My parents would sit on one of the stone benches outside the lodge and order drinks and fried chicken.

I suppose my father had an understanding of where my mother

came from, unlike most people in the village, because after all American ways are not that different from English ways. And although he has a rather serious outlook on life, my mother seemed always to know how to tease him. She wasn't offended by his sweeping comments on the evils of Europeans, for example – she would just laugh and make some damning comment about Batswana.

So they became a regular sight at the lodge, and in the village too. Of course in a village everyone knows who is lovers with whom. Apart from going to the lodge, my mother would cook meals in her tiny concrete house and invite my father to go round. And so it all started. 'It seemed we had known each other all our lives,' my mother used to say when she was in a fanciful mood.

Shortly after they met, my mother moved out of her house in the school compound and in with my father. No doubt this gave her access to some of the creature comforts she had been missing. But that's not really fair because my father's family was, and still is, poor and my mother took responsibility for them too. By poor I mean they had no paid jobs, they had no water, they sometimes had no food. The reason my father lived alone was because he worked for the government, some drought relief project I believe it was, and was given a house with the job. Of course my mother didn't move in until she had met my father's relatives many times and they had then offered goats and so forth for the slaughter.

My father's house was concrete and it was near where he worked, some distance from his mother and grandmother who were always moving around finding ways to get by. His grandfather had died down in the mines in South Africa and his father had died a few years before from TB. My father had several brothers and sisters, all younger than him. As the eldest, it often fell to him to provide for them all, though his uncle was in effect the head of the family. The women in the family had several plots of land, the way you did back then: the cattlepost where the cattle were kept, the lands where they ploughed if they could hire a plough, and the residential plot where they lived.

The house my father lived in had three rooms and a long porch shaded with a crumbling green mosquito net. The house is still there today, totally decayed. I think it used to belong to a missionary who died of malaria.

Considering my mother was such an outsider, my father's family took her in with open arms. Then she became pregnant, thus proving her womanhood, and things got easier and easier. I was born in 1976, the year we got our own currency, the end of the South African Rand and the introduction of our own money. 'Pula! Pula!' we shout at official gatherings and end-of-term assemblies. 'Pula!' It means rain.

When I was a baby, my father's family petted me and spoiled me because to them I was a bit of a toy, being light-skinned with a strange-shaped nose. This gave me a mistaken belief that I was something special. Before I was born I suspect some people mistrusted my mother, perhaps fearing that she was only 'playing' with my father and would soon return to where she came from, although wherever exactly that was no one was quite sure. Marriage and children would prove that they were serious. So first they got married and my mother officially became Mrs Kenosi. Then they had me. My mother would have been twenty-six perhaps, my father a couple of years older.

Two pay cheques every month meant my parents lived well, but it was still not enough to support the rest of the family and to save. My father grew frustrated with his job, the way a lot of people returning to Botswana from overseas studies did, and still do. They come back home only to find they're not going to be treated properly in their own country. The department he worked for was headed by a British man who mistreated his staff and who hated to be contradicted. My father was not, on the whole, one to keep his mouth shut if there was something to be said. He began to think he was never going to succeed in Lephane and he started making other plans.

In the eyes of the family my father's years in America had been a success because he had completed his studies, learnt very good English and come home. But for him his years abroad had been a great disappointment. And if those years had been disappointing, then coming home was an even greater let-down. He wanted to provide his family with the sort of things expected from a son who had gone to America.

My mother meanwhile, though settled at the school, was having difficulties too. Each year the intake increased and so did the workload until she found herself working evenings and weekends too. Because she found it hard to say no, and because she was neurotically well organized, anything she suggested at the school she was put in charge of.

She had by then decided that Botswana was to be her home. She wrote letters to her mother explaining that she had married and was not coming back to England, and she did not go back when her father died. My parents lived on in the ex-missionary house, reasonably comfortable but unsure of the future. For my mother the novelty of no restaurants, no cinemas, no baths, no hot water, no tar roads was beginning to wear off, I suspect. While my father, who had returned from the States expecting a highly paid job, was growing even more frustrated. Relatives were round at the house most every day asking for food, provisions, firewood, school fees and clothes, and because they were family it never entered my father's head to refuse.

Despite this pressure from the family I know that my parents could afford to go on holidays sometimes, holidays being a British sort of thing that my father partially adapted to since a government job meant also having holidays. I know they did have holidays because I've seen the photographs. There are piles of badly taken pictures of animals I've seen in an old box under my mother's present bed in Poloko. If she herself features in any of them, she is looking nervous or extremely pissed off. Which is not surprising, considering in those days she was afraid of a creature as small and usually harmless as a spider, which my father found very funny.

I suspect my mother wanted holidays in hotels and such – as a teacher she had the time and the money – and compromised by agreeing to go into the bush. I also suspect that my father set these holidays up as some sort of test, making sure to camp as near as he could to any lions that might be around. My father is all for what he calls confronting your fears. In the photographs my mother is wearing tight cotton dresses or flared trousers that she brought with her from England and her hair is short but gathered in what they call a pony tail, presumably because this style resembles the tail of a horse. She is a tall woman but she has a habit of slouching down to one side, which is what she is doing in all of these photographs. She has a long face and a slightly crooked nose that is only visible from one side, so she always tried to ensure photographs were taken from what she called her good side.

I remember once in Jamestown I was in my parent's bedroom and my mother was dressing to go somewhere for the evening. She allowed me to search around in her small box of jewellery and then I watched her apply her make-up. 'I only use a touch, Dimpho,' she told me. 'I can't stand it when women cover their faces with war paint.' I nodded, understanding that the way my mother applied make-up was the best way. 'I might have a crooked nose, but I do have a nice bone structure, if I say so myself,' she added.

'And me, do I have good bone structure?' I asked.

My mother considered for a moment and then said, 'It's too early to tell.'

In these holiday photographs my father looks serious and is standing to attention. It is almost impossible to take a photo of him looking normal. On his head is his beloved baseball cap he bought in the States with a picture of a bull on front. My mother, with all her animal fears, must have been in a state of permanent tension on these trips, so it's even more surprising that she eventually agreed to set up home in Poloko and not stay down in Gaborone where most of the wild animals have gone.

My father, growing up in Lephane, was well versed with wild

animals. When he was a child, and this used to be one of my favourite stories, he once spent a night in a tree with my grandmother hiding from lions. As far as I remember the story, my father and his mother and my great-aunt and her child were hitching to some fields outside Lephane and mistook the path they wanted. It was November, the height of summer, and a hot afternoon in the bush, and they had been dropped off at the wrong place. They realized it was the wrong place, and started to walk in what they hoped was the right direction. My father was just a small boy and struggled to keep up with the women. As they continued, night fell and my great-aunt heard some lions in the distance. They travelled on, not knowing whether to go forward or whether to retrace their steps until they reached the home of some crazy white man who lived in the bush.

Something happened then to make them turn back. Either the white man refused to allow them to stay or his dogs chased them off, and they headed back the way they had come. It was then that they heard the lions again. So the four of them climbed up into a nearby tree, one of the largest acacia trees in the flat sandy bush all around, and it was there that they spent the night. I used to get chills listening to my father tell this story and, like my mother, I begged for more details. How many lions were there? Did they try to climb up the tree? Weren't you pricked by thorns? What were you thinking about?

'What is there to tell?' my father would say, getting annoyed. 'There were lions and we slept in a tree.' But after some prodding he would agree to go over everything again, explaining, for example, that when there are lions about you don't *choose* a tree to hide in, the nearest big one will do. Perhaps I just wanted to know that he had been afraid.

The morning after their night in the tree my great-aunt and grandmother had to make the terrible decision about whether it was safe to come down and continue on their way, or whether the lions were going to get them. Obviously, they made the right decision. I have found out since then that quite a lot of people in the States are under the impression that we actually live in trees, have bones through our noses and big bottoms to store water in. While I was in the States just a year or so ago, a college student asked me, puzzled, where the Queen of England would stay if she came to visit. I replied in a tree.

Ever since that night my father has had the ability to sleep anywhere without moving an inch. My mother always joked that he slept like a soldier, body straight out, or like a corpse, hands folded on his chest, or like a donkey simply closing his eyes and drooping his head slightly when it was time to snooze.

So my parents went on holidays until my mother was cured of the habit, most likely by fear. One of the attractions of going out into the bush was coming back to Lephane, where she was beginning to feel at home. What she loved most about the village was that when she went out and about she always met someone she knew, which apparently doesn't happen in London.

Though my mother did know people to stop and pass the time of day with, she had no close friends until she met Oabona. Oabona was 'going out' with my father's brother Bopadile. My mother and Oabona took to each other immediately. Bopadile on the other hand, though my mother liked his company, was a Bad Apple and very different from my father. Bopadile was always on the move, quite often thieving, whereas my father still had the idea that because he was a Motswana, because he was educated, and had been to America, the nice life would fall eventually into his lap.

Bopadile's attitude was that things were corrupt and the way to benefit from this was to be corrupt yourself. And once Bopadile had completed his current plan of corruption, my father would hear about it only when someone came to our house to complain and ask for compensation. 'Bopadile has taken my car,' someone might say. 'What are you going to do about it?' Or, 'Bopadile has borrowed money from me and he says you are the one that will return it.'

My mother was reassured by having Oabona as a close friend, for there were some in the village who were suspicious of my mother and by extension my father. Actually by that time there were a couple of other what they called mixed couples, and in Lephane there is now an area where Batswana women married to white men live. The men for the most part behave appallingly, but that's another story.

My mother would have met Kennedy about that time, the man who now manages the chicken farm in Poloko. Kennedy was a poor relative of my father's who was getting into trouble for his constant drinking. My father provided Kennedy with odd jobs, and sometimes gave him clothes or money. But then my father would care for anyone as long as they were Family. This must have been novel for my mother because she came from a real disjunctional family, to coin a term. I say disjunctional because really I can't understand how someone can so successfully divorce themselves from their family, and it worried me that though my mother did write to my grandmother, she clearly didn't like either of her parents.

My father wanted to move out of Lephane to try and succeed elsewhere and my mother was all too willing to take a break. She didn't like a 'stranger' looking after me when she was at school. She thought that a mother should be with her child, even if it wasn't always the norm around her. On the other hand, she gave birth to me at the local hospital, which was only slightly better than it is now. People blamed my father for that, thinking, I suppose, that a white woman should give birth somewhere nice.

My father began threatening to give up his job every day. My parents had married the year before I was born and had disappointed the family by holding only a small party when what my grandmother wanted was to sing all night long. Then my parents disappointed the family even more by moving all the way down to Jamestown, although my father's only aim in life was to provide for his relatives.

BOOK TWO

Chapter Three

In 1979 my father got a job at a salt mine some 500 kilometres south-east of Lephane and my parents moved while I was still a toddler. My mother was all for moving – after all, hadn't she just packed up and come all the way from England? What was another 500 kilometres? she thought. I blame my parents' habit of moving around for the fact I can't seem to settle down – though, having said that, moving does not mean you are not settled. My father's mother, for example, is a very settled sort of person and she is constantly moving around from the cattlepost to the lands and so on.

People were excited about the Jamestown mine at that time. We had diamond and copper mines, but the salt mine was brand new and people innocently believed things were looking up for our country, for hadn't the money from diamonds given us schools and tarred roads and hospitals? School children were taught to be proud of our developing nation, which was peaceful and prosperous compared to our neighbours. But there were already those like my father who wanted to know where the rest of the money from the diamonds had gone when most people in Lephane had no water or electricity or toilets.

My father was in accounts, though it's hard to say what he did exactly. But he is a numbers man, he likes the orderly fashion of playing around with numbers, as if they are divorced from everyday life. He still likes to stroke his chin and talk about numbers, and this usually leads into one of his favourite topics, which is the nature of logic. The worst thing he can say about something or someone is that they are not logical. This image of him stroking his chin is an apt one, for he's a thoughtful man and not taken to making rash, impetuous decisions the way my mother is. And I would say that we Batswana like to consider things before we act. That's why we call Kgotla meetings so everyone can express their views. These days, of course, decisions are made from above and then they trickle down to the people they affect.

Looking back, it was crazy for my parents to have moved. They went straight from a close village and the bosom of the family to a new-built town that still today has an artificial quality about it. Someone must have known even then that the mine might not survive, but off the government went erecting a town and spreading the god of development. Surely my father, having studied in the States, was under no illusions about how he would be treated at the mine. Though the government were partial owners, everyone knew that it was run by the Boers, and it was South African multinationals who were the major shareholders.

So in a truck provided by the mining company, one of the perks of the job, my parents and I moved to Jamestown. My father's job was part of the company's localization scheme, a scheme that was never to materialize the whole time my father was there, nor afterwards when we had left and moved down to Gaborone. According to the multinationals, the Boer management was only temporary and Batswana would be trained to replace them. They said the mine was a highly specialized operation and that no Batswana knew how to run such a place. But however much the mining company said they wanted to give the 'locals' jobs, you know some jobs are always reserved for the white people.

We moved in September, the time of year when winter has faded and summer begins. Lephane was still green when we left, while Jamestown was dry, dusty and unwelcoming. There were only a few hundred inhabitants, nearly all working for the mine. A lot of them were contractors and so-called experts who were supposed to go back to South Africa or England or wherever they came from once their jobs were done. Because the town was so new, there wasn't yet a council in place, so it was a settlement of mine employees, mostly men. The flamingo population on the pans was several times that of the people, and when the flamingoes came for breeding the horizon was a pink, squabbling mass of birds.

The pans are a huge, flat area of open plain and bush. The salt-encrusted grasslands around Jamestown were cattle country. The cattle, which were owned by politicians down in the south, would roam freely over the limitless land. The colours of the land are not sharp the way they are up in Lephane, rather they are pale, pastel shades of brown and yellow. Many, many years ago the area was part of a vast inland lake where people must have gone to fish and hunt. Further west of Jamestown, the open flatlands fill with water when there's a good rainy season and then thousands of zebra and springbok make their journeys, followed by lions and other predators.

Although presumably people had always known there was salt on the pans, the government had only just decided to make a business of it. So first they had to get rid of the people who stayed around there, people whose land this had once been. Then the mine was built on the pans and, finally, some ten kilometres away, the town. In a large clearing in the bush government workers were busy grading sand roads and eventually tarring them. Houses were built at an alarming rate.

Jamestown was set out on a grid and all the houses were white with green roofs. One road, less than ten kilometres long, encircled the town, and inside it was the grid divided into plots for houses and more roads. All around us was bush, sandy land and small trees, and along the tar road towards the mine were the salt pans. You could walk around the whole town in a couple of hours.

When we first arrived in Jamestown, we lived in a tiny house in the central area. No furniture was provided, though the expatriates were given beds and curtains. There were no shops and everyone ate in a huge tent except for the contractors, who lived in mobile homes some ten kilometres away at the mine itself. The tent was erected where the council offices are today. That was the only access to food, for the nearest town, Thabeng, was two hundred kilometres away and the roads were still pretty bad.

Jamestown lay about twenty kilometres from the turn-off to the road heading up north to Lephane and down south to Gaborone. This north–south road was finally tarred a few years ago. Stories told that a leopard visited the Jamestown turn-off every evening. Why a leopard should choose to do this I have no idea, but there would have been plenty for it to eat at that time.

Jamestown, unlike other urban areas being built in Botswana then, was set out in such a way as to make neat class division of people. On one street, for example, were all the low-cost homes, small squarish structures in small bare yards. Inside these houses there were showers but no baths, and the stoves used gas not electricity. There were no cupboards, shelves or wardrobes, as if earning less meant you had less need for space than the high-cost people, the mine managers who had more rooms and more amenities, being higher on the scale of evolution than their low-cost counterparts.

It was no wonder then that there was an 'us versus them' mentality in Jamestown. The Boers really rubbed our noses in it as they hired maids and gardeners, built swimming-pools and drove brand-new cars. But those down at the bottom of the money scale in Jamestown were still doing much better than the people in the villages around us, for everyone in Jamestown had a roof over their head and at least one person in the household had a pay check every month.

As the mine was managed – or rather mismanaged – by the Boers, this system of housing also divided people in terms of what is known as race. So one street would be low cost and only black people lived there. In the yards were bony dogs, maybe some chickens, maize in a small regular patch of sandy soil, some biltong strung up outside, babies playing on the sand. And right around the corner in the high-cost area were big houses in big gardens, with white inhabitants who rarely left their domains except when the men went to work and the women went to Thabeng to shop. In the high-cost streets every house had a mean, well-fed dog and usually a gardener or a maid or both. This is because when you have money the point is to pay someone to do all the jobs that you don't want to do, and don't have to do any more.

The jobs created by the mine for Batswana were, of course, the low-paid, low-status ones. The multinationals which owned the mine and the Botswana government which had a big share in it promised that employment opportunities would open up in James-town, as shop assistants and petrol pump attendants and so forth, which I presume we were meant to be grateful for. Some six months after we arrived a small, expensive food shop opened up in a dark, plastic-smelling trailer. When you went inside, you found yourself sliding slowly down the sloping floor to where the half-rotten veget-ables were at the back.

The first real shop was, not surprisingly, a bottle store which sold alcohol, soft drinks, cigarettes and ice. So you couldn't buy fresh meat or vegetables in Jamestown but you could get drunk. The food shop provided three jobs and the bottle store two. There was also a garage that usually had no petrol, but provided three more jobs. Apart from working for the mine itself, or being a maid or a gardener, that was about it. Which made people like my father question how exactly our country was meant to be benefiting from this mine.

It's not that we Batswana are stupid, but we do tend to talk to ourselves about bad situations and, while we are still talking and weighing things up and getting everyone's opinion, before you know it some multinational has moved in and we've been taken over. It seems to me that we take a lot of shit before we actually do anything about it. But then perhaps that is true of people everywhere. Jamestown was a small place and people were just not prepared for what was going to happen.

In the medium-cost houses were people like my father who was about as high as a Motswana could be at that time without being a lackey for the Boers. There was a big gap between the medium-cost houses and the high-cost houses, though later on new types of medium-cost houses were built and these were grander. Our house was small and rather dark. It was cold in winter and hot in summer. We had two bedrooms, a kitchen, living-room and a bathroom with a bath.

We had enough money for food every day and with a loan from the bank my parents bought a small pick-up truck because the one my father had had in Lephane had finally died. The rest of my father's income went back to the family in Lephane. What we didn't have was money to buy luxuries like a fridge – and of course a video or telephone were quite out of the question.

Also in the medium-cost houses were one or two South African Indian men who were a sort of buffer against theblacks as the Boers called them. Like the Batswana, the Indian men were static when it came to their jobs and the Boers were as likely to have an Indian person promoted to any position of authority as they were a Motswana.

Within their groups of colour people kept very much to themselves and rarely stepped across the great divide. All the time we lived in Jamestown hardly a single conversation could go by without a Motswana complaining about the whites and the mine. So here we were in an isolated town in the middle of a salt pan with firmly separated groups of people.

This was one of the reasons my mother was so isolated. Some Batswana were suspicious of my father, thinking that if he had a white wife, then perhaps he didn't consider himself a Motswana any more, perhaps he was on the side of the Boers and other whites. And while my mother tried hard to be friendly, Batswana in

Jamestown were having bad experiences with white people and so they were wary.

For my mother it wasn't good enough to chat with people in the street and then not see them for weeks. According to her scheme of things, when you made a friend you invited them round for tea, then they invited you round for tea and it went from there. Some Batswana made overtures to my mother because they thought her whiteness would rub off on them, and then maybe they would have all the things the white women seemed to have. Another way of doing this was to get yourself a white man, but the white men had white wives, and if they didn't, or even if they did, they wanted Batswana women for just one thing. No Boer in his right mind was going to marry one.

Those in the high-cost houses in Jamestown quickly surrounded their houses and gardens with some sort of barrier. This meant constructing either hedges, reed partitions, thorn bushes or in some cases even electric fences. Although their servants' quarters were the size of the low-cost houses and would have been reasonably comfortable for anyone to live in, they were usually empty. 'The Boers don't want us to see all the goodies in their houses,' my father would say and waggle his finger in and out of his ear, which is what he does when he's joking but pretending not to care, or when he's so irritated he doesn't know what to say.

One of the strangest things about Jamestown was that it was so untypical. I realized this years later when my parents and I told people about life in the township and they were staggered and amazed. There were not many newspapers at that time, so news still travelled by word of mouth. All people knew was that we had a new salt mine and everything was going to be developed.

Every day for the first few months my mother and I went off to the tent, where everyone stared at us as we lined up to be fed. Like refugees, you could say, although much more like refugees were the people in the squatter camp which sprang up almost as fast as the town only a few kilometres down the road. I never saw this camp, but I have seen many since then and people lived mainly in homes made of cardboard and plastic sheets. Of course once the town had a council in place, they soon got rid of the squatters. Government workers went down the road one summer morning and burned the place to the ground.

The uncle of the present chief in Jamestown went along, no doubt hoping to ingratiate himself with the mine managers, the infamous Boers. He made the right move, for he got a small pick-up truck, which was filled up and serviced at the mine for free. All he had to do in return was make speeches at Kgotla meetings and introduce the mine managers to the community, which he thoroughly enjoyed anyway. Unlike the present chief in Jamestown, this old chief did not have his people's interests at heart.

Once the mine really got going, once the land had been cleared and the roads tarred, the expatriates were allowed to choose the plot where they wanted their house built. My father made a huge fuss and said he should be allowed to choose a plot too. Both my parents remember choosing their plot for the sole reason that it had two large Mophane trees. When the house was built, however, the first thing the builders did was to hack them down and my parents were left with a deserted plot on which their medium-cost house was built. Jamestown was hot and exposed enough as it was, and once the trees were cut down there was no shade at all. I swear that it was so hot in Jamestown that sometimes you could hear our house creak with the agony of it all.

One day, when the houses were first being built, a wildebeest ran through the township. One of the builders, driving a cement mixer, went after it and killed it there and then and that must have been some feast. It's hard to imagine that there were once so many wildebeest around, let alone leopards, for in our quest for development first we moved the people out and then we killed the wild animals. It was a bad way for a township to begin. The people who had been cleared off the land set up home in the bush and were refused drought relief when they came begging to the council. The council said they didn't fall under their jurisdiction and advised them to apply to the authorities of a large village some hundred kilometres away.

If Lephane had once been hard for my mother, life in the township of Jamestown was hell. She had nothing to do, knew no one and was shunned on all sides. During the day the township was silent because the men had gone off to the mine. It was hot and barren and there were frequent dust storms. In the summer months when people eagerly awaited the rains there were afternoons when the whole sky would fill with a whirling grey. At first, as it darkened, you would think the clouds were bringing rain, but it was just a salty dust that coated the few small plants with white and then whipped in through the windows.

Those expatriates who didn't work in the mine stayed inside their houses and wondered what on earth they were doing in Jamestown. It took over six months before the shop in the trailer, the bottle store and the council were in place, though the mine quickly built an English medium primary school for the younger children of its expatriate employees. 'English medium' is the euphemism for private, for English is our official language and everyone should have been learning it anyway. Before independence children like me would not have been allowed to go to the white schools at all.

Once the council was in place a Setswana primary school was built, but I was too young for school and stayed at home with my mother. That is, until the pre-school disaster. We did need a pre-school, that was true, but my parents got involved in the scheme thinking it was something other than what it turned out to be. They were tricked by people they thought were their friends and in some ways they never really recovered from the whole episode.

My mother must have been glad of me at that time, though bringing up a small child in Jamestown can't have been fun. I was someone she could talk to and play with, and as an ex-teacher she was used to having an audience. But then again when you have only a very young child to talk to, it can sort of turn your mind. I have seen white women, isolated wives of men with paid jobs over here, carrying around their children and talking to them to remind themselves that they exist. I have seen them walking into shops and saying to their small children whom they carry on their hips, 'Are you hungry, then? Well, we just had lunch, didn't we? Yes, we did. We just had some nice soup, didn't we?' Or, 'Is that the time? We'll have to get going, won't we, because Daddy will be back soon, won't he?'

In banks and post offices I've seen them let their children roam around, climbing up on desks and holding on to bars, while Batswana exchanged glances because their children would soon have been told off if they had behaved like that. And their children always seem to be complaining and demanding, 'Mummy, I want this. Mummy, when are we going to go home? Mummy, I'm tired,' and so on. There now, here is a part of me that hates them too.

My parents clung to the idea that it was good that they had moved to Jamestown. They would make money, they would save, they would return home to Lephane and provide for the family, which would finally be able to live a standard of life expected from a son who had been educated in the white peoples' place of America. And my mother, who had few people to talk to in the early days, must have been a bit hopeful about the arrival of the white wives. At least some of them would speak the same language and would be sort of in the same boat as her. Also their arrival signified that more amenities would be established. Soon the mine would build a swimming-pool, a 'community' hall, and then a restaurant and bar which they called the Baobab Club.

I had many children to play with at that time, so though my mother didn't have friends I did. I was about four years old and could walk and talk and so on. That period of my life in Jamestown is clear in almost every aspect and there was a time not long ago when I really believed I could account for those couple of years week by week, if not day by day.

I had begun by playing with the other Batswana kids out in the street. We had a neighbour, Beauty, who worked as a secretary at the mine and she had several children, one of whom, Thebe, was my own age. Beauty came from Lephane and was a distant relative of my father, which made it all the more fitting that I should play with her children. Thebe and I played together nearly every day, either in my parents' yard or Beauty's. Beauty, who was a kind woman, had given Thebe and me a pink plastic doll each. So we set up an area of the yard for our dolls. We would put our dolls under an old piece of car roofing and say it was their house. Or, alternatively, we would tie them on our backs with pieces of cloth and pretend we were women. We would brush the dolls' yellow stringy hair, plait it, decorate it with bougainvillaea leaves, wash it, dry it and finally pull it out.

Unlike me, Thebe was a very easy-going child. She always replied to her elders, did what she was told with good grace and was very interested in food. She encouraged me to take food from my parents' house and then we stored it where our dolls slept. Thebe was eager – that is the word that really describes her. She never sulked, the way I did, she never refused, the way I did, she took every opportunity and made of it what she could. The couple of times my mother took us to the Jamestown swimming-pool, for example, Thebe threw herself in even though it was her first time to see a swimming-pool and she couldn't swim. I would refuse to take off my clothes and would walk around the edge peering into the water, or sit and sulk and dream in the shade of the tree.

When the white wives arrived with their small children and my mother made some brief friendships, I found myself playing with the white kids. On the whole my mother didn't like me to be playing out of her sight, so when she was invited to the women's houses she always took me along. And the things these children had in their houses! And the nonchalant way they treated those things! Soon my mother would fall out with one or other of these white women and I would find myself back in the yard with Thebe or out on the street with the other Batswana kids, my mother watching at the kitchen window. When the children of the white wives started at the mine's English medium primary school, my mother tells me, the women stayed home and cried all day. They were that lonely.

Those who made friends with my mother urged her to visit South Africa, which they said was a beautiful place and not at all what you heard about in the news. Where we live, they told her, it's not like that at all, and they would tell her how well they treated black people. 'I had a maid,' they would say, 'and I treated her like an equal, you know. She ate with us, she even had a bath at our house, yes! And there was no dirt in the bath afterwards.'

Yet many of these women were terrified of returning to South Africa. 'If anything happens to the children,' they told their husbands when they learnt they were moving back, 'I will never forgive you.' My mother remembers all these sorts of conversations and quotes them when I ask her about what Jamestown used to be like. But though the white women were afraid of life in South Africa, they were also afraid of life in Jamestown, or rather they were afraid of this faceless horde called 'theblacks' who, they thought, were just waiting to pounce.

My mother spent that first year or so in Jamestown doing the domestic jobs which she hated so much, taking care of me without the help of any relatives, and she developed a passion for our yard. Within that first year she had managed to hedge herself in so the house was partly obscured from the road. By the end of 1980, the year our President died, the hedges grew bushy and frantic and the bougainvillaea at the corners of the yard shot out their branches and showered us with purple and red flowers. Hedges, bougainvillaea and paw-paws were about the only things that could grow in Jamestown. The soil, a salty sort of sand, was not a welcoming place for plants.

In general this was all my mother did during the day. I say all not because looking after me and a house wasn't work but because it was not what she wanted to be doing. She had resigned herself to coping with Jamestown, and also she thought there might one day be an opportunity for her to teach again. Meanwhile, she cared for me and wrote letters to England.

Chapter Four

After that first year in Jamestown, life settled into a routine and my mother was a great one for routines. In the mornings the alarm rang at 5 a.m. and my father called me and got up. He always called me when he woke and urged me out of bed because he thought it was very wasteful not to get up with the sun. My mother dozed while my father had his shower and then made coffee. He had picked up the coffee habit during his time in the States and with his love of gadgets had brought a coffee-maker back with him – not to mention a hi-fi, an electric shaver and a small camera, none of which he liked anyone else to touch.

My father had used his living allowance in the States to buy fancy things. Then he had hauled them all back to Botswana, where they were totally out of place and suggested that we were much better off than we were. Although there was electricity in James-town, there were frequent power cuts and for whole days none of my father's gadgets could be used. But I think he liked to look at them, to have their presence remind him that he had got something out of the States. It was common for returning Batswana to bring back such things as blue jeans and cameras, just as later it became common to see someone park a brand-new pick-up truck outside a relative's mud house.

My father had trained me well. In the mornings I would not disturb my mother but get myself up, wash and dress while my father made some soft porridge on the stove. He then inspected me for cleanliness. We ate the porridge in silence while standing up. This habit infuriated my mother who would cry, 'Sit! You're making me nervous,' so we did it when she was not around. A meal to her meant sitting round a table and talking, which is what she said people in Europe did, with the implication, my father responded, that sitting and talking while eating was the best way to go about these things.

So we stood outside and ate our porridge and listened to James-town waking up. From the high-cost houses round the corner we heard maids and gardeners opening gates and the white people starting up their cars. We heard people walking by on the way to the mine's bus-stops and we heard the giant black and white crows that bounced along our metal roof. Sometimes we heard cow bells as some rib-thin cattle moved past on the small lane behind our house. We heard cockerels in nearby yards, donkeys laughing by day and jackals by night.

But on the whole life in Jamestown was much quieter than it had been in Lephane, and once the mine employees had gone to work there was a lull that lasted until 5 o'clock when they came home again. The giant birds, which my mother said were crows and could be found in England, made the most noise in the morning and I was always a bit in awe of them. If I woke early, I would lie in bed and listen to them running along our roof and then jumping off with great squawks.

After we had eaten, my father smoked a cigarette outside, went off to work, and my mother got up. Sometimes, especially in the early summer when the mornings were clear and fresh, she got up before my father had left to give him a kiss goodbye. 'We're in public!' my father would say appalled and gesture outside to people strolling by to the mine's bus-stops in no hurry to get to work. After my father had gone, my mother had what she called her 'peaceful first hour' when she made tea for us both, inspected the garden closely and finally got dressed, choosing with great care between her three or four dresses.

Then she worked in the house. I only realized this much later, but though she was a great one for cleaning and putting away, in fact she only maintained a veneer of neatness and cleanliness. As long as things *looked* okay on the surface, she was more or less satisfied. So she might harangue me to clean my room, but she never checked under the bed where I believed the monsters lived. She might tell me to sweep the floors, but she never bothered about the spiders' webs lining the window sills, although she was afraid of the spiders themselves. The stove had to be clean on the top, but inside it could be pretty filthy.

Although my mother always looked clean and tidy herself, underneath her clothes were fastened with safety pins and on close inspection you could see small tears in her clothes. She was also a messy eater and was forever wiping crumbs off her front, whereas my father lifted the plate carefully to his chest and ate without dropping a thing.

She tried to get me to help her in the house, but often I made a fuss and pulled faces and sulked. And I was an expert at being what my mother called a Difficult Child. She said Difficult Child as if questioning why she of all people had to be landed with one. She could call me until she was blue in the face and I'd just ignore her. 'Mma?' I would then say innocently when she finally tracked me down. For that was how my father had trained me, a woman was always Mma and a man Rra. To answer in any other way would have been rude. I always came immediately when my father called.

There is a photo of me under my mother's bed in Poloko that is badly taken and faded, but I remember the posture well. I am standing at the doorway to the kitchen scowling, holding myself very straight and tall, my eyebrows taut in defiance. My grandmother says I looked just like my father when he was a child.

My mother, as part of her routine, went for her morning swim at about 10 o'clock depending on the season. I was usually left playing with Thebe next door. Though I was under strict instructions not to leave our neighbour's yard, there was a small triangle of bush behind our house where cows sometimes attempted to graze in the late afternoons. Thebe and I and some other small children gathered together some big plastic bags, which we tore open and used as a roof for a house we had built from loose branches. We sat under our shelter and played with cans and things in the intricate way children do.

Other times we played the sand game. My mother was always questioning me about it because she couldn't understand the rules or see the point. In the sand game one team tries to fill a big empty Coke bottle with sand and wins points every time it manages to fill the bottle and then empty it again. Everyone on this team helps to fill the bottle as best they can. Two people from the other team throw a ball to each other trying to hit a member of the opposing team. If you are hit by the ball, which was usually an old sock, then you are out. If you are the one holding the bottle, then you drop it and another member of the team takes it up and continues. There were no clear winners or losers in this game, which was why my mother couldn't follow it, and it could go on for hours, be interrupted for an afternoon and then simply begin again.

However much my mother had established a routine, she was not happy in Jamestown, and so Christine's arrival was a welcome relief. After a year and a half in Jamestown and a few not very successful friendships, she finally had a friend who spoke the same language and understood the complex rules of friendship and hospitality of my mother's people.

Christine was married to Frank, who was a boss at the mine. That meant he earned more than the Batswana, though it was people like my father who knew everything and did all the work. Frank had been trained as a teacher, I believe, so I don't know how exactly he ended up being in charge of Stores. But then if you're a Boer, it doesn't really matter. Only Frank was English, as was Christine, but they had lived the past ten years in southern Africa and had picked up a few tips on how to treat black people. Yet they saw themselves as different from the other whites in the township because of their liberal attitudes. Christine and Frank Fish. I still laugh at that surname. Just imagine being addressed as Mrs Fish. But it never seemed to bother Christine.

Christine was a short, breathy sort of woman. Her breathiness was partly a result of the fact she did things frantically, invoking an element of drama in the most trivial things, and partly because she hardly ever had a thin cigar-like cigarette out of her mouth. She was a bullet of energy, and if this energy had been directed to something useful she could have changed the world. But she was only out for herself – a British trait as my father would say. She had a passion for organizing: when her husband told her he had accepted a job in a small new town in Botswana, she must have rubbed her hands in anticipation. Like a lot of expatriates, in Botswana Christine was to find an importance that she would never have achieved at home.

Frank seemed to be his wife's opposite, especially in his relations with other people. Where Christine was loud and pushy, Frank was quiet and calm. Where Christine was talkative and welcomed people on board immediately, Frank was reserved and slightly formal. He seemed to defer entirely to Christine. He made women comfortable because he appeared so gentle and interested. He made men comfortable because there was no need to compete with him. And I think they rather liked feeling sorry for him in his persona as a Henpecked Husband because it made them feel so much better about themselves, restored their manhood as it were. But Frank was not all he seemed, and nor of course was Christine.

One morning in May, just as the weather was beginning to turn into winter, my mother met Christine. I remember it was about that time because whenever we had our first cool night my mother would announce, 'Winter is coming,' and then she would spend all morning making soup. 'It's sock weather,' she would announce next and start pulling out my winter clothes. But by the next day the sun was hot again. 'It's going to be a scorcher,' she would announce as she did her inspection of the plants, and she said it with a touch of surprise as if it wasn't a scorcher every day.

This particular morning in May my mother took me to the pool with her and she appeared appalled to find someone else already there. The pool was a short walk from our house and lay in an area of cleared bush about half a kilometre from the Baobab Club. It seemed vast to me and it was strange to see this sharp rectangle of blue in the middle of dry brown bush. The pool was not just for anyone, you had to pay a monthly amount to use it, which meant that most Batswana never went there. This was precisely the point in charging the fee.

Most of us couldn't swim anyway, unless we came from some-where where there was a river, where we might have learnt to splash around while our mothers washed clothes. Many white people didn't use the pool either because they had built their own in their gardens. If, walking around Jamestown, you passed a high reed or hedge fence, then you could safely assume there was a pool behind it.

So my mother had the Jamestown pool mostly to herself and she was always promising to teach me to swim, but at that time I didn't like water at all so I took up my position in the shade of the tree to watch. Arriving that day, my mother ignored the strange woman in the pool, undressed quickly and dived in. She swam as she always did, with long, steady strokes, overtaking the other woman. When my mother got out for a rest, the woman, who was now holding on to the side of the pool, called out 'Hello!' for all the world like a cockerel. My mother turned round.

'Hello!' the woman said again, this time in my direction. I just stared. 'Have you just arrived?' she continued.

'Sorry?' My mother fastened the towel around her waist.

'Just arrived in Jamestown? What a place!'

For some reason my mother nodded. She has a habit of lying if you give her an easy opportunity. To answer 'Have you just ar-rived?' with a no would have meant having to give an explanation.

'Me too!' the woman in the pool cried as if this should establish an immediate friendship and she got out of the water. 'What a place!' she said for the second time. When they had finished dressing at opposite ends of the pool, the woman came over to introduce herself.

'Christine,' she said. 'I'm Christine and . . .'

'Rose,' my mother replied and then, pushing me forward a bit, she added, 'And Dimpho.'

Christine seemed to hesitate for just a moment. 'She's yours?'

My mother stiffened. 'Yes, she is.'

'What a beautiful child,' Christine said.

'Are you from South Africa?' my mother asked when she could get a word in.

'God, no!' Christine said loudly. 'We've been living there of course, but I can tell you I've had enough of that.'

My mother nodded. 'What did you do in South Africa?'

'Well' – Christine paused for a moment – 'I'm a teacher by profession.'

'Same here,' my mother smiled.

'We ran a school actually . . .'

'Oh, yes?' My mother looked vaguely interested and bent down to gather up her clothes.

'They don't really welcome you here, do they?' Christine complained – 'You should come for tea!'

I think my mother was amused at someone being so keen to know her. Sometimes this had happened with other white women, but then they met my father and that was the end of that, because you couldn't really be *friends* with someone married to ablack.

That afternoon Christine appeared on a brand-new bicycle with a small fluffy white dog stuffed in the children's seat.

'Just thought I'd come round to say hello!' she announced gaily from the gate, straddling the bike and leaving the dog perched a bit precariously. 'I heard you lived here. Would you believe we're just round the corner!'

My mother invited her into the yard and introduced her to my father who had just come back from work and was standing outside smoking a cigarette. Christine leant from the bike as she held out her hand, laughing slightly as if embarrassed. My father shook it in the European way and said, 'Mompati.'

'Christine,' she said and laughed again. 'Well . . .' she began, taking a look round the yard and then back to my father, 'and how are you finding the mine?' She spoke slowly: white people always assumed my father couldn't speak English well, or perhaps they were just used to speaking slowly to maids and gardeners.

My father shrugged.

'That bad?' Christine asked.

'I met Christine at the pool today,' my mother explained and leant forward to pat the dog panting in the seat on the back of the bicycle.

'And this is Snowy,' Christine said, then she turned her attention to me as I stood straight-limbed by the doorway. I scowled, still shy. My father indicated that I should greet our visitor properly.

'Dumela,' I mumbled, barely audible.

'In English,' my mother said, so I shifted and said, 'Hello.'

'Hello,' Christine beamed.

'Fine,' I said because I thought that was what came next and she laughed.

They stood in the yard, my father offering Christine a chair, which she refused, saying she couldn't stay long. They talked of this and that, and then Christine rode off to make more friends. That was the last time I saw her on a bike and although she did come round afterwards, it was always by car and she stopped outside our gate without turning the engine off. Actually I don't recall a single time Christine ever came into our house – she always said she was in a rush, which she always was.

My father was pleased that my mother seemed to have a friend and he was polite to Christine. He wasn't good at making small talk with white people, it was only when he was with Batswana that he talked a lot. He had realized, I suppose, that there weren't many women in Jamestown and few of the Batswana could speak English well enough to make friends with my mother.

'She seems nice, doesn't she?' my mother asked for reassurance once Christine had gone, and my father said, 'Mmm,' which is the noise he makes when he can't be bothered to actually form words, another habit that used to infuriate my mother.

'She says she's just arrived,' my mother went on. 'Tomorrow Dimpho and I are going there for tea,' and she smiled at this establishment of friendship. The British, in my opinion, seem to have all sorts of complex and petty rules for friendship and hospitality. To complicate matters they also seem to have a way of saying no when they mean yes and vice versa. In Botswana the British are known as hypocrites, though I don't think this is quite the right term. 'Shall I help?' my father might ask my mother while she was cooking, and she'd say, 'No, you're fine,' and so he would continue what he was doing and my mother would crash around in the kitchen, furious that he hadn't got up to help. Or he might say, 'Do you mind if I . . .' and she would say, 'No, fine. Go ahead,' which meant, Yes, I *do* mind. When things got bad, my father would always say, 'In Setswana we have an expression: the wheel that squeaks gets oiled.'

'Yes I know that, Mr Africa,' my mother would say and go back to her tasks.

Another source of minor conflict was time. Now my mother, being British, had very strong ideas when it came to time, and even though she herself sometimes admitted that they were ridiculous, she couldn't shake them off. If, for example, someone said, 'I will be at your house at 10 o'clock,' and then didn't come until the afternoon, she would open the door expecting an apology, which we Batswana would never give because in our view we had done nothing wrong. 'I said I would come and I have arrived,' would be our way of looking at the situation. 'The fact that I said 10 o'clock is really neither here nor there.' Often too we Batswana say what we would *like* to do, and Europeans take this to mean what we are *going* to do. Back in Lephane my mother was frequently upset with my father's relatives who never did what they said they would, for example come on time. Now British people find this the height of rudeness, but it goes deeper than this for they believe you can't really trust such people. It's a sign that they are shifty, lazy, unreliable and so forth.

And another thing – my mother always had the door locked, or at least the screen door. 'I come from England,' she would say when my father got annoyed. Batswana were always very perplexed as to why they couldn't just knock and walk straight in to our house but had to wait for the door to be unlocked. My mother was forever instructing me to check that things were locked and turned off, and she would hound my father about whether he had fully put out his cigarette.

There were a lot of conversations between my parents which began, 'You people . . .' Sometimes it was affectionate, sometimes not.

Chapter Five

The day after meeting Christine at the pool, my mother said we would go and see our new friend, who as luck or later misfortune would have it lived in the very next street. Now my parents and I lived in a two-bedroom house. By Jamestown standards we didn't have much, but in terms of how people in the villages lived we did. We had a bath, hot water, electricity and even a ceiling fan, which as a child I spent many hours watching. We also had a tiny 'servant's quarters', as the mine called it – it was in fact just a small square room more like a garage. But all this was nothing compared to what Christine and Frank had, and my mother with her love of creature comforts was entranced by Christine's abode. It wasn't so much that she wanted what Christine had, but that her childhood in England had accustomed her to just about everyone having things like inside toilets, baths, hot water, electricity and television.

But she was also careful to point out to me that many people in England had nowhere to live and unlike in Botswana you couldn't just apply for some land and get some relatives together to build a house, rather you had to be very rich to have land. She told me some people in England lived on the street without shelter, that they had to beg strangers for food and money, that old people died because it was too cold and they couldn't afford to pay for warmth, that people rummaged in rubbish bins to see what they could find to eat. She drummed this into me so that I wouldn't be under the usual impression that all white people were rich. But all the white people I ever saw were, so I don't think I really believed her until much later. Certainly every single white person in Jamestown was rich, much richer, I assume, than they would have been back in their own countries.

Christine's house, and it was hers because it was her domain, was huge. It had four bedrooms, only one of which – the *master* bedroom – was in use. The house had a large well-equipped kitchen with space for about three people to work in and two bathrooms, which Christine called His and Hers, putting a plaque on each door of either a girl or a boy urinating. There was also a dining-room and a living-room that had glass doors opening on to the garden and a concrete patio. Christine had set to work almost immediately upgrading their surroundings, creating the sort of living circumstances the Fishes were apparently used to.

The mine gave the expatriates a huge amount of money as an 'incentive' for coming to Botswana and another huge amount for 'settling in'. One of the first things Christine did was to get a roundavel built in the back garden. This was not for living in, of course, but for show – a traditional house on display in the garden of Christine's mansion. She immediately employed a gardener to look after all the plants she had ordered from Thabeng and he spent the mornings watering the place while Christine's fluffy white dog, Snowy, fussed and yapped around his ankles. She owned a second dog, Butch, a huge dribbling creature, for she wanted one dog to be a toy and the other to scare people away.

Coming from our medium-cost house with its small poky rooms, its tiny 'servant's quarters' and its garden struggling to exist, you can imagine how it was for my mother to visit Christine. In those days my mother travelled by bicycle, a second-hand one my father had bought in a government auction, and she put me on the back. In Lephane, she says, she had been known as the Tall White Woman on a Bicycle because bikes were not a common sight in the north and nor, of course, were white women. And wherever she went, children called to her and knew her to be a teacher. In Jamestown they called to her too. 'Goodmorningafternoonteacher!'

young children would cry, tearing out of their yards after the bicycle. This embarrassed and confused me no end.

As Christine's house was only round the corner, it wasn't much of a journey, but for me it might as well have been to another world. Petrified by Christine's dog, Butch, which was the size of a small cow, I refused to enter the gateway and took up my difficult child posture instead. But when Christine appeared, I soon grew alert. Here was something interesting to look at, I thought, as Christine came wafting down the walkway wearing a near see-through sort of wrap-around thing. She may have thought that that was what the 'local' women wore, but even so the women of Jamestown didn't walk around in their wrappers the way they might have done in a village. If they worked in the mine, then they wore nice dresses and suits, and if they were maids they were usually provided with a uniform made from pink, scratchy material which resembled cardboard more than cloth.

Christine was heavily perfumed, and today I always associate her with the smell of sour milk, although I'm sure she would never in a million years have drunk sour milk. So perhaps it was the perfume mixed with the smell of her thin cigarettes. She came wafting down the path with one of these in her hand, checking that her hair was in place with the other. She wore her hair tightly pulled back in what they call a bun, presumably because it resembles a type of bread.

'Oh, what a day I've had!' she said in welcome, as if my mother had just come in time to rescue her from some trouble. She turned and went off back to the house expecting us to follow. But Butch and I were staring at each other, both transfixed. Butch began barking and then leapt at me. He would have easily knocked me to the ground had Christine not shot out her free hand, hooked it on the dog's collar and yelled, 'Butch!'

The dog relaxed slightly, but I didn't until Christine locked it away in the dog house, a little wooden structure with a pointed roof and a painted-on window which I had mistaken for a watchman's house. Butch had a scary face. Its lips were permanently turned down in a slippery scowl and its eyes were sunken and bloodshot. It breathed heavily like a dragon in a cartoon. I say 'it' because my father said it was ridiculous to go around referring to animals as 'he' or 'she'. In Setswana we make a big distinction between people and other animals.

Snowy, the toy dog who lived inside the house, came to the doorway and yapped at me, ignoring my mother. It was small and clean and fluffy with a strange muscly erect tail. Christine used to wash it herself in the bath and it always smelled of apple shampoo. Snowy was one of those small fussy dogs that you just want to squash with your foot, and it had two sharp little teeth that for some reason grew upwards out of its mouth and straight over the top lip so it always looked as if it were going to bite you. These teeth presented a bit of a problem when Snowy ate, because it had to stop frequently to wipe them off before diving once more into its personalized food bowl. Snowy's eyes bulged as if someone poking sharply at the top of its nose, where there was a big dent, had caused them to pop out. Still, Christine thought it was a beautiful dog.

We sat in the living-room, Snowy taking up its perch on a large soft chair, me as quiet and obedient as befits a Motswana child until Christine suggested I go and 'play' in her children's room. Her children were away at school in South Africa because they were too old to go to the mine's primary school. Christine made coffee for my mother. Not having a maid yet, she did this herself and shouted through to the living-room as she continued the conversation. My mother sat and said, 'Uhuh,' when necessary and looked around. One whole wall of the living-room resembled a library, but of videos not books. On the other walls were belongings the Fishes had picked up during their ten years in southern Africa – woven baskets and animal skins, landscapes and weavings done in garish colours, strange, distorted wooden sculptures. On top of the huge TV were photos of Christine looking happy and Frank looking abashed. Above the pictures was a large silver cross with a man in pain.

Christine finished making the coffee and re-entered the living-room. She carried a tumbler of what looked like Coke for herself and a plate on which little chocolate-covered biscuits were arranged in the shape of a fan.

'God, I haven't had these for *years*,' my mother exclaimed reaching forward to help herself.

'What a day!' Christine said again as she sat down and began a dramatic story – drama being the way she lived on a daily basis – about their moving to Botswana. 'It's so nice,' she said at last, 'to be here and settled with our things. They took a *week* to arrive. You know how it is when you come home to your own washing machine.'

'We don't have one,' my mother said and then laughed, a bit embarrassed.

'Oh! How on *earth* do you manage? You must come and use ours,' Christine said sweetly. My mother must have been making a mental note of what else she could make use of.

'We've been here *weeks* without any of our things. And when the freezer did arrive, the lock was broken.' Christine took a sip from her drink and looked genuinely upset.

I was finally ushered out of the living-room and into Christine's daughter's room, which resembled a sort of padded cell, being as it was taken up by a huge bed covered in all sorts of sheets and blankets and duvets and pillows and soft toys. On the walls were pictures of pop stars and giant friendly-looking elephants and hippos. I wasn't sure what I could and couldn't touch so I sat on the carpet in the middle of the room and stared, making a note of what I would tell my friend Thebe later. After some time I wandered back into the living-room.

My mother was warming to Christine, who was complaining about South Africa and talking about the move to Jamestown. My mother drank her coffee and pointed out that though some of

Christine's furniture had been slightly damaged in transit, it was lucky there was so much more tar road now than there had been a year ago. She eyed the TV screen as if hoping to be invited to watch it at some later date. There had been no one in Lephane with a television, and so for my mother, as for most people in the early 80s, it had become a symbol of real luxury. Nothing was actually broadcast but you could watch videos. Today we're still waiting for our own channel, which the government says is in the pipeline. For now we have South African channels and programmes from the States. But more people have TVs and there are whole shops devoted to videotapes.

'So, you lived in Lephane,' Christine was saying.

My mother nodded, she seemed surprised that Christine had heard of the place.

'And do you know the De Villiers?'

'No,' my mother admitted, 'I didn't know many –'

'Oh.' Christine lit a cigarette. 'What about Robby Pretorius? He owns some safari company. Oh, what's it called . . .?'

'No,' my mother said again, shifting slightly on the sofa and putting her coffee cup down. It was a beautiful pottery mug glazed with green, which she had noticed and admired earlier.

'Well, what about the Van Zyls? They've just moved there.'

'No.'

'My dear, who *do* you know?' Christine gave a shrill little laugh.

My mother was annoyed and tapped her finger on the edge of the sofa.

'Joke, Rose, I'm joking,' Christine said, leaning forward, and my mother relaxed.

'Yes, it must be so interesting' – Christine began on a new tack, stressing the word interesting – 'to really know about life in Botswana. I do find the whities separate themselves so much, and what about your husband's family?'

'Well, there's so many of them!' my mother laughed. It seemed she wasn't quite ready to give out personal information.

'And what do you think of this place?'

'Terrible!'

And they both laughed.

'Aren't they just so *racist*?' Christine said suddenly, and my mother nodded enthusiastically.

'These Boers,' Christine continued, 'you must have to put up with a lot. Lord, their attitude . . .'

My mother murmured her agreement.

'I am sure you are quite famous in the village already,' Christine said. She had this strange habit of calling Jamestown a village when it was so obviously not.

I came further into the living-room then and Christine reached out for me. 'She is just so cute,' she said to my mother, as if congratulating her on a new dress. I stood obediently until she had finished petting me, though I was working up to my difficult child posture.

'I'm asking for water,' I mumbled, holding my hands behind my back.

'"Can I have some water, *please*?"' my mother corrected and I nodded.

'Do you know what I think we should do?' Christine said after she had fetched my water, which was cold and straight from the fridge. 'I want to take you out for lunch! Just a sec while I change.'

My mother leant back in the real leather sofa and sighed. Taking advantage of her mood, I crept up and sat beside her. There was only one place we could go for lunch of course, the Baobab Club. We both longed to go there, but my father said he had enough of the Boers all day long at the mine. The last thing he wanted to do was go and drink with them in the evenings, even though one of the managers had recently told him he had 'potential' and advised him to drink at the club and take up golf. My father probably just waggled his finger in and out of his ear in response, which wouldn't have gone down too well.

My mother agreed with his attitude, but the Baobab Club was her only chance of what she called 'a night out'. It cost quite a bit to become a member, much more than it did to use the pool, and if you weren't a member you couldn't go. Christine, of course, was already a member.

Christine reappeared after some time wearing a mini skirt and a tight T-shirt that I stared at in fascination, having only seen children wearing such an outfit. She dangled her car keys in the air and off we went. She drove like a woman possessed, turning her head one way to talk to my mother, and steering with the hand that wasn't holding a cigarette. As we drove through the small township she waved to people she seemed to know already.

In a storm of dust we drove up the driveway to the Baobab Club and screeched to a halt. The club – it was my first time to see it up close – was a large, oval building beautifully thatched with a stone porch running all the way around. Tiny new trees had been planted outside and two men were engaged in building what looked like a giant heart from painted stones. Not a real heart, of course, but what my mother called a 'love heart'.

Christine strode in and looked around for servers.

'Harold!' she cried to an elderly man, who came through one of the doors leading out to the porch. Harold did a sort of small bow. 'Madam, good morning.'

'Yes, yes, good morning,' Christine replied.

'And how are you?' Harold said. He wasn't going to be distracted from completing some sort of proper greeting.

'Fine, fine . . .'

'And I am also fine.'

'We want a table for lunch, Harold,' Christine interrupted, getting to the point. 'We'll just have some sandwiches, I think?' She raised her eyebrows at my mother to see if she had anything to add. My mother was looking down to avoid Harold's eyes.

'Perhaps you'd like to go and play on the swings . . .?' Christine suggested to me hopefully. 'What *is* her name again?'

'My name is Dimpho,' I offered, feeling bold.

'Oh, gift, how nice,' Christine said and I could see my mother was surprised at Christine attempting to translate my name. It was strange about Christine, just as you were about to label her in some way she said something that threw you off line. I think in the beginning my mother just went along for the ride.

'Actually, it's *gifts*,' my mother said, but Christine was already leading us outside.

I was urged off to a grassy area where there were shiny new climbing-frames and suchlike donated by the mine. In the distance I could see a couple of white people walking slowly with sticks over their shoulders. Some small boys followed them clutching big bags. I learnt later that this was a game called golf where you spent several hours or even a whole day walking around the cleared bush hitting a ball into holes. White people in Jamestown had so much leisure time to entertain themselves in.

My mother and Christine settled themselves down at a table which Harold brought out from inside the club. They made a nice pair, my mother resting back on her chair laughing, her face smooth and open, her touch of lipstick fresh, listening to Christine who was leaning forward telling a story. I realized that I had not really seen my mother with a friend since we had left Oabona back in Lephane.

Afterwards as we went home I could sense that my mother was on a sort of high. She was playful with me and once home hummed as she did her domestic chores. She turned on the hi-fi, which my father always told her not to because she never handled it gently enough for his liking, and we danced around sweeping. Maybe that's why I like sweeping so much to this day. Unlike my mother who hated, but hated, all housework, I have always liked sweeping.

When my father came home that day, he too was in a good mood. It was probably a Friday because that was the only day he was cheerful, as if a great weight were about to be lifted from his shoulders.

'I got the dog,' he said, getting himself a beer from the kitchen – in those days he still drank beer – and he did a little dance in front of the cooler box. Because my mother liked things to be cold, coming as she did from a cold country, I always thought this a bit strange, we had a big blue and white cooler and we filled it once a week with ice that we bought from the bottle store.

'Dimpho, you hear? We're getting a dog,' my father repeated with a little dance. One of the nicest things I have ever seen is my father dancing, for he did it so rarely and it's a dance the way only people around Lephane do. His expression, permanently serious, was such an odd contrast to his dancing legs.

'What dog?' my mother called from the bathroom where she was washing clothes.

'Excuse me but weren't you the woman who wanted a dog?' my father mocked, and my mother laughed in a muffled way from the bathroom. It was true, she had wanted a dog. I was stiff with excitement and made myself not ask my father questions, as that was not befitting a child and if I interrupted I would learn nothing.

'So how was your day?' my father said, sitting down with his beer and putting a jazz tape on the hi-fi, and adding as he often did: 'This is Real African Music, and don't let those Americans tell you any different.' After a moment he muttered, 'Someone has been playing with this,' but my mother pretended she couldn't hear.

'We went to Christine's,' she said, coming into the living-room with wet hands.

'And?'

'And,' my mother laughed, 'we went to the Baobab Club. She took me and Dimpho out for lunch.'

'That was nice.'

'Mmm. Dimpho, what do you think of her?' She turned to me.

I shrugged in a fine imitation of my father.

Later a friend of my father's turned up with a puppy and announced proudly that it was a greyhound.

'It is not,' my mother hissed, but she didn't say it loudly because after all the friend was older than both my parents and she knew better than to contradict an elder. Instead we all thanked him and after the man had gone we took a closer look at the puppy. It was skinny, black and white, with outsized ears and feet and it was frantic for our approval. 'If that's a greyhound then I'm the Pope,' my mother said. Greyhounds were the dogs to have at that time. I'm not sure why, but it was understood they had them in South Africa and that they were therefore something special. So any skinny dog was a greyhound. My mother, who had always wanted a dog, was all for it coming into the house but my father was firm. 'It's not a child,' he said, 'it's a dog.' That reminded my mother again of her day with Christine and so she filled my father in on what had happened and all that she had done and seen. I stayed outside and taunted the puppy until it bit me.

Chapter Six

'Christine has invited us for dinner,' my mother announced one evening in June. She popped her head round the wall dividing the kitchen from the living-room to see how my father took this news. 'And she's given us this,' she added, holding up a tin-foil package.

'Mmm.'

'Is that all you have to say?' she prodded. My mother always liked someone's attention when she was talking to them.

'Mmm?' My father roused himself.

'Argh!' my mother yelled, standing in the doorway with the tin-foil package in her hand.

'I saw her on the way back from the pool today, then I went there for tea and she gave me this. You know, you should see her house, it really is something.'

'When?' my father asked grudgingly. As a rule he didn't speak much for the first few hours after he came home from work. In fact he didn't even remove his shoes for the first hour. And woe betide me if I bothered him.

'You mean when are we invited for dinner? Saturday night,' my mother said brightly because Saturday night meant something to her and it was usually on a Saturday night that she most moaned about life in Jamestown.

In Lephane, she told me, they had often gone out on a Saturday night. They went around visiting relatives like Bopadile and Oabona or occasionally to the safari lodge outside the village. In those days quite a few of the villagers went to the lodge because there weren't many tourists from overseas then and the people enjoyed themselves without bother. Sometimes my parents went to a bar in Lephane or to picnics, where, my mother tells me, my father always urged her not to dance, because if she did everyone would watch her. But in Jamestown there was nowhere to go except the Baobab Club.

'Well, I want to go,' my mother said warningly, which made my father laugh because my mother usually preferred other people to make her decisions for her if it involved going somewhere. She was always asking my father and me, 'Shall we go here? Shall we do this? What do *you* want to do?'

'But what shall we wear?' my father asked, bending down to carefully untie his shoelaces.

'Well, I thought . . .' my mother began before she realized he was joking and she retreated back into the kitchen where there was only room for one person.

My father got up. 'What's in that?' he asked pointing at the package my mother had placed on the living-room table.

'Biscuits,' my mother laughed from the kitchen. 'But it was nice of her,' she added and she came out of the kitchen to unwrap the tin-foil package. She handed me a biscuit.

'Food of the white people,' my father said, munching his way through several of them before wrapping the package up again.

'Here come the vultures,' my mother said half an hour later as my father and I squeezed into the kitchen to see what she was cooking.

My mother looked forward to dinner at the Fishes because it seems that's how social relationships go where she comes from. You meet someone, they invite you to tea and you become friends. Then you invite them to tea and you are invited to dinner, where you do a lot of drinking and sit around a table eating and talking and so forth. If it's a real occasion, then for some reason you end the meal by eating cheese. Then it's your turn and you must invite them back. If you don't invite them back, it could be considered very rude. My mother missed this sort of arrangement. In Botswana if you come to someone's house and they are eating, then of course the food will be divided up and you will be given some. An arrangement is hardly necessary for something so simple and straightforward. And of course you don't talk while you eat or your tongue will grow as long as a cow's, at least that's what my father always told me.

But my mother never really got the hang of our ways of hospitality, and if she went to someone's house and found them eating, she would apologize for coming at a bad time. When they offered her food, she would nearly always refuse, saying she wasn't hungry even if she were. This made people very puzzled, and sometimes rather offended. And they didn't think to press her until she finally accepted, the way people in England like to do.

And while I'm on the topic of eating, we Batswana don't mind too much about whether food is hot or not, but my mother would not touch anything she called 'luke warm'. In a household it is normal for the person doing the cooking to lay the food out on plates. If a person doesn't turn up, then you simply cover that plate with another one and wait until the food is wanted later. But my mother said that food that had been sitting around had germs. I was terrified when I first heard about these germs. She said that because of them cooked food that had cooled was dangerous.

'Do I look like I have suffered from this?' my father would ask and my mother would have to say no. But all the same she had this amazing ability to think she was always right in such matters. I don't know what made her believe she knew best but she was convinced that she did. She was always making snap judgements on things according to her ideas of good and bad. She would never hesitate, for example, to say a film she had once seen was rubbish, or that the way someone had decorated their house was tasteless. I inherited from her this absolute confidence in my own opinions. I found out later that this is not usual in a woman because we are expected to defer to a man first.

Usually if my parents went somewhere, which was rare, I would be sent next door to our neighbour Beauty. My mother and Beauty got on well because they left each other alone except when one could be of use to the other. In a different place perhaps they would have been friends, but working at the salt mine was such a disheartening job and people like Beauty were so tired when they came home that they just wanted to rest. And when Beauty and my mother did have conversations, it was all about how terrible the mine was, even though they were always promising each other not to talk about it any more.

There was also a cousin of Beauty's who had recently moved in next door, a man called Listen. 'Listen! Is that Listen I hear?' my mother used to say when she saw him and it never failed to make her laugh. Listen was quite amusing for us children, seeing as he was often drunk and would then tell us incredible stories, rivalled only by my father's mother.

She of course still lived in Lephane, so we didn't see her much at that time except for during my father's holidays, which were few and far between. At first we had returned to Lephane every month end to enable my father to give his mother and other relatives money. But this ritual had been broken because my father hadn't had a pay rise in eighteen months and the journey from Jamestown to Lephane was expensive. 'I am quite prepared to hitch,' my mother always said, which was the way most people travelled then, and it was safe and cheap, but for some reason my father didn't want us doing this. I think he thought it wasn't quite befitting for my mother to hitch.

The Saturday night that my parents had been invited out for dinner, Beauty was not around. She had gone with Thebe and Listen to a funeral, and because my mother didn't like leaving me alone I was taken along to the Fishes' house. In the afternoon my mother bathed and then dressed herself up, because, she said, there was such little opportunity to do so in this God-forsaken place. She also dressed up my father, who could look stunning when he put his mind, or hers, to it. He is a tall man, a little thin but graceful, and clothes hang nicely on him. He is measured in his movements and clothes never seem to crumple on him the way they do with me.

I put on a party dress that a relative in Lephane had given me for Christmas one year. It was my favourite – all white with a bow in front, a ribbon around the waist and little bits of lace around the sleeves and neck. I had grown too tall and the sleeves pinched, but I was in love with it. I had never been given a chance to wear it before, and when my mother saw me coming out of my room she was not amused.

'You're not wearing that, Dimpho,' she protested.

I scowled.

'Mompati, come and see what she's put on.'

'Yes it's very nice,' my father said, coming to have a look.

'It is not,' my mother said. 'Take it off. You can't wear that and who's going to clean it, anyway? Put those trousers on. It's going to get colder.'

We had quite a struggle until in the end I gave in.

We arrived at Christine's house and Butch, on seeing my father for the first time, went wild. So we hesitated at the reed fence Christine had just had constructed while Butch threw itself with great slobbering moans of longing against the gate. Finally we heard Christine's voice from inside the house yelling, 'Frank!' and then Frank appeared down the walkway. He chained up Butch and let us in.

Frank was not dressed for the occasion, if indeed it was an occasion, but wore only a pair of shorts. He had a flabby body the colour and texture of soap that didn't go at all with his face or what you would have guessed his body looked like without clothes, and I suppose it was all the drink he consumed. It was a habit with the white men in Jamestown that when they came home from work they stripped down to just a pair of shorts and then pottered around washing their company cars or playing in their gardens in

65

full view of anyone who walked past. This didn't go down well with my father, who thought you shouldn't really go around displaying yourself like that in public.

'Aha,' Frank smiled and closed the gate behind us. 'You do look lovely,' he said to me and I looked down, embarrassed. 'Come in, come in,' he said to us in his rather formal fashion. He clapped my father on the shoulder and obediently we followed him. On the concrete forecourt Frank stopped to point out a plant he said he had just put in and Christine appeared at the doorway waving my mother urgently to come in.

'Oh, you're here, Dimpho,' Christine said as she saw me. 'You couldn't get a babysitter? Shame, it must be difficult in this place. Anyway, come in, come in. Frank, you know Mompati, and this is his wife, Rose.'

My mother shook Frank's hand. My father had already given her his impressions of Frank, saying he behaved well at the mine and treated Batswana respectfully. But this had sometimes happened before: a new white man arrived, behaved well and then was co-opted by the other white people and realized that to get on at the mine, he had to belong to just one group of people.

Frank stood by the new plants with my father who made some genuine noises of appreciation because gardening was something both he and my mother loved doing. And, after all, it was extremely hard to get anything to grow in Jamestown.

Inside the house Christine, who had dressed for the occasion in an off-the-shoulder black dress, was rearranging some furniture and puffing with the effort. Snowy the inside dog was sitting defiantly in the corner and barked half-heartedly at me. My mother sat down at the opposite end of the room and Christine yelled, 'Frank!' because he was still outside.

'Yes, yes.' Frank ambled in smiling apologetically, whether for his wife or for himself it wasn't clear. Then he disappeared down one of the corridors and came back with a T-shirt on, the same grey as his hair, and he looked more presentable.

He went over to a beautiful wooden drinks cabinet and asked my parents what they would have, again in his formal sort of way. It's funny the way the English say, 'What will you have?' whereas we tend to say, 'What will you take?', especially considering that historically the English have been rather good at taking.

Frank had kept his English accent, but Christine sometimes broke into a South African accent and used expressions like, 'Is it?', 'Just now' and 'Agh, shame'. My father brightened up perceptibly at Frank's offer of a drink and the four of them settled down. Frank then offered a cigarette, which my father took politely.

'Sit well,' my father said to me as an aside, for I was perched uncertainly on the arm of the sofa.

Christine asked my mother if I would like a Coke. 'Perhaps she can go and play in our daughter's room . . .' she suggested, but my mother didn't make a move to send me out, she knew I was still too shy.

At first the talk was general. My mother admired the glasses they were drinking from and my father inquired politely about one of the landscape paintings on the wall. Then they got on to the subject of Jamestown and the mine. Christine was furious that they had only been given a high-cost house and not a 'special' high-cost house which the very top people got. Frank murmured that really what they had was fine, which earned him a smile from my mother.

There were other sources of Christine's fury too.

'They said it was a *town*!' she laughed. 'That it had shops and amenities and all that, ha! Call this a town!' And my mother agreed.

'They said they would fly us here to see the area first, but Frank was given the job before I had set a foot in the place,' Christine explained. There was a slight pause until Frank said, 'Your whisky,' and handed over what looked like a glass of Coke. Christine bristled almost imperceptibly as it appeared this was a little secret of hers.

After a while Christine ushered my mother into the kitchen to help and I followed. The men were left alone. Now my father will get on with anyone no matter who they are, as long as they are civil and seem good. And Frank did seem good, he was interested and gentle and soon brought my father out of what my mother some-times called 'his shell'. Frank made a few disparaging comments about the Boers at the mine and at the way things were being managed, and my father was not slow to voice his opinion on that. He was probably enjoying looking around at the things Frank had because he also wanted to have those things. He admired things that were expensive, always thinking that this meant they were the best, and even if he couldn't afford it, he wanted the best. For men I suppose they had a lot to talk about: they worked at the same place, they both liked electronic equipment and so on. Little more was required than this.

My mother meanwhile was instructed by Christine to prepare a salad. It seemed she had been invited over to help rather than be waited on, but obediently she set to work, though an evening out should have meant she didn't have to cook for once.

'I do admire you,' Christine said, struggling to cut up big chunks of beef while Snowy sat on the floor watching and panting slightly. I leant near the doorway and fiddled with the magnets Christine had on her fridge.

'Oh?' my mother asked.

'I mean it must have been very hard not speaking the language and everything. How *did* you live in Lephane? Did you have a nice house?'

'Yes,' my mother lied because that was the easiest answer, 'but the electricity often went.' She didn't mention the house she had first lived in, perhaps because she didn't want to complain or maybe because she didn't want to confirm Christine's belief that life in the 'real' Africa was rough and harsh. But she gave in to the temptation to pretend she had been, and still was, worse off than in fact she was. 'And I haven't seen a TV for years,' she said – a complaint she would never have made to a Motswana, but with Christine they were talking from similar backgrounds.

'My dear!' Christine laughed. 'You must come round and watch films with us. I have the latest film with . . .' and she was off listing which films she had and which people were in them and whether she liked them or not.

My mother got on with the salad.

'Does Mompati cook?' Christine asked.

'Oh yes,' my mother said.

'That's unusual, for a Batswanian to cook, isn't it? I mean African men are rather macho, aren't they?'

'It's not Batswanian, it's Motswana,' my mother said. 'Someone from Botswana is a Motswana.'

'Yes, please correct me, I do so want to learn.'

My mother smiled at Christine's humbleness. 'Yes, he can cook. I would say, actually . . .' – she hesitated – 'that men around here know domestic things. I mean as children, you know, they can cook and wash and so on, boys as well. And I really don't agree with this African men thing, I mean I don't think this is an *African* thing at all, and –'

'Really?' Christine said, not fully concentrating but slapping sauces on the meat.

'Frank!' she yelled, 'Get the braai started.'

'He is *useless*,' she said of her husband in a stage whisper, 'I suspect he can cook, he certainly says he can, but when you're married, why bother?'

'Exactly,' my mother said as she set out the salad. 'So it's not an African thing –'

'Well, that does look nice,' Christine interrupted, covering the salad and heading for the fridge that was so large it took up one whole corner of the kitchen. I moved quickly out of the way.

'It is nice to have a fridge,' my mother said a trifle enviously.

We all gathered on the newly expanded patio outside. 'Beautiful part of the world,' Frank said as he sat down and surveyed the cool June sunset before us. It was winter already and the days though sunny were cold. The bush around Jamestown was dying and night came early.

'Yes, isn't it a beautiful sunset?' Christine said.

My father wiggled his finger in and out of his ear because this was a bone of contention between him and my mother, and he constantly mocked her approval of sunsets. Frank got up to fetch some beer and my father, who finds it hard to restrain himself from taking charge when meat is being prepared, stood up to get the fire going on the Fishes' shiny new braai stand.

Christine put down a tray of snacks on the large wooden table. 'Don't stand on ceremony, help yourself,' she urged and eagerly my mother and I leaned forward.

'Oh, god, Christine,' my mother cried, 'where on earth did you get *prawns*?' and she picked one up, cracked its skin and lovingly popped it into her mouth. Then she peeled one for me. I pulled a face as the meat went down. 'All the more for us,' my mother said happily and asked my father if he wanted a prawn.

He shook his head with a look of disgust and I examined the prawns with dismay, pink leggy creatures with a pungent smell.

'Have you ever tried these Mophane worms the locals eat?' Christine asked.

'Yes,' my mother said.

'And?'

'Oh, well, they were just crunchy, really.'

'Imagine eating worms!' Christine laughed.

'Actually,' my father joined in now, 'you do know that prawns are related to cockroaches?'

Christine gave a peel of laughter.

'Now tell us all about Lephane,' she ordered and, before my mother could answer, continued, 'Elephants, for example – have you seen many? Of course, we've seen everything in the game parks down in South Africa, but in Botswana it's rather different, isn't it?'

'Oh, yes,' my mother said and she started one of her animal stories.

I think the arrival of Christine and Frank made her aware of how much she was settled in Botswana. Her role was to sort of initiate them, and Frank at least was extremely good at paying attention, or at least appearing to, which my father on the whole was not.

'The first time I saw an elephant,' my mother began as Frank leaned forward to listen, 'it charged us.'

Christine laughed, excited. 'Do tell.'

'Well . . .' – my mother settled down, she loved to have some attention – 'we were on the way to Moremi . . .'

Christine and Frank listened attentively. Though they had seen plenty of animals during their ten years in the region, these were mostly in small game parks, while in the early 1980s Botswana was just becoming known for having lots of animals and lots of space to see them in. The fact that we had such a small human population and such a big country meant tourists could come and see our animals without having to see each other or meet the people. And like a lot of expatriates Christine and Frank Fish cared more about our wild animals than us. I have rarely heard of a white expatriate setting up anything to relieve our poverty, unless perhaps they work for some aid agency, but when wild animals are in danger they can move mountains.

Before my mother had quite finished her story, Christine had gone back into the house. She was forever moving round, and now she yelled 'Frank!' for him to come inside. 'There's a woman out there rattling the gate,' she said standing at the patio door.

'Oh,' said Frank.

'You think she's a maid?'

'On a Saturday night?'

'Yes on a Saturday night. Go and see what she wants.'

So Frank, giving my parents a long-suffering look, went off round to the front of the house. Christine disappeared back inside.

'Isn't the garden lovely, Dimpho?' my mother asked, sighing and stretching out her legs.

I nodded that it was.

'We now have a maid!' Christine said triumphantly as she came back to the patio shortly afterwards.

My father waggled his finger in and out of his ear, he didn't agree with the idea of maids.

'Of course I don't really *want* a maid,' Christine said, sensing some disapproval, 'but Frank insists. And,' Christine continued, still not getting any response from my parents, 'at least then we provide a job, don't we?' Still getting no response, she added, 'Do you have a maid, Rose?'

My mother laughed. 'No, and we don't want one.'

'Oh?'

'We are perfectly able to wash our own floors and our own underwear,' my father said rather pompously.

Christine giggled as if he had said something very funny or very rude.

'*We?*' my mother asked, but my father didn't rise to the bait.

'I agree absolutely,' Christine said suddenly, 'but I just can't do everything, all the upkeep of the house, when what I want to do is start a business.'

'Oh, yes?' My father sounded interested, he was always on about how he was going to start his own business and the idea probably occurred to him that here were some people with money who might be prepared to spend it.

But Frank broke the train of talk when he reappeared with a small bone in his hand. 'Just found this out front,' he said, holding it up like a quasi-scientist demonstrating soap powder on TV.

Christine lit a cigarette.

'It was buried and I just happened to unearth it with my foot.'

'Yes our puppy buries bones all the time,' my mother said.

'Oh, no!' Christine cut in. 'We don't give Butch bones. He chokes on them, you see. How very strange. I *told* that gardener to clean up all the rubbish.'

My father laughed at the idea of a dog like Butch not being

given bones, he was already throwing bones to our puppy. Then he put his head down to lay the pieces of meat lovingly on the fire.

'We're being bewitched, then, a spot of black magic?' Frank offered and Christine gave a wild little giggle.

'I wish someone would bewitch my father,' she said. 'A plane crash would do. He has announced he's coming here to visit us.' She turned to my mother: 'Imagine!'

My mother gathered that there was no love lost between Christine and her father, and perhaps she warmed to Christine because she herself wouldn't have dared be so explicit, at least not in public, about her father, whom she similarly despised.

The meat was soon ready and Christine instructed my mother to go inside and help her bring out the plates and salad and so forth. Christine liked to divide jobs according to sex and my mother found it hard to refuse. Christine had a way of bustling people around. All she had to say was, 'Shall we girls get the utensils?' for my mother to reluctantly follow. My mother strongly believed that when you were a guest you had to be polite and being polite meant not causing waves.

We continued to sit outside though night had fallen and it was getting cold. Frank put on the patio lights and flying creatures threw themselves up against the glowing bulbs. Above us the Southern sky stretched clear and magnificent and no sooner had you counted some stars than more appeared.

Christine and Frank chatted away, while my father, sitting down for once, ate his meat with relish and in silence. Christine had brought out some wine, and I noticed my mother drinking several glasses. Her face became slightly flushed, her movements freer and her voice louder. I scowled, I didn't like her like that. Butch meanwhile had been allowed out of its watchman's hut to join the fun and it lay like a huge cow on the patio, permitting Christine to drop choice, lean morsels of beef into its great slobbering mouth. My father looked away, he couldn't bear to see animals being spoiled.

My parents and I left soon after we had finished eating, I was half asleep and my father had something or other to do early the next day. With her stomach full of 'good' food and her head light from the wine and the promise of videos and washing machines, my mother seemed happy enough. Though she didn't exactly pine for material things, I think she was looking forward to using all the fancy pieces of equipment that Christine had. We walked the short distance to our own little home, just round the corner from the street lights and the barking dogs of the high-cost houses.

I heard my parents that night giggling over their evening. From listening to them the next day, it was unclear whether they actually liked their new friends. They loved to discuss people, and Christine and Frank kept them going most of Sunday. My father said they must have money and wondered what sort of business they were thinking of setting up.

Sunday was the quietest day of the week in Jamestown. In the late morning people could be seen out and about, going to the shop in the trailer to buy half-frozen meat and yellowing cabbages for Sunday lunch or heading off to a church meeting in the bush. But by midday everyone retreated inside their houses or yards and the men slept off their Sunday drinking or perhaps washed their cars. In the late afternoon people began moving sluggishly around again. Football games would begin in a clearing in the bush, where young men ran around with the ball and slightly older men parked their pick-ups in the shade, sat in the back and drank more beer. Beauty usually turned on her music on a Sunday afternoon and my father would hum along to the Country and Western songs she liked to play.

'Stand by your man ...' my father would stand outside and croon.

'Oh, please!' my mother would yell from the kitchen window.

'Oh, well,' my mother said finally that Sunday evening, 'they're not that bad, are they? And it will be nice to use the washing machine. What a relief that will be.' She looked at my father and me accusingly.

'As long as we don't have to go round there all the time,' my father said, protesting as my mother took his plate away before he had quite finished eating.

'Who said we have to go round there all the time? And I didn't notice you complaining last night,' my mother said sharply. She gave me the last of the biscuits Christine had given her before and I went outside to relish the food of the white people, which like the clothes and cars of the white people was something to aim for. If we want to describe how lavish something is, we just say it's a white people thing.

Next day my mother bundled up all our washing and we walked with it over to Christine's house. Christine was lounging in a silk dressing-gown on the sofa complaining of a headache, but she soon came to life. As my mother was to discover, for all her rushing around and plans to start a business, Christine rarely left her house.

'Thank you for the other night,' my mother said politely. She had been well brought up as she was always telling me, and being well brought up over there in England seems to mean saying 'Please' and 'Thank you' all the time regardless of whether you are grabbing something or lying. I can be bitter, just like my father, when I want. He may have seemed an easy-going man, but when he wanted to characterize a group of people, be they British, American or South African, he made no hesitation in doing so.

Christine showed my mother how to work the washing machine which she kept in her servant's quarters. 'Do you know what this was like when we first moved in?' she asked, waving her cigarette round the small house. 'The place was knee-deep in dog shit.'

'No!'

'Yes, whoever stayed here before, well, he didn't want dog shit on the lawn so he made his dogs shit on the floor in here.'

My mother made a face.

'I mean, did he really expect a human could live here afterwards?' Christine asked and my mother nodded furiously.

'So I told those housing people to clean it all up,' Christine said as she led us back to the main house.

Christine said she was going to have a bath and did my mother mind but could she look after herself for a while. My mother obviously felt she couldn't exactly leave now we had put our clothes in the machine, so we went into the house to wait. Inside the kitchen we were surprised to see a young woman busy washing down the walls. Embarrassed, my mother greeted her and then began backing out.

'Joy!' Christine yelled from somewhere in the house, 'I thought I told you to – oh!' She was marching into the kitchen when she remembered my mother was there. 'You've met Joy, our new maid, Rose?'

'Yes, we just met,' my mother said.

'Joy,' Christine began again, wheedling now, talking to her maid as if telling a very small child some crucial instructions they must understand, 'Could-you-please-hoover-the-floors-in-the-children's-bedrooms?' and not waiting for an answer, Christine hurried out with a quick smile over her shoulder to my mother.

My mother stood there looking unsure. I don't think she wanted to be identified with Christine in this manner. So she chatted to Joy as best she could and waited for the washing to finish, much as she finished her own chores at home and waited for my father to return.

'Joy!' Christine yelled again. 'Get the madam a drink.'

'I'll get it myself,' my mother yelled back after she realized it was her that was the madam. Joy continued washing the stainless white walls and I stood quietly watching her.

Chapter Seven

Later that day my mother and I came back home with our clean washing. My mother told my father that she wasn't going to Christine's again because she had been called a madam.

'That won't be any great hardship,' my father said.

'Oh, come on,' my mother immediately changed tack, 'she's not that bad, I feel rather sorry for her in a way, and just look at the colour of these trousers,' and my mother held up my father's clean washed clothes.

But my father had other things on his mind – in other words, work. He still hadn't had a pay rise, the management training he had been promised hadn't materialized and he had all manner of tales of corruption to tell.

For some reason my mother would usher me out of the room when he started talking about the mine because, I suppose, she knew I listened very carefully to everything going on around me, although my father didn't seem to think I was paying attention. Perhaps it was because when he was a child he wouldn't have been allowed to interrupt his elders or ask questions. But I was increasingly beginning to ask questions, and it was something that for the most part my mother encouraged.

At that time I would have been about five years old, I was speaking a mixture of English and Setswana and when I tried to speak in just one language I usually picked the wrong one. I had already spoken to Christine, for example, in Setswana and didn't quite believe that she couldn't understand me. As I grew up and later when I attended school, I used English almost all day long and I regularly dreamt in English too. I remember one night in Jamestown, when I woke myself up shouting in English.

Later at secondary school I failed miserably in Setswana, it was the reading and writing I couldn't do. But most of us at school did badly in Setswana, perhaps because what we speak is often so different from what has been written down for us to learn and be examined in.

At home my father spoke English to my mother and Setswana to me. At the mine he spoke both languages interchangeably. After his years in America he spoke English perfectly, the only give-away being just that – he spoke it too perfectly. At least, this was the sort of English he spoke to expatriates. To Batswana he spoke another type of English – that is, he pronounced the words in a different way and sometimes put them in a different order.

My father hated working at the mine. His face would grow stony as he prepared to leave in the mornings and our puppy, who hadn't yet been named, would whine in sympathy and shiver in the cold as the gate was opened and my father drove off. The mine itself was about ten kilometres from Jamestown and the tarred road travelled through sandy plain and bush. People on their way to work in the company buses, which were in fact converted cargo trucks, sometimes passed wildebeest or ostriches on the way to and from their shifts.

My father had his own car, but he was never resented because he was always giving lifts. In the morning a little crowd would gather outside our house and then pretend to be strolling by and stop to ask for a ride to work when my father drove out of our yard. My father actually hated giving lifts because often he would be asked to stop in at so and so on the way and pick up this or that, and before he knew he was heading way out of his way. Sometimes we Batswana have an attitude that the world owes us a favour.

The South African managers all had their own company cars and car allowances that enabled them to avoid having to travel with the peasants. They never stopped. If they passed a black person look-ing for a lift, they would speed up and glance the other way.

Although my father had a medium-cost house and a car, he was known for not taking any shit from the Boers, who almost to a man distrusted and even hated him. Unlike what I have seen of American people, for example, who can turn a smile off and on at demand, we Batswana don't smile as a rule unless there's some-thing to smile about. And working at the salt mine run by the Boers meant there wasn't usually anything to smile about.

So among many of the managers my father got a reputation for being bad-tempered. He told us that the managers would say, 'Cheer up, Mompati,' as they breezed in and out of his office. 'What's wrong with *you*?' they would ask. I suppose it made them uncomfortable not to be smiled at. They had no idea my father could be playful if he chose.

God knows what my father actually did all day at the mine, but it tired him out. I suppose he kept track of the amount of money going in and out, which would seem to be a pretty important thing to do. I carefully followed the conversations my parents had about whether he would be trained to be a manager as had been promised when he was taken on. My mother, very clear-minded on some things, told him repeatedly that he would never be manager, that the Boers would simply never allow it. And this was part of the reason why they toyed with ideas of starting their own business. My father, I think, would have considered it a defeat if he had simply returned to Lephane.

The mine itself, although 'mine' is a misnomer as people didn't work underground, was there to produce salt. It was then sold to South Africa, but there was stiff competition and things weren't going well. For some obscure reason Botswana bought its own salt from South Africa and that was just one way that the mine was of almost no benefit to our country. The government, who owned a big share, said that the project provided jobs, but, as I've said, those jobs were hardly anything to write home about.

One time I went to the mine at night because my father had to collect something or other. We drove along the tar road lit up by a winter moon and suddenly in the flat distance the mine buildings threw themselves up from the land, illuminated and humming like a boat on a huge dark ocean.

Another time I went with my father on a tour of the mine. He worked in the office section where white men strode around purposefully with walkie-talkies on their hips and instructed their secretaries to make coffee. Because he worked in the offices, at first he knew very little about what went on outside.

The salt pans that surrounded the mine were vast – whole fields of salt that gave an inch when you walked on them. I remember my father telling me that these fields were like snow, that when he had been in America it had snowed in the winter, which is when it is summer here, and that the roads were often covered in ice, just as the roads around the mine were covered in salt. As the midday sun bounced off the pans it almost hurt to look around and there was an eerie atmosphere because the workers, the conveyor belts and the pipes, and everything but everything were all dusted in white.

The water we got in Jamestown was salty too, but the powers that be spent a lot of energy denying that it was harmful. The expatriates drove two hundred kilometres to Thabeng to get their water, and sometimes they even bought it from the bottle store.

Even now there are those who cling to the theory that there's nothing wrong with the water in Jamestown, and indeed it has improved over the years. But back then the township clinic did a roaring trade in people with stomach problems from the water and eye problems from the dust.

That time my father showed me round the mine, we popped our heads round the control-room door, where six white men lounged in front of huge screens chatting to each other and smoking cigarettes. It was here presumably that they organized their golf games and their drinking sessions and criticized the Batswana for being lazy and never coming to work on time.

Like some of the other mines in the country, we had little control of the profits or the share our country received. Instead we trusted the British and the South Africans to decide for us how much our resources were worth. Why trust these people who were plundering our natural resources? This was the sort of question my father would ask of an evening as he held court outside by the winter fire when his friends dropped by. His friends, some of whom were distant relatives, often came to ask his advice and to try out my mother's cooking. He would smile as they took the plates they were given and looked with surprise at the half-cooked vegetables my mother offered.

The problem with the mine, as I see it now, was expectations. When our government told us it was opening a salt mine, we expected to benefit. What we didn't expect was that we wouldn't be in charge and that those who were in charge would go around so blatantly feathering their nests. The Boers and the other white people were usually not qualified or experienced in their jobs and it often seemed that we were getting the dregs from South Africa. How they kept on getting work permits I have no idea.

The Batswana were eager to work, to be trained and to get a good life, but we were being denied the opportunity. So we had to sit back and watch the Boers driving round in their new cars and building swimming-pools in their new houses and hiring us to do their dirty work. On top of that, the mine was not making any money and already the government had had to put in millions to keep it going. While the management said they couldn't afford to increase everybody's salary, they bought themselves company cars. Then they would hold a meeting for the Batswana in each department, give out free booze and award little certificates for good behaviour. As if to say, 'There now, that should shut them up.'

The mine had two sets of rules, one for white people and one for black. If, for example, a Motswana was ill for the day, he or she would return to work to find a warning notice. But if a Boer took a few days off, no one said a word. A Motswana found drunk at work would be immediately fired, while a Boer would be bundled home by his friends to sleep it off. The Boers acted as if Jamestown was *their* town, with a primary school for their children and a club for them to drink and eat at. Which raises a question I thought of only the other day – who on earth was James, anyway?

My mother, as far as I know, never visited the mine until the month we left Jamestown, but she knew the other side of things – of what the women left back in the town did with themselves. Even at that time the constant topic of talk was whether or not the men were going to get a raise, be allowed more overtime and, more importantly, whether or not the mine was going to close.

The white women who were there to provide comfort at home were bored out of their minds. They didn't like Jamestown and they didn't much like each other. From the way my mother tells it, they were like schoolchildren, back-stabbing and constantly breaking up and reforming into new groups.

The Batswana women did their domestic chores and then a lot of them did domestic chores for the white people too. Some liked being at the beginning of what was promised would be a proper town someday. Those who already came from small towns found it peaceful and they thought they would be able to save money, seeing as the only things you could buy in Jamestown were the most basic items, although these were vastly overpriced. Those who could afford to made monthly trips to Thabeng, where the real shops were. But most people had to make do with the small shop in the trailer. The shop employees spent a lot of time wrapping up things like tomatoes in little packets making sure to put the rotten ones at the bottom so you didn't see them until you got home and opened the package up. They also spent a lot of time going round the half-empty wooden shelves writing individual prices on each squash, orange or apple with a black pen. I remember my mother being furious when I once spent the morning going through our kitchen writing made-up prices on all our food.

Attempts to open other shops always failed because the rents were so high, and there was no land available on which to build your own shop. There was briefly a hair salon in Jamestown, for example. Big posters advertised 'Gents White Hair' and said 'Come One Come All!' but the white people never had their hair done there and soon it closed. There were no clothing shops, so again you had to travel far away, if you were able, to buy a school uniform or jumpers for winter. For someone like Christine, who was used to shopping, there was nowhere to go and nothing to buy. Her problem was not saving but finding things to spend all her money on.

While there were no shops to go to, there were various church groups which flourished in Jamestown. So though you couldn't buy nice tomatoes or clothing, you could praise the Lord. The church group the white people went to was held in a hall near the Baobab Club, the rest of Jamestown just met in the bush as no permanent structure was built for at least a year. In the evenings you could hear the church people singing, and most of the followers were women. But it was the men of the Zionist Christian Church that my friends and I loved to watch. They wore pale brown suits and some carried knobkerries. They would stomp up and down on a Sunday morning in a clearing in the bush and then march back home through the empty streets of the township.

My mother, as I've said, stayed at home and did her domestic jobs with bad grace. Having always had carpets and hoovers and washing machines and dishwashers when she was growing up in England, it had taken her a while to adapt. I have a clear image of her standing in our bath in our house in Jamestown treading, or rather jumping up and down on, our dirty washing with a look of fury on her face. It was my father who enjoyed and was good at work in the house, when he got round to doing it, and it's a shame that he had to be the breadwinner because he would have run the house very smoothly. In a perfect world he would have remained at home while my mother went out to work.

My mother tried for over a year to get a teaching job at the recently opened primary school in Jamestown. Then she even tried for a job at a secondary school about a hundred kilometres away in a village called Kgadi, but every reply from the ministry in the south said, 'Your application is under consideration.' Then, as now, there were few trained Batswana teachers, at least not nearly as many as were needed. And no one wanted to be posted to Jamestown, not after having seen the place – and here was my mother all eager again to teach and already living in the township. But the government did not seem to be bothered that it was opening so many schools when there weren't enough people to teach in them.

My mother relayed these employment troubles to Christine, who had said she was a teacher too. Like many of the white women in Jamestown, Christine had left paid employment to follow her husband to a country where officially she was not allowed to work. Jamestown was full of women, expatriate and Batswana, trying to earn a living on the side. Batswana went down to South Africa and came back with clothes and shoes and perfume to sell. The white women went to newly independent Zimbabwe and came back with household things to sell. Every now and again the housing people made a swoop on the white women busy turning their homes into little industries, but of course this didn't stop them at all. Christine had several such plans and was very interested in whether my mother, as the wife of a Motswana, could get away with having a business. This is still a common ploy expatriates use. They get a Motswana to lend their name to an enterprise so as to receive loans and other help from the government.

Chapter Eight

After our evening at the Fishes' house we sometimes 'popped round', as my mother put it, to see Christine. She always welcomed my mother like a long-lost friend.

'Oh, Christine, you shouldn't have,' my mother would say as Christine offered freshly ground coffee, smoked salmon and cucumber sandwiches, the coffee beans and fish flown up from South Africa on the company plane.

Christine seemed to spend her days thinking up business schemes and improvements for her house, and she was already exhausted by trying to establish the kind of life she thought she and her husband should be leading. She managed – and this is one example of her amount of push – to get a telephone installed within only a few months, though she had no one really to ring except some people back in South Africa and Frank at work.

'This is Mrs Fish. Put me through to my husband, please,' she would say when she rang the mine. My mother was embarrassed to discover that Christine did not know that Frank had a private line and instead always went through the switchboard. Christine repeatedly urged my mother to apply for a phone so that she could call her too.

My father rarely saw Frank at work, which is probably why they remained friends for as long as they did. Frank was in charge of stores which meant he had considerable power when it came to supplies and sometimes he let a car part go to my father for a fraction of the cost. Frank had heard what a whiz my father was in accounts and asked him to teach his two children maths when they came to Jamestown for their school holidays. My father agreed to teach them what he could, though the winter holidays were a few weeks away. Frank confided that his son was about to fail his exams and needed all the help he could get.

'Have you told him it'll cost him?' my mother asked when my father told her this piece of news, because she was always on the look-out for him being ripped off, and they could do with any money they could get. But my mother was better at giving advice than taking it and she was just as likely to do something for free herself. She couldn't bring herself to ask Frank to pay, but she wanted my father to.

'So, have you told him?' she asked.

'Yes.'

'You've told him?'

'Well, not exactly . . .'

'Mompati!'

'I know, I know, it is something I will do, I'll work out how much to charge him.'

'You do that. And, anyway, I thought you said Frank was a teacher himself?'

'That's what he said. He said he was a headmaster at a school in Rhodesia.'

'Oh, really? Christine said it was a school in South Africa.'

Once a decision had been made, my mother was all for acting immediately. No time like the present, she always told me when I was resisting doing something. To my mother it was more or less a crime to be Doing Nothing. Doing nothing meant not being Active, meant just sitting and resting or sitting and thinking, both of which I was extremely good at. So if my father said he was going to do something, she always tried to get him to do it straight away. But we Batswana are careful people and don't like to be rushed.

The conversation about teaching the Fishes' children ended when my father suddenly remembered that his brother, Bopadile, was coming to Jamestown. My mother was worried about where he would sleep and so on. 'But why didn't you *tell* me?' she wailed.

'I am telling you,' my father said patiently. He never came home and told us news immediately, he always waited until he was settled first.

'So when's he coming?'

'Mmm?'

'And how long's he staying?'

My father shrugged. If someone said they were coming to visit you, the last thing you would do is ask them how long they were staying.

I adored my uncle Bopadile. He had an air of excitement about him. Whereas my father was reserved and could sit for a long time stroking his chin and thinking, Bopadile was always on the go. And he always seemed to be dirty, with dust in his hair and car oil on his hands, which with my mother's mania for being clean was excitement in itself. Bopadile, who had been working for a brick-making company in Lephane, was coming to Jamestown to look for a job. This much my mother managed to get out of my father.

Like many people, Bopadile was under the impression that something exciting was happening in Jamestown and he wanted a piece of the action. But most people found out this wasn't easy and, after a fruitless few months, they packed up and went off somewhere else. None of us thought Bopadile would stay, because even if he did get a job he never liked to stay in one place for very long. He was one of those people who had many skills, none of which could ever be put to full use, so he hopped from one type of job to another, but always getting on with everyone.

Though white people often mistook them for each other, Bopadile was a few years younger than my father, shorter and with a lighter complexion. While my father was careful with his plans, Bopadile was impetuous and wanted to make money NOW. He looked up to my father, because he was older, because he had been to America, had a white wife, a car and what appeared to be a nice job. But he also used my father, thinking that because he was his brother it was acceptable to take advantage when he could.

After that first evening at the Fishes' and once we had used their washing machine and 'popped over' a couple of times, we didn't see Christine or Frank for a little while. Frank appeared to be working long hours at the mine, though not as long as my father, and Christine was in a frenzy of what she called 'getting the house ready for the children'. You would have thought royalty was visiting the way she fussed on, and 'the children' took on mysterious proportions in my eyes. Christine was convinced that they would be bored in Jamestown and she was determined to show them a good time.

Meanwhile, we had Bopadile to contend with. One winter weekday evening he came whistling up our driveway with a bag over his shoulder and a big smile on his face. We all rushed out to greet him.

'Whosit!' Bopadile said, laughing and shaking my parents' hands. Unlike my father, Bopadile used expressions gleaned from being at heart a city boy and from having worked for a year in South Africa.

My mother asked him how he was and told him to come in.

'Sharp!' Bopadile beamed.

He was one of the few of my father's relatives who my mother didn't mind providing for at all. 'He might be a bad apple, but he gives as much as he receives,' she would say. I think she enjoyed having him around because unlike my father he was chatty and a social animal. People who knew him had the habit of saying, 'Oh, Bopadile!' with affection but exasperation as well.

Bopadile settled himself into our servant's quarters which my mother had made me help her clean up, though it had never really been dirty. Of course it wasn't exactly a servant's quarters, but she had fixed a small table and a curtain for the window and put all the necessaries in the toilet. For the first week or so Bopadile went off with my father in the morning to the mine to see what he could get in the way of work. Then in the afternoon they came home together, allies against the Boers.

'They have arrived,' I would say each day as I heard my father's car outside. Then Bopadile would spring out, open the gate and usher my father through with a wave of his hand.

'Whosit!' he would say to me and tweak my ear or pull my nose as he went by. For some reason, annoying as the tweaking and pulling was, I could never maintain my Difficult Child pose with Bopadile. If you sulked, he appeared not to notice and went happily on with what he was doing.

'Nice shoes,' my mother said one day when Bopadile came home.

He looked down at his shiny leather mine boots with pleasure.

'Where did you get them?'

'The mine.'

'Well, I know that. I mean how did you get them? Have you got a job yet?'

Bopadile just laughed. 'That smells nice,' he said, peering around the kitchen. My mother flicked him with a tea towel until he went outside.

That was the thing with Bopadile, he was always turning up with things and no one could ever work out where he had got them from.

Once or twice my mother and Bopadile went to the Baobab Club together, while my father looked after me. Although you had to be a member of the club even to get a glass of water at the bar, this wasn't a problem for Bopadile. Within a week he had made friends with people throughout the township and was already managing to get free food at the mine even though he didn't work there. By the second week he had made friends with all the people who worked at the Baobab Club, and one Sunday he presented my father and mother with two roasted chickens and a box of strawberries which he insisted were 'left over' from the Boers' Sunday lunch at the club.

The first time my mother and Bopadile went to the club together it was because Bopadile had heard a little party was going on, and somehow or other he had wangled an invitation. My mother spent the afternoon dressing up, applying her make-up and changing in and out of her three or four dresses. I rushed into my bedroom and put on my white silk-ribboned party dress but my mother was having none of it. When she told me I couldn't come, I sulked for the rest of the afternoon.

Bopadile emerged from our servant's quarters in an array of finery. He wore shiny new leather shoes, green trousers with sharp creases down the front, and a yellow shirt with the top few buttons undone. He paused in front of the kitchen window to admire himself.

'Are you sure you won't come?' my mother asked my father, who was lying on the sofa peacefully listening to a jazz tape. I don't know why she asked him because it had all been arranged that he would stay and look after me.

'Mmm?' My father raised his head slightly.

'Right you are. See you later, then,' she said and off they went.

Bopadile was also an enthusiastic cook and, as long as my mother pointed him to the kitchen and provided the ingredients, he would cook up a storm. But then, as is the habit with many men, he wanted a round of applause for his efforts and he left the kitchen as if a bomb had hit it. My mother would then have to clean it up. My father would insist that it was me who should clean it up, as I was a child.

My parents had some fallings-out on how to raise children. I think my father, who had been brought up as a well-behaved Motswana child, wanted his turn to be an elder and reap the benefits that position gave. After all, he had been ordered around for so many years on the understanding that once he was an elder the tables would be turned. So it annoyed him to see my mother apparently coddle me, and he believed that, as with dogs, a good slap was the best way to teach a lesson.

My mother was livid if she saw him hit me. When he did – usually when she wasn't around – I would retreat to an area of sand under our one paw-paw tree and play with my old tea box of treasures – scraps of material which I would take out carefully, smooth out, then fold up and put back again. This kept me busy for hours. My father approved of this activity because it kept me outside and quiet, and he often said the best toy for a child was a cardboard box.

My mother never hit me. She said in England people didn't hit their children, which of course is a lie. I can't say my father or my grandmother hitting me ever did me any harm, because I was bred in part to believe it was a way to get respect, and I certainly respected my father and grandmother. At secondary school we played up the teachers who didn't hit us, but there were few of them. I find it hard to sort this out in my mind now I know that in other countries teachers are not supposed to hit their pupils; it's worrying that our notion of respect involves violence, especially considering that until recently we were such a peaceful country.

Nowadays I don't think you can justify hitting a child, or anyone for that matter, but I didn't think any the worse of my father or grandmother for having given me the occasional thrashing. My grandmother would even boast about how great a beating she had given someone and would have me laughing with pleasure at tales of beatings she had given my father when he was a small boy. 'Now I'm not going to buy you a train when I grow up!' my father would cry when his mother beat him.

Once my parents' different ideas of punishment came to a head when I went off to play although they had told me not to leave the house. My mother had gone to the shop and my father was fetching firewood. I went next door to see Thebe. She wasn't at home and I roamed around the small area of bush behind our house looking for her. When my parents came back to find the door open and the house empty, they were very angry. But when my mother said, 'Right, no supper for you,' my father was outraged.

'How can you deny a child *food*?' he said. So they spent the whole evening arguing over how a child should be disciplined and quite forgot to punish me.

Because Bopadile brought a bit of fun to the house, my mother didn't begrudge looking after him and she even gave him money when he asked for it. Although she was in theory very careful with money and was always on the look-out to make more, she could be extremely gullible when it came to people borrowing, because she just couldn't say no and her way of saying no was never understood.

At the school in Lephane my mother had been known as a push-over and people from the school – the secretary, the gardener and so on – used to come to her house and say, 'Madam, I'm asking for money.' My mother, feeling guilty that she didn't have to go borrowing money, would hand it over. Then she would be surprised when she never got it back. So the next time someone asked for money, she would say, 'Well, I'm afraid I don't have much at the moment,' as if that would make them go away. Instead they just stood there until she finally found some.

My father soon put a stop to this, saying people were taking advantage of her and she was a fool to continue to be used. 'Who is the idiot here?' he would cry, 'the one who is borrowing or the one who is lending?' But my mother was never quite convinced, and as they both had this weakness when it came to lending it was slightly comic the way they tried to reform each other. He would tell her off for lending to the gardener and then give half his wages to a relative. This he defended because it was family.

After Bopadile had been staying with us for a couple of weeks, one day, unbeknown to my father, Listen from next door came round to ask for money. Listen, like Bopadile, had come to Jamestown looking for work and had ended up living with his cousin Beauty, trying to get odd jobs so he could go out and drink. He was very respectful when he greeted people and had a slightly hunched way of walking that suggested he was about to ask something from you. Which he usually was.

When he spoke English, it was flowery and complicated. He had gone to school down in Thabeng, enjoyed his courses but failed his leaving exams. He looked around and realized there was nothing for him to do but to go back to the family and be a farmer. This seemed like a great humiliation. The promises that education would give him a good job had been revealed as a cruel joke, a joke that would grow crueller as the years went by. He kept up his English, however, and improved it by reading the government newspaper that reported officials' speeches in the type of English he aspired to. Yet the fact that a word even slightly mispronounced is impossible to understand meant my mother couldn't always understand him. This embarrassed her and she would nod in agreement when really she wasn't following at all.

This time Listen stood outside on the road and rattled our gate a few times until my mother left what she was doing and went outside.

'Dumela, mma,' Listen said respectfully, leaning on the gate.

'Dumela, rra, o tsogile jang?' my mother replied. If there was one thing she knew to perfection it was greetings.

'Ee, ke tsogile sentle, mma,' Listen said and he waited until my mother pushed our puppy out of the way and opened the gate. 'Wena, o tsogile jang?'

'Ke tsogile sentle, rra,' my mother replied.

Listen said 'Ee' a few times for good measure and then paused by our bougainvillaea bush.

'Madam,' he said finally.

My mother snorted, embarrassed.

'I am asking for that which I need because I am going to Kgadi.'

'Oh,' my mother said, a bit at a loss.

'Again, I am thinking I need provisions,' Listen added – we Batswana do love to have our provisions on road trips – 'or I will be hungry,' and he pointed to his stomach. My mother sighed and went inside. She came out with perhaps a pula in change, which she handed over, thinking this would resolve the situation. At that time this would probably have bought quite enough food for one person on a long road journey, and probably filled their stomach on the way back again too. In my grandmother's household thirty pula would probably be all they saw in a month.

'Farewell, madam,' Listen said and he went back next door.

My mother didn't mention the episode to my father and when I tried to she shushed me up.

The very next day Listen came round again. This time he rattled the gate and entered as my mother came outside to see what our puppy was barking about.

'Dumela, mma.' Listen bowed his head respectfully.

'Dumela,' my mother replied.

'O tsogile jang?' Listen continued the greetings because my mother had left them hanging in the air.

My mother just said, 'Ee.'

'Ee,' Listen echoed and, smiling, he bent down to pat our puppy. 'This is a good dog,' he said approvingly.

'It is?'

'Yes, accordingly, it is not a Tswana dog.'

'It's not?' My mother appeared puzzled. 'How can you tell?'

'Because it is not brown.'

My mother looked down at our puppy, which, grateful for the attention, jumped up and pawed her legs.

'No, it is not a Tswana dog,' Listen repeated, for everyone knew Tswana dogs were scrawny bush dogs and non-Tswana dogs were those found in Jamestown which had full bellies and got washed with shampoo.

'Madam,' Listen said after a suitable pause. 'I am thinking that you want your yard cleaned,' and he gestured in a leisurely fashion to the area on the road in front of our gate that was a mess of stones and straggling weeds.

Now my mother had a thing about giving people jobs. She

would give out money and food, but she couldn't stand the idea of hiring someone to do what she could do herself. So when Listen asked to clean up the area outside our fence, she didn't know what to say. So she became a wife and said, 'Ask when my husband is home from work.'

Listen hovered for a moment. 'O a re eng?' he asked me.

'Me, I'm not saying anything,' I replied. Listen laughed because I had spoken in English.

'And when will you be going on your trip?' my mother asked him.

Listen looked puzzled for a moment and then he smiled. 'Shortly,' he replied.

Sure enough at about 5 p.m. there was Listen hovering outside our house waiting for my father. No sooner had my father parked the car than Listen came up. He and Bopadile greeted each other like long-lost friends and then Bopadile went inside the house. Now my father always received visitors outside the house, a hangover from how he used to live in Lephane. So my mother busied herself in the kitchen keeping an eye out of the window. Usually if my father talked to someone outside, she would berate him afterwards with, 'Why didn't you ask them in?' To her it was the height of rudeness to receive someone outside, but the custom also had its uses in that she never had to let anyone into the house if she didn't want to. To both my parents their house was their haven and there were times I saw them both cowering behind a curtain pretending not to be in.

'What did you tell him?' my mother asked as my father came back into the house and Listen jumped happily over the fence connecting our yard with Beauty's next door.

'I said he could.'

'Could what?'

'Mmm?'

'You heard me.'

'I said . . .' – my father talked slowly, he hated to be questioned – 'I said he could clean it up.'

'But we don't *need* it cleaned up!' my mother exploded. 'It's not even *in* our yard. I can clean it up myself!'

'What are you so excited about?'

'I gave him some change yesterday,' she sighed.

'Rose!'

'I know, I know.'

My mother went outside and started watering the plants, but the conversation wasn't finished. 'Mompati!' she yelled and my father came out and stood quietly with a toothpick in his mouth.

'So what are we paying him to do, exactly? Perhaps he'll clean it as payment for what I've already given him?' she suggested hopefully.

'Mmm?'

My mother waited.

'Well, he'll move the stones and so forth.' My father wiggled his finger in and out of his ear.

'Oh.' My mother continued the watering and I waited for her to say, 'Mompati, the ear is a delicate instrument,' which is what she usually said when he started wiggling his finger in and out. 'So do we have to pay him separately for moving the stones?' she asked instead.

'We didn't discuss it.'

My mother moved off to water the plants at the back. 'Sometimes,' she said over her shoulder, 'I think you're soft in the head.'

My father laughed and sat down for a rest, telling me to fetch him some water.

A few days later as Christine was finishing the countdown to her children arriving for the school holidays, she invited my parents once again to a Saturday night dinner, this time with a video thrown in.

'Christine's invited us over,' my mother told my father on the Friday evening.

'Mmm?'

'Do you want to go?'

'Don't mind.' He was taking off his work shoes.

'Really . . .' my mother began, appearing at the doorway to the kitchen looking worried, 'really, we should have invited them here.'

My father didn't reply.

'Shouldn't we?' my mother prodded.

'Whatever.'

'I mean it's our turn. We went there already and –'

My father laughed. 'Your mother's people . . .' he said to me, leaning back in his chair with his shoes finally off and his feet free.

'Mompati! They stink,' my mother yelled from the kitchen. 'Is Bopadile around or what?'

'I don't know. Why?'

'Well, obviously, what are we going to do with Dimpho?'

'She can play here.'

'But you just said you don't know if Bopadile is around. I'm not leaving her on her own.'

'If she's next door, she won't be on her own.'

'So you know that Beauty is around?'

My father shook his head.

'Then she'll have to come with us.'

I pushed between them and scowled.

We set off to the Fishes' house slightly more subdued than last time. Neither my mother nor father had bothered to dress up, but my mother had insisted on buying a bottle of wine and taking it along.

'Frank can afford a crate of this stuff,' my father complained as we went to the bottle store on the way.

'That is not the point,' my mother said firmly.

In England, she told me, when you are invited somewhere, it is polite to take a present. But if Batswana are invited anywhere, they expect everything to be laid on for them. My mother was always sort of stumbling on to differences like this and only when it was pointed out did she realize how many times she had been offended when she'd invited a Motswana over and he or she had appeared empty-handed. She never got invited back, either. Perhaps that's why she got on so well with Christine in the beginning, because they operated according to a similar set of petty rules.

When we arrived, Christine locked up Butch who was straining to get at my father and took us on a little tour of the improvements she had made. A reed fence had been built around the roundavel, so now there was a mini compound within her yard which looked just like my grandmother's place. The fencing had been badly done and my father told her so. Christine decided to bow to his greater knowledge on these things. She was in a hyped-up mood and the strain was showing on her face. Although it was evening, for some reason she was wearing dark sunglasses. She told us that her maid, Joy, had left a few days ago. Her father was due to arrive any day now and shortly afterwards her children would be coming too.

That evening my parents and Christine and Frank discussed business for real. It was Christine who was most full of plans. She told my parents that every day she could see where a business could be made. She had, it seemed, decided on a school, or a newspaper, or importing goods from South Africa, where, she assured them, things were cheap. My parents who had had countless such conversations between themselves listened, ate the food and drank the drinks.

It was July and midwinter, so they sat inside this time. Christine got my mother and me to help her prepare the food and then afterwards to clear up all the mess. Then she brought out a huge shiny book which contained pages and pages listing all the videos they had. She gave it to my father so he could choose a film, but then she constantly interrupted him with. 'Oh! This *is* a good one!', 'I love *this* one', and 'I've seen this one nearly twenty times!'

Christine instructed Frank to turn the lights down and they settled down to watch. At this point I fell asleep and eventually had to be carried home. My mother later complained that Christine talked all the way through the film and even stopped it to replay bits she especially enjoyed. Frank took no part in the proceedings, except to fetch more drinks when Christine told him to.

Chapter Nine

The following week my mother decided it was high time that she and my father return the dinner favour. The scales were unbalanced, she explained, because we had been to the Fishes' a couple of times and yet they had never been for a meal at our house. So Christine and Frank were duly invited over, along with Christine's father who had just arrived. It wasn't so much that my mother wanted them to come for dinner, she explained rather defensively, but that she felt she *owed* them.

We spent the day cleaning the house and cooking, me trying to shoo our puppy out of the way. When my father was not around, my mother was always allowing it into the house and talking to it as if it could understand. My mother shuffled around in socks because the mornings were still cold. Unlike her, I was always barefooted and my childhood is summed up by the sound of bare feet padding on a smooth concrete floor. Bare feet on a bare floor is a hot country sound and for me it conjures up open doors and sunshine.

My mother seemed to think that Christine would be inspecting our domestic arrangements, and she set me to do all manner of things like collecting hairs from the plug-hole in the bath even though nobody was going to be washing themselves. To help us clean she put on the hi-fi and we opened all the windows and I danced and swept and picked up hairs. My father had gone off to collect firewood so we could all sit outside, keeping ourselves warm and roasting meat at the same time. My mother said there wasn't enough room for us all inside the house. Bopadile was meant to help my father, but he had disappeared early and had not returned.

In the afternoon my mother washed and dressed, and for once she allowed me to wear my party dress. Perhaps this was part of her effort to keep up appearances, for when I asked her, 'Why do we have to clean the house?' she said, 'Dimpho, what would someone *think* if they came here and found everything dirty?' So she wanted me looking presentable too.

After we had dressed, my mother made salads, prepared some vegetables and marinated the meat. By the time it was dark she was beginning to fuss.

'They should be here by now,' she kept on saying. 'What time is it?'

'To seven,' my father said, using the short-hand familiar to Batswana. If someone asks the time, it is usual to say either 'past' or 'to' the hour. We don't usually feel the need to be specific.

'Would that be ten to seven or an hour to seven?' my mother asked. She was always very precise when someone asked *her* what the time was.

At the last moment Christine sent Frank over to say there was an emergency and would my parents go to their house instead.

'It's Frank,' my father called from outside as my mother was turning off some vegetable dish in the oven. As he entered the kitchen, Frank was his usual apologetic self. But my mother was annoyed. 'What about the food?' she asked him rather bluntly.

'Um . . .' he hesitated, smiling. 'Christine suggested you could bring it with you?' He put it as if it were a question to make it sound less like an order.

'Oh, yes,' my mother mumbled and she started to take the salads out of the cooler and cover them up. Frank went back outside and hung around talking with my father. My memories of Frank are always of him coming to our house with some message to relay and then standing, uncertainly, outside. He was such a nondescript sort of adult. Friendly but removed, unlike Christine whom I felt uncomfortable with but who couldn't be ignored. He was the sort of adult who would say hello, pat your head and then pause because he couldn't remember your name.

The emergency turned out to be that Christine was expecting a phone call from her children. She welcomed us at the door of their mansion half-dressed, saying she hadn't spoken to them for two days and must wait for their call. The winter holidays lasted a couple of weeks and the Fishes' children had spent the first few days with friends.

'They *need* to talk with their mother,' Christine said with a strange sidelong look at Frank.

The children would be coming up to Jamestown in the company plane, and it was the company that paid for their incredibly expensive private schools down in South Africa. Christine was waiting to see what their travel arrangements were.

She ushered my mother and me into the living-room where the TV was on. Every time we went to her house there was a video playing, often children's cartoons turned up to top volume.

'My father,' Christine announced, waving in the direction of a white-haired old man sitting in the corner of the sofa absent-mindedly patting Snowy. The old man got up with some effort and came over to shake my mother's hand.

'Her husband, Mompati,' Christine added as my father and Frank came into the room. She spoke like a butler announcing guests at a ball.

They shook hands in the European fashion and sat down. I stayed close to my mother.

'Lovely part of the world,' Christine's father said approvingly to my father.

'You came all the way from England?' my mother asked.

Christine's father nodded and was about to speak when Christine got up and said, 'Who will have what?' Then she nodded to Frank that he should take the drinks orders.

'It's a very long journey,' my mother continued. She seemed quite eager to talk to someone from home.

'You're from England? You have a slight accent . . .' the old man said.

'Oh, father, I *told* you just now.' Christine sounded annoyed. 'Get down!' she yelled at Snowy, who was trying to get on to her lap.

'Yes I'm from London, originally,' my mother continued.

'Really?' The old man seemed interested and he nodded a few times. 'Whereabouts?' My mother told him and he appeared to know where she was talking about. 'We used to go to those parts, when we were younger of course . . .' and he gave a little laugh.

'Oh, get out the violins,' Christine said sarcastically.

My father coughed.

'And when was the last time you were home?' the old man asked my mother, ignoring Christine, who was pushing a dish of peanuts towards him.

'I haven't been,' my mother laughed. 'The air fare . . .' and she tailed off.

My father smiled, looking a bit apologetic. 'Is it your first time here?' he asked the old man. Despite the patronizing comment about Botswana being a beautiful part of the world, my father knew to be respectful to an old person.

Christine, annoyed that she was no longer at the centre of things, called my mother into the kitchen so they could reheat the food my mother had made. As she left the room, Christine called to Frank to start the fire on the patio.

'Totally gaga,' Christine said of her father as she opened the fridge door. Her fridge door had a little keyhole on the top left-hand corner, which I suppose was to lock away the food from the thieving maids. Every fridge I ever saw at that time had a lock on it, for the fridges came from South Africa, a place presumably full of thieving maids.

'I mean what would happen if. . .?' Christine continued. 'He's an old man. What he wants to come here for I've no idea. He says he wants to see the children.'

'It is a long way,' my mother said, waiting for further instructions. 'Dimpho, stop playing with those things on the fridge.'

Back in the living-room the old man patted the space next to him for my mother and I to sit down.

'And how old are you?' he asked me. I was surprised, usually people didn't ask me questions directly.

'Me. I am five years old,' I said in careful English.

Snowy tried to jump up at me and I drew back.

'Don't you like dogs?' the old man asked. Now, I had been trained by my father to be respectful to my elders, though it is hard to tell the age of white people, and I thought it might be rude to say I didn't like dogs. But I couldn't help saying no because I had still not established the relationship I would have liked with our dog.

'Nor do I,' the old man laughed and slapped his thigh. 'But Christine tells me they have souls, so we must be careful.'

I had no idea what he was talking about, so I just stared at his white hair and at the spectacles hanging on a string around his neck.

'Drink, father,' Christine said and she placed a glass with a slight bang on the table in front of him.

'Now, Christine, you know, always wanted to be a missionary.' The old man leant back on the sofa with a smile.

Christine sat down and for once she appeared to be embarrassed. This was strange to see and a red flush spread over her neck and face.

'Really . . .' she began.

'No,' the old man dismissed her protest, 'she did, you know.'

My mother laughed and splattered her drink down her front.

Frank ushered my father outside to help control the fire.

The old man leant back in his seat, relaxed now. 'Can't you turn the TV off?' he asked Christine. 'I can't hear a thing. Now,' he continued to my mother, 'when my daughter was a little girl, she used to say her prayers every night. She would kneel by the foot of her bed and say, 'Please, God, take care of my mother, father, the heathens and give me somewhere nice to live.'

Christine made a sort of choking noise.

'And then she went to South Africa and achieved her dreams.' The old man paused and then added a trifle sadly, 'And it all went well, didn't it, Christine, if you forget about a certain husband and his certain ways?'

Suddenly the atmosphere in the room was electric. My mother leant forward for the peanuts and began munching on them distractedly.

'Christine was always the leader, weren't you, Christine?'

'I really don't think . . .' Christine began.

'No, let me continue. She was the head girl at school, you know, and didn't we all know it! I remember once she beat up two little girls and their parents came round to complain.'

My mother coughed on her peanuts and reached hurriedly for her drink. Christine got up to put a new video on the TV.

The old man raised his voice. 'Men don't take responsibility for their families, do they, these days?' he said to my father, who was just coming back into the room.

'Pardon me?' my father said, hovering by the doorway. He always said, 'pardon me,' because he had been taught at school that it was disrespectful to say, 'What?'

'I was just saying, men have to take responsibility, don't they?'

'Definitely,' my father said, glancing at my mother to see what was going on.

'You don't find a family man these days, do you?' The old man didn't seem to want a reply.

'Frank!' Christine yelled. 'Is the meat ready or will we be here all night?'

'Ah, yes, Frank,' the old man said, and he seemed to drop into his own thoughts.

A little later my father carried in the meat from the braai outside and we all moved to the dining-room table to eat.

'So,' the old man began to my mother, 'has Christine told you all about what happened in South Africa? Not very welcome there, were they, my daughter and Frank?' and he chuckled to himself.

My mother held her fork halfway to her mouth, politely confused.

'Oh, for crying out loud,' Christine said and she handed a knife to Frank.

My father looked appalled and he frantically wiggled his finger in and out of his ear. 'Frank has told me about when he was head-master in old Rhodesia, about the teaching they did over there,' he offered.

'Teaching was it?' the old man said and he chuckled again.

When he chuckled like that, it occurred to me that he might be Father Christmas. I knew Father Christmas was a white man with white hair who chuckled, so it seemed to be an obvious connec-tion. My mother had told me, when we got sent Christmas cards from her friends in England, that Father Christmases could be anyone really, but that they dressed themselves up and everyone pretended not to know who they were. One of those quaint Euro-pean rituals, my father would add.

'Will you be travelling around while you're here?' my mother asked the old man.

'I hope so. I have always loved Africa.'

'You've been here before?'

'Oh yes, many times.'

'Rose,' Christine cut in, 'this salad here really is delicious.'

My mother thanked her.

'Oh' – the old man seemed to come to life – 'she got you to make the food, did she?'

Christine got up, pushing back her chair with a loud scrape, and hurried off down one of the corridors.

'Now what about this case at the mine?' Frank said to my father, referring to something that had happened that week.

We ate duck which had been freshly flown up from South Africa.

But no one paid much attention to the food and the old man seemed to be having a running battle with Christine, as my mother put it later. They sat at either end of the table and my parents were caught in the middle. The old man's energy seemed to flag towards the end of the evening however, and he kept on asking when the children would be arriving. He even had photographs of them in his wallet, which he showed my mother and me.

It was about this time, a few months after she had arrived in Jamestown, that Christine established what she called 'Ladies' Night'. Dissatisfied with the Baobab Club, probably because those who frequented the place were refusing to take her into their circle, she had decided that once a week, usually Friday, would be Ladies' Night. To begin with the ladies in question were my mother and Christine, and they met in Christine's house. The gentlemen – that is, Frank and my father – were left to their own devices. It was a chance for Frank to be allowed out, for usually Christine didn't like him to go anywhere on his own. It also meant she had the house to herself and her friends, of which she had so far only managed to make one, namely my mother.

On Friday night Frank would be sent on his way with a case of beers to my father. Often my father's friends from the mine would also come round and sometimes there would be quite a gathering. I usually busied myself playing with Thebe next door, while the men drank beer. Later on, when he was completely drunk, Frank would sing. Frank's repertoire was, oddly enough, mostly hymns and my father's friends would teach him church songs that they knew. To me and Thebe it was a funny sight: Frank, his eyes blood-red, slumped over the outside table, and my father, loose-limbed and sloppy, singing along.

Up until this stage in their friendship my father had been quite defensive about Frank, saying he had it rough with Christine. But my mother didn't buy this idea at all and was rather sarcastic about him. I think it was the comments of Christine's father which coloured the way she felt. 'He's playing a role,' she would say, but my father never bothered to ask her what she meant.

My mother was equally defensive about Christine, saying she might be a handful, but she was kind, she meant well, she was bored and lonely and she wasn't as bad as all the other expatriate women that were around, was she? I think she was trying to find a way to explain why they were friends. Certainly Christine had introduced order and social events into my mother's life. My mother liked, I suppose, to have day-to-day contact with someone and to listen to all their daily dramas. She liked to be invited to tea and to have someone to visit. She also had a feeling, which she voiced to me, that something was not quite right with Christine, and for some reason she blamed Frank.

One Friday evening my mother set off for Ladies' Night carrying the usual offering. Bopadile was away for the weekend, as was Beauty next door, and my father and Frank had said they wanted to go to a bar that had just opened. It was the first public bar to open in Jamestown, and not surprisingly it was packed. Frank must have been the only white person there. So I went along with my mother to Christine's, my mother promising that I could watch videos with them.

We arrived to find Christine in bed. 'Rosie,' Christine called from along the corridor in a wispy voice, 'I'm in here.' She had taken to calling my mother Rosie, and though my mother complained to my father about this, she didn't know how to tell Christine to only call her Rose.

We made our way down the corridor, stepping fearfully over Butch, who couldn't find a space big enough to lie comfortably in except the hallway.

Embarrassed, my mother stood at the door to the bedroom. I came up and stood behind her, looking around Christine's bedroom. The air was close and there was a sour milk smell. On the wall directly in front of me was a man on a cross, just like the one in the living-room.

'Come in, come in,' Christine called, so my mother did, but she hesitated about where to stand.

'Oh, you've brought Dimpho too,' Christine said and she didn't sound too pleased.

'Yes, it's just that Mompati and Frank said they wanted to go to the bar and –'

'Did they, indeed?' Christine sat up in bed and then sank down again.

'So I thought, anyway, that . . .'

Christine motioned that my mother should sit down on the bed. Christine didn't look her usual cheerful self. Instead she appeared rather vulnerable. She was wearing a thin red nightdress and she had a sort of scarf wrapped around her naked neck. On the pillow next to her, on Frank's side of the bed, was a huge pale brown teddy-bear sitting up as if it were a person.

'This place is getting me down,' Christine complained.

'Yes, it does that.' My mother sat perched on the bed and I sat beside her. 'When are the children coming?' she asked, to brighten things up a bit.

'They need me,' Christine said. 'How can they be down there without a mother? I've told Frank . . .' She heaved herself up further, cradling her Coke glass.

My mother made as if to stand up, but the phone rang and Christine shot out a hand to answer it.

'Hello!' She beamed into the phone and gestured that my mother should remain on the bed. 'Oh, me, I'm just getting along, same old things. Is it? Agh, shame. Yes, I've got my best friend here,' and she reached out for my mother, who had now stood up. 'Here she is . . .' and Christine handed over the phone.

My mother took the receiver cautiously. It had been several years since she had used a phone and she didn't know who was at the other end. Whoever it was must have been equally confused, because after a bit of small talk my mother handed the phone back to Christine, who was busy looking for her cigarettes.

'Where's your father?' my mother asked as we were led along the corridor and back to the big room.

'Hmm?' Christine seemed distracted and she tugged at the scarf round her neck.

'Is he gone already?'

We reached the living-room, where the TV was on.

'Yes. He had to cut short his visit, what a shame,' and Christine smiled sarcastically.

'Oh, Christine, you shouldn't have,' my mother said when Christine brought out a tray from the kitchen with a bottle of champagne and little nibbly things to eat.

My mother said later that she was puzzled that Christine had referred to her as her best friend.

'What did you make of her father?' she asked my father, as if they hadn't discussed the whole thing countless times already.

'He seemed a nice sort.'

'Well, I suppose so but you never can tell. He didn't seem to like Frank though, did he?'

'Mmm?' My father had drawn back ever so slightly from Frank since that evening with Christine's father. Though they still drank together, the suggestion that Frank was not a family man, that he had somehow mistreated his family, troubled him.

'There's something sad about Christine at the moment,' my mother went on.

'Are you the Jamestown social worker?' my father mumbled.

'Oh, for god's sake, do you have to be a social worker to feel bad for someone? What happened to the wonderful African way of life, the community that cares for everyone?'

'It was destroyed when we built places like Jamestown,' and my father laid down on the sofa and closed his eyes.

That evening a distant relative who lived in a village about half an hour's drive away came round. He brought the sad news that my father's uncle had passed away. It had taken so long for this message to get from Lephane that the uncle had already been buried.

My father was upset by the news of course. When his father had died, the uncle had taken over much of the responsibility for the family and my father realized that he would now have to provide for the woman and four children his uncle had left behind. The next day he got out a small book and began trying to work out how much money we had.

Chapter Ten

A couple of days later the big event occurred and Christine's teen-age children arrived. But strangely enough, considering all the trouble Christine had taken over their arrival, she soon became bored with them and sent Frank round on Sunday morning with a message asking my parents to come for lunch to meet the children. For once I was included in the invitation and of course I saw it as a good opportunity to don my party dress. I was instructed to clean myself up and put on clean clothes, though not my party dress, and Frank went back home to wait for us. But my parents, though they had accepted the invitation nicely enough, spent the rest of the morning arguing. A duplicity common with adults.

'It's my weekend,' my father whined, 'I don't want to go over there and be entertaining. I just want to hang out here,' he added, using one of his favourite American expressions.

'And do what, exactly?' my mother turned on him. Because she spent every day in our house, at the weekend she wanted to get out, while my father, who spent every day at the mine, just wanted to sit quietly at home.

'If you didn't want to go, then you should have said so, shouldn't you?' my mother said.

It was a hard situation to solve, but because my parents had said they would go, they did.

So off we went, me holding my mother's hand tightly in my usual fear of Butch. I now enjoyed our own puppy, who was still nameless because my mother chose English names that my father disliked, and my father chose Setswana names that my mother couldn't remember from one minute to the next. But though I now liked our puppy, Butch was an unknown entity. The fact that it barked furiously at my father made me terrified. This time my father encouraged the dog by rattling the gate and insulting it in Setswana. 'Your father's asshole!' he shouted in Setswana, which was the height of insult, and he would normally never say such a thing in front of me. I giggled, but didn't let go of my mother's hand. My father got annoyed with me because I was too afraid to enter Christine's yard.

Christine's children were pale-skinned giants and they stared pointedly at my father. There were two of them, a girl called Lizzie who I suppose was about thirteen and a boy called Peter who was a couple of years older. Lizzie was dressed up to match Christine's fantasies in a ruffled blue mini dress that I secretly admired, although I knew my mother would have a few scathing comments to make about it later. Lizzie's skin, like Frank's, was the colour of a blonde bar of soap. Peter was slightly redder in the face, with spots on his forehead and a rather aggressive way of standing. I was pushed off to be played with but was uncomfortable the whole time, wondering if my parents were going to abandon me to these two.

With my friend Thebe I was used to being the leader, but here my role was minimal. Lizzie treated me as if I were a new doll and showed me everything in her room, which of course I had already seen. In Peter's room was a Bible the size of which I had never seen before and he let me touch its newspaper-thin pages reverently.

'How can you live in such a boring place?' Lizzie said, lying down on her brother's bed. 'It is *so* boring here.'

I didn't know what to say.

'Get off my bed,' Peter said, but his sister stayed where she was.

'Do you think we can leave soon?' she asked no one in particular.

'Let's ask Daddy,' Peter said, saying the word Daddy as if it were something nasty.

'Why? Because Mummy's too drunk already?' Lizzie said and she leapt up and did a twirl around the room.

'Mummy,' I heard her asking Christine later in the kitchen, 'is Dimpho black or does she just have a sun tan?'

Christine shrieked with laughter. I went to look for my mother to see if we could go home.

During lunch, which as usual consisted of things flown up from South Africa, Peter and Lizzie spent most of their time trying to get their parents' attention. They were loud and demanding. I didn't know many children of their age and I was mildly shocked.

'This place is shit,' Peter said halfway through a strange, clear, cold soup, 'I don't want to stay here.'

Christine ignored him.

'When are you going to get that video I asked for?'

'Soon, darling,' Christine said. 'Stop moaning.'

'I am so bored,' Lizzie said, playing with the hem of her dress. 'Dad?'

Frank patted his daughter on the head, poured more wine and promised they'd go to Sun City in the next holiday.

'But we've *been* there,' Lizzie said.

'Dad, I need a hundred rand,' Peter said and he got up and started rifling in the pockets of Frank's jacket that was hanging on the back of a chair.

'I want to go Sun City,' I joined in.

'I want to go *to* Sun City,' my mother corrected me.

'No, you don't,' my father said firmly.

As we had all sat down to eat lunch, Christine asked Frank to say grace. I was intrigued by the ritual, but sensed that my father was uncomfortable. I looked around the vast table at Christine and her family with their heads lightly bowed and felt privy to something secret, something to which I thought I would rather like to belong. When they had finished grace, they started handing out bowls of soup. I took what I was given and ate in silence, but Lizzie said, 'Ugh,' and pushed her bowl away.

'She used to be such a good eater,' Christine said to us as we moved on to the main course.

'That's a lie,' Lizzie said.

Christine gave her a furious look. My father twirled his finger in his ear. To say to an elder that they were lying was unbelievable.

'You always exaggerate,' Lizzie said, but she pulled the plate a little nearer.

'There's no fat there, so eat,' Christine ordered, but she hardly touched her own food.

'"There's no fat there, so eat,"' Lizzie imitated her.

I watched, fascinated, and was about to join in when my father warned me that if I didn't shut my mouth my tongue would grow as long as a cow's.

Later, after lunch when the atmosphere was slightly calmer, Christine tried to get her children to show off their accomplishments. First she told her daughter to go and get her recorder. Lizzie slouched off down the corridor and came back with a small wooden pipe with holes in it. Then she set up a metal music stand, put some sheets on it and began to play. But she kept on making mistakes, and every time she made a mistake she stopped, went back to the beginning of what she had been playing and started again. Although Christine had told her daughter to perform, she didn't take much notice of what she was doing and even began clapping before she had quite finished. Then Christine sent her son off to his room to get his sporting trophies and photographs of him playing rugby.

After Christine had ordered the children away, the adults began on the idea of a business once again.

'I just think,' Christine said, looking at my father, 'that people around here deserve a good education for their children while they're still young.'

My father agreed.

'And if your child is young, like Dimpho, where can they go? There's no pre-school for two hundred kilometres, is there?'

My parents shook their heads.

'They need a good start and it's never too soon to start educating someone, is it?'

Frank, who usually took a back seat in the social proceedings, suddenly began outlining the plan as if he had had it up his sleeve all along.

'Rosie here . . .'

My mother flinched at being called Rosie again.

'. . . is a teacher. As you know, she can't get a job, we want to start a pre-school. It's perfect!' Frank offered my father a cigarette.

'But I'm a secondary school teacher,' my mother protested, 'though I did think I could work in the primary school here . . .'

'I really don't think that matters, Rosie,' Frank said and he handed my father a glass of cognac, which my father took in silence. Frank was quite firm for once and I wonder in retrospect whose idea the pre-school actually was. It seemed the plan was to convince my father, as if my mother had already agreed, but she was sending my father eye messages to say this wasn't the case at all.

'And of course,' Frank continued, 'there are enough expatriates already running businesses here, and with you in charge, Mompati' – he lifted his cognac glass for cheers – 'that won't be the case. We'll put in the time and the money and when it all gets going we leave.'

My father began nodding and stroking his chin. He realized, I suppose, that the reason the Fishes wanted a school was to make money. He also realized that they needed him because in theory expatriates weren't allowed to set up such a business on their own. And with a Motswana involved an expatriate could always say they were contributing to local development. The idea that Frank would put in the money and eventually hand over the school to him was exactly his idea of foreign aid. 'The aid we need,' he often told my mother and his friends, 'is not this British aid with strings attached, it's not this Peace Corps aid with its CIA contacts – it's responsible, skilled people who *give* us money, *train* us and then bugger off back to their own countries.' The fact that he swore during this sort of talk showed how angry he really was.

'So we would start a pre-school?' My father stroked his chin some more in a businesslike fashion. 'We'd need premises of course, but it is a good idea. We have often thought of starting something ourselves. Money is a problem, however,' and he looked to my mother for confirmation.

'I don't know about education being a *business*,' my mother began.

'It would be a community school of course,' Christine interrupted, 'and we'd charge fees just to keep it going.'

'Fees?' My mother stretched her arms along the back of her chair.

'Yes,' said Christine brightly, 'for those who can afford to pay, and God knows there're enough of them here in Jamestown. For the locals we would offer scholarships, we would offer –'

Although she seemed to be talking sensibly, by this time both she and Frank were pretty drunk. Christine, her whisky masquerading as Coke and with a cigarette in her hand, was trying to shoo away her daughter who was attempting to ask her something.

'My daughter,' Christine confided to us loudly, 'refuses to believe her periods are going to start soon. She just refuses.'

Her daughter flushed crimson and my mother, equally embarrassed, changed the subject. We talked instead about elephants and the safaris the Fishes had been on.

As we were leaving, Frank, prodded by Christine, brought up the subject of my father teaching their children maths, and it was agreed he would do so on the remaining two Sundays of their stay. That is, my father didn't exactly say no and he didn't exactly say yes.

'Of course,' Christine said hurriedly, 'we will pay you for your troubles,' and she smiled sweetly.

My mother gave my father a satisfied look.

This meant, however, that my parents' weekend was now almost full. On Friday it was Ladies' Night and on Sunday my father would be teaching the children. The net had been cast. It seems amazing in retrospect that my parents didn't just say no and ignore the Fishes' demands. My father, after spending any time with Christine, whom he had started calling Her Majesty, would withdraw once we got home. And I noticed that my mother, when it came to defending Christine, seemed more and more uncertain about whether she really wanted to defend her at all.

But, none the less, my parents were drawn to the Fishes. My father, who continually worried about supporting the family back in Lephane, was intrigued by the idea that he might be able to get the Fishes to set up a business that he would be in charge of. My mother felt she had got in so deep with Christine, had accepted her food and used her washing machine, that, ridiculous as it now sounds, it would be too complicated to withdraw. And, as I've said, she liked having someone to visit.

'Christine has asked me to go round for tea,' my mother would sometimes say.

'So don't go if you don't want to go,' my father would answer.

'And how do I tell her that?' my mother would sigh.

Then Bopadile would come into the house with his usual cry of 'Whosit!' and the atmosphere would change.

On that first Sunday of teaching the Fishes' children my father was lying on the sand outside on an old rug smoking a cigarette and thinking.

'Are you going to Christine's, then?' my mother asked, wiping her hands on a tea towel.

'Mmm?'

'You heard.'

'Later,' he said and shifted on the rug.

'You did say you would go.'

'Yes, I did say so.'

'Well, it's 12 o'clock already.' My mother washed some dishes for a while and then began again. 'It's not that I think you *should* go,' she said, coming outside, 'but you did say you would.' She seemed greatly troubled by the idea that my father wasn't going to stick to his word.

Bopadile came out and joined my father on the sand. 'They have money these people?' he asked casually.

'Ee,' my father replied.

'So what's this business you're going to do with them, then?'

'A pre-school.'

'A what school?'

'A pre-school, where you send your child before primary school.'

'So they will learn English?'

'Among other things.'

'That's good,' Bopadile said. 'Give me a cigarette.'

My father handed over the packet.

'So they've got money these people,' Bopadile said again.

'Your uncle always sees an opportunity when he wants one,' my mother said to me, half admiringly.

In August, after the Fishes' children had been sent back to South Africa, Christine got into the habit of sending over food with Frank, which for my mother really unbalanced the scales. She didn't want Christine sending over food parcels, but she said she didn't know how to refuse them. My father, who would eat anything, couldn't really see what the problem was. But my mother found it a burden and made a big fuss about cleaning up Christine's plates and plastic containers and sending them back promptly. One time Christine sent over a whole smoked salmon which she said she didn't have room for in her freezer.

'Oh God, think of the cost of this,' my mother said in awe.

One morning in early September Christine drove up to our

house and beeped the car until my mother came out. 'Emergency,' she said gesturing to the back of the car. 'It's Butch.'

'Oh, what's wrong?' My mother peered into the back of the car.

'Sick as a dog,' Christine laughed. 'No, seriously, I think he's got arthritis.'

'You're taking him to the vet?'

'Yes. Not here of course, I'm off down south, we had a vet there and he's very good.'

'Won't that cost a fortune?' my mother protested.

'It's the company car, Rosie,' Christine said as if my mother were mad. 'Anyway,' she continued over the noise of the engine while she took a drag on her cigarette, 'what I wanted to ask you was whether you'll keep an eye on things.'

My mother nodded. 'Frank's going with you? Do you need Snowy fed?'

'Oh no. Frank's staying here, I've left him instructions, but you know what men are like,' and Christine gave a little laugh.

'Hello, Dimpho,' she called to me. 'Did you like that chocolate cake I made?'

My mother pushed me to reply, but I pulled a face and then Christine drove off.

It was about this time that Bopadile landed himself with a temporary construction job at the mine. He came home one day with my father and proudly told us the news.

'Well,' my mother said, very surprised. 'That's great. How did you manage that?'

He just smiled and went to look in our cooler for something to drink. 'Boers,' he announced, 'are easy to handle.'

My parents laughed.

'What will you get paid?' my mother asked.

Bopadile named a sum and my mother looked appalled. 'The Fishes spend that amount on meat for their dogs for God's sake.'

Bopadile shrugged.

My father was earning six times more than Bopadile, but once we had paid rent, bought food and petrol and telegraphed some money back to the family in Lephane, we were broke.

Bopadile moved out of our servant's quarters and into a tiny house, which he shared with two other construction workers. Despite this he still used my parents' postal address and mail came for him every week. My father, who had learnt to be suspicious of his brother, opened the letters and they were always bills. It seemed Bopadile had been to Thabeng and had bought, among other things, a bedroom suite on hire purchase. My father collected the bills and gave them to Bopadile when he came over to eat at our house, but Bopadile always said, 'Oh, I've paid those,' and managed to leave without taking them with him.

One afternoon Listen from next door came round to get paid. He had spent most of the morning finally clearing the stones from outside our gate and generally making the area neat and tidy. My mother told him to ask my father as she didn't have any money. So as usual Listen hovered around outside until my father came home from work.

'Did you pay him?' my mother asked when my father came into the house.

'Yes.'

'Well, how much?'

'Oh, a couple of pula.'

'Nice work if you can get it. And what happens to the stones now?' She pointed outside with her eyebrows, in a gesture typical of my father, to where the stones lay in a pile beyond the gate.

My father laughed, a bit embarrassed. 'Listen says he needs a wheelbarrow to move them and he hasn't got one. He will do it next week.'

'Oh yes,' my mother said. Through the kitchen window she watched Bopadile and Listen who were deep in conversation across the fence.

Chapter Eleven

My father said Frank was a different man with Her Majesty away and one night he invited him to come to the salt pans and have a braai with us. But it didn't turn out to be a happy evening, at least not for my mother. In Lephane it had been common to go into the bush for the evening, usually to the bank of a river, and braai goat meat on old oil drums cut in half. Sometimes people got together and bought drinks from the wholesalers and then held a party and sold the drinks. There would be American and South African music on a borrowed cassette-player, and with a bit of luck someone would bring a generator and electric lights would be strung up in the trees.

In Jamestown the bush was an unwelcoming place to picnic, so people went to the salt pans instead. According to my mother, the pans looked exactly like a beach. But then she always compared things she saw to things she had known before. If the sky was a deep blue with the promise of rain, for example, she would say it was just like the Mediterranean sea. This habit annoyed my father, who would say, 'You mean your sea is just like our sky,' or, 'You mean your beaches look just like our pans.'

It was so hot there that the land before you shimmered. The heat played tricks on the eyes. I would think that before me was a vast lake and I would walk towards it endlessly on the sand, the water always just out of reach because it existed only in my imagination. But in the right season, when it rained, the pans did become a vast lake and flamingoes would gather in their thousands to eat and breed. And then I could walk knee-deep in salty water, mud oozing between my toes, pausing to pick up a flamingo feather or a shell.

There was little shade on the pans – just one big baobab tree that had become a favourite place for the Boers to braai. It stood on a slight grassy incline, which led down to the pans. When my father suggested we go out one evening to picnic, Frank insisted on the baobab tree.

After work we picked up Bopadile and then went to the Fishes' house to collect Frank. We found him sitting at the dining-room table looking around with wonder at the mess the place was in.

'Lord, she's going to eat me alive!' Frank said. He laughed, but he looked worried and a little bewildered. I saw my mother's hands itching with a repressed desire to clean the place up.

My father sat down at the table and pushed to one side a row of empty beer cans.

'I'll have to clean this lot up, I suppose,' Frank said vaguely.

My mother tutted quietly. Bopadile, who had been standing out-side annoying the dog Snowy, came in. He greeted Frank, whom he knew from work, and joined the men at the table.

'Are we going or what?' my mother urged.

My mother sat in the front of the pick-up truck with my father, while Bopadile and I sat in the back. Frank followed us in his car, for the Fishes now had another car besides the one Christine had taken down to the vet in South Africa. I sat with my back to the cabin of our truck and Frank waved at me as he drove behind us. He veered a little and I suppose he was already drunk. His mouth was opening and closing and it looked like he was singing while he drove. We stopped briefly at the bottle store to buy drinks.

Then we drove through Jamestown and along the tar road that led to the mine. After about seven kilometres we turned off to the right and bumped up and down on the sand until we reached the baobab tree. Then Frank set up the braai while Bopadile and my father went to gather firewood. My mother unpacked a small fold-ing table and laid out the drinks and the salads she had made.

When they returned, I said I needed to go to the toilet.

'She needs to go to the toilet,' my father told my mother.

'So?'

'Aren't you going to take her?' he asked.

She sighed and off we went, leaving the three men enjoying themselves by the fire. I suppose she thought it was going to be a night out and instead she was stuck with me. When we came back, we found the men discussing the mine as usual, a subject my mother said she was sick and tired of.

Later, as we all gathered round to eat our meat, my mother said it was a shame Christine wasn't there. 'She would have liked this,' she said, leaning back in the chair she had brought with her and looking up at the stars. In the distance glowed the lights of Jamestown.

But no one answered her. On the pans in front of us we heard the jackals laughing. The men stood together licking their fingers while Bopadile continued to entertain them with stories from the mine. My father picked up the dishes and handed them to my mother.

'What am I supposed to do with these?' she asked.

'Ah, women!' Frank said and the men laughed.

I could sense my mother getting annoyed.

'When is Oabona coming here, then?' she asked Bopadile. She missed her friend. Bopadile looked vague. 'I will ask her. She will be bringing my child,' he said proudly.

'Child?'

'Yes.'

'But I didn't even know Oabona was pregnant!'

'You have a son?' Frank asked Bopadile.

Bopadile beamed. 'A girl, she's just a small girl.'

'Why didn't you *tell* me?' my mother went on. She couldn't get over the fact that she hadn't known. But of course no one we knew in Lephane had a telephone and apart from my mother people didn't really write letters.

'Hey, I miss her,' Bopadile said.

My mother snorted at the idea that Bopadile could miss the child when he hadn't even mentioned that he had one. She could never get over our ways of family, where a child doesn't necessarily have to live with its immediate parents. Already we were used to families being separated, the men away perhaps at the mines in South Africa. If someone was a teacher, it was quite usual to be posted over on the other side of the country from his or her husband or wife. And as for children, well, the person in the family most capable of looking after the child does so. Whatever is in the child's best interests, as my father would explain. A child, after all, used to be a family child.

My mother took it upon herself to pack all the braai things away. The men were getting a bit drunk and she was tired and wanted to go home.

Christine returned the next day with a rejuvenated Butch and then we didn't see the Fishes for a while. Sometimes it was like that – we would see Christine every single day and then suddenly we didn't see her at all for a week. It was mid-September, and everyone was complaining about how hot it had become. Occasionally we got dust storms just when what we wanted was rain.

In the following weeks Christine became something of a pillar of the community, though Jamestown was never really a community. We heard of her activities through what Frank told my father at the mine. Christine had joined a township development committee, we heard, and had been voted secretary. We also learnt that she had made several women friends and that once or twice they had gone to the baobab tree for a braai. My mother was hurt that we hadn't been invited.

'Do you want to go out with their Boer friends?' my father asked.
'No.'
'Well, then.'
'But how can they have friends like that?'

For someone who never seemed to leave her house, Christine had made a number of contacts and one day she sent Frank over with the news that she had got accommodation for the soon-to-be pre-school. At that time in Jamestown most everything was set up in residential houses. The customary court, the police station, the water utilities and the post office were all set up in medium-cost houses and this leant a relaxed air to official proceedings. When you went to buy stamps, for example, you felt you were visiting someone in their home.

'Yes, Dimpho,' the post-office woman would say to me. 'O a re eng?'

'Me, I don't say nothing,' I would reply and she'd laugh and slap the counter with her hand.

In the winter the government employees hung around outside getting warm in the sun. This made the expatriates mad because they'd drive around the corner to pick up their mail or pay a water bill and find no one at their desks. In the summer the employees would move back inside and then the expatriates would demand to know why there was no air-conditioning in any of the buildings.

There was also a bank which was open part-time, but no one was quite sure when. The bank employees would drive in two or three times a week from Thabeng and customers had to wait for them to arrive from their long trip. So the Boers would stand outside, always in a line, and complain to each other and consult their watches. Then when the employees did arrive and opened the doors, the Batswana would rush in and the expatriates, who had been so patiently queuing, would get pushed to one side. One even sent a petition about the matter to bank headquarters in Gaborone. She never got a reply.

As part of her township development plans, Christine volunteered herself to teach a group of Batswana maids. Once a week, sometimes twice, a handful of expatriate women at the Baobab Club would hold meetings at the hall near the club, where they taught the Batswana women to knit, crochet and so forth. This, the madams promised, would teach the maids a skill and allow them to make a bit of money on the side. But seeing as the maids had to pay for the lessons, it didn't really work out like that.

A bone of contention between Christine and her first maid, Joy, had been that Christine had offered to pay for Joy's lessons and Joy had shown no interest whatsoever. This was before Christine joined the group herself. But when she did, she didn't stay long. Finding herself without a supervisory role in the knitting circle, she soon gave up and threw her energies into the pre-school instead. She 'stole' two women from the knitting group and co-opted them into her pre-school plans. She got Frank to print out posters at work, me to go round with my friends to put them up, and my father to translate them into Setswana. Soon Jamestown was plastered with notices about the new school.

I thoroughly enjoyed putting the posters up, as it gave me a leadership role in my group of friends, all of whom, apart from Thebe, were younger than me. We strode around the township, me holding the posters and Thebe holding the tape, putting them up wherever we felt like it. Some we put up outside the post office, police station and customary court. Others we tried to stick on the street-light poles in the roads with the high-cost houses. The giant black and white crows perched on the top of the lights and squawked down at us menacingly.

It was rather a let-down when we had finished our little job and Thebe suggested Christine might give us some food as payment. So off we went to Christine's house, but after rattling the gate for half an hour and being barked at by Butch we eventually gave up. As compensation I told Thebe that we would play our snake game, in which we took a branch and dragged it carefully along the sand to make it look like a snake had gone by. My mother almost always fell for this joke and shrieked in alarm, but my father never did because he had done exactly the same thing when he was a child.

A day or so later Christine did give me something as a thank-you for putting up the notices – a little cloth book called *Jesus and You*.

My mother came upon me one hot windy afternoon reading it under the paw-paw tree. For some instinctive reason I tried to hide it from her, knowing, I suppose, that it would become the subject of a long conversation.

'What have you got there, Dimpho?' She bent down. This was her main concession to children, bending down. Otherwise she treated me more or less like she treated an adult. So if we played a game like snakes and ladders together, she played to win. It was an insult, she thought, to make allowances because I was only five years old.

'Christine gave it me,' I told her.

'Gave it *to* me,' she corrected.

I nodded and turned over one of the pages, hoping to entice her into the pretty pictures.

'Dimpho, where do you think you go when you die?' my mother asked me seriously. She liked asking me these sort of questions.

I pointed up to the sky.

'What's up there, Dimpho?'

I squinted into the sun to see if this was a trap. 'God,' I said eventually.

'Who told you that?' she asked me.

I couldn't remember, so I pointed back down at the book. But the seed of doubt had been sown: the seed of both religious doubt and doubt that my mother knew everything. According to the book and what I had gleaned from conversations held between adults, you went to heaven when you died. That is, if you had been good. This sounded to me like a nice idea, but my mother didn't seem to believe it, and so I wasn't sure what was right.

Neither my mother nor my father believed in a god. For my mother it had never really been an issue because she said she hadn't had a religious upbringing. But for my father it was different, because when he was a small boy his mother had become a Christian and had taken him along to church meetings and so forth. So he had believed in God, and then he had stopped. So while my mother was slightly intrigued by ideas of God, my father was angered by what he saw as a conspiracy to convert the heathens. At school, he said, he had been somewhat of a singer and as the opportunity to sing came mainly with the church he had learnt all the relevant songs. That was why he had been able to join in when Frank got drunk and started singing.

Sometimes my father would sing a church song if we were going on a journey, but always with a touch of bitterness. He would sing and I would sing along and then he would stop suddenly and mutter about what he had been singing. But apart from the hymns Frank had sung and the book Christine had given me, the Fishes hadn't really introduced religion into their conversations at all.

In October the winds died down, though we still got dust storms some days. My mother had finally packed away my warm clothes and the creams she used to stop her skin from cracking – in the winter she always complained about her elbows being dry. There was this one type of cream she used on me that I haven't been able to find anywhere since. It came in a white plastic jar with a picture of a woman on front and it smelled of coconuts. Only I had never smelt a coconut at that time, so maybe it was just a chemical thing. When I was a baby, my mother used to smear me all over with this cream until I was shiny like a wet apple. She must have picked this habit up from my father's relatives. The cream is one of the smells I have several times come close to smelling, but have never found exactly again. I asked my mother recently about this cream and she said it came from England, but I don't see how this was possible unless my grandmother sent it.

Because of the heat, even my mother left the doors unlocked for most of the day, hoping in vain for a breeze. Once she tried shutting the doors and windows and turning on the overhead fans, but they just blew hot air all round the house, so she gave this method up. She had been on at my father to get mosquito nets put on the windows, like the high-cost houses had. The nets were not so much to keep out the mosquitos as the other things that come at that time of year and mostly do you no harm at all. But mosquito nets cost money of course, money we didn't have.

One evening my mother was sitting at the table writing to my grandmother. My father and I were outside, when we suddenly heard a scream. Rushing into the house, we found she had turned over the table in her haste to get away from whatever it was that had frightened her so much.

'Mompati!' she said breathlessly.

'What is it?' he said urgently, looking round the room.

'One of those . . .' – my mother looked round frantically – 'things . . .'

'A nasty *black* thing, was it?'

'No. It was a pink thing, actually,' my mother snapped.

'Oh, one of those,' and my father relaxed.

My mother looked silly now and I bent down to pick her letter up from the floor. 'It's that time of year, I suppose. But . . .' – and she remembered her fear – 'I just looked up . . .'

We all looked at the small ventilation shaft on the wall up near the ceiling.

'I don't know what made me look up – some movement, I suppose – and then whoosh! It came tearing in and down the wall.' She finished her story and shrugged. 'Now I'm going to have to find it and kill it, I suppose.'

My father began to leave the room.

'I told you,' my mother said, 'I told you we needed mosquito nets,' and I do believe she was close to tears.

'But you don't put a net over that thing, do you?' my father asked patiently, pointing up at the ventilation shaft.

'No, but next time it will crawl in through the window.'

This attitude of my mother's to animals and insects confused me. I wasn't actually afraid of the pink spidery thing that had frightened her, though it always gave me a surprise to see one because they moved so fast. What bothered my mother, she always said, was its colour – the transparent pink yellowy legs – and the fact that when you did catch up with it and killed it a sack of brownish liquid on its back burst like urine on to the floor. And these creatures would rush like lightning into the house, tiny whispery things, and hide themselves in cracks and crevices. Then a few weeks later they would reappear ten times their original size. I would just have been curious if my mother hadn't been so afraid.

What I was afraid of, I remember, were things of the mind like familiar objects which turned into ghosts in my room at night. But I rarely said anything to my mother because she would have started a heavy conversation about what ghosts are and so forth. I remember the sheer *terror* I had about going to the toilet at night in case some Thing was going to get me. There was also a part of the bush behind our house that I was afraid of. Thebe had told me a witch caught children there and rode about on them all night long. One night I actually did see a ghost. I was coming back from a fearful trip to the toilet and had just got to the door of my bedroom when I saw an old man sitting in shadow in the corner of my room. I stood there paralysed with fear and then ran for the bed, took a flying leap on to the mattress and shut my eyes.

The next morning, as my father and I were eating our soft porridge outside, I mentioned this to him.

'Did he ask you anything?' my father asked gently.

I shook my head.

'He didn't ask you anything?'

'No.'

'Well, if he does, just answer him. Perhaps he has a question to ask.'

I was reassured by my father's casual response and promised that in future I would do just as he said, but I never saw that ghost again.

Still, at night familiar bundles of clothing took on mysterious proportions and I never let my arm hang down from the bed in case the monster beneath grabbed it and pulled me into the unknown.

A couple of days after the episode with the spider, my mother decided for once to go to Christine's uninvited and she took me along. We found Christine sitting on the floor of her mansion while a new maid washed the walls. Christine was absolutely absorbed and shrieking like a child over two kittens on the floor. Snowy the dog sat at the other end of the room, looking on in a superior fashion.

'Rosie!' Christine cried as she always did, with great drama. 'Look, aren't they so adorable?'

My mother, to my complete amazement, immediately got down on the floor and began playing too. 'In England we like cats,' she said to me softly. I stood apart from the women, watching the kittens uneasily, then finally I made a grab for one and it scratched me.

My mother laughed. 'It's just a tiny scratch,' she said dismissively. 'Where on earth did you *get* them from, Christine?'

I suppose she was surprised to see them because we Batswana are not that fond of cats, which we associate with witches, and there weren't that many around. One or two expatriates in Jamestown kept cats, but these stayed mostly indoors. Some people in the villages also had cats, but they didn't pay half the attention to them that the expatriates did.

Christine didn't answer my mother's question because she was shrieking again at the antics of her new playthings.

'Christine?'

'From Carol.'

'Carol?' my mother queried. 'Who's Carol?'

But again Christine was too busy to answer. One kitten was tearing its way up her night-gown and she was laughing like crazy.

My mother shifted nearer to the kitten on the floor. Christine picked it up and put it on my mother's lap and my mother immediately began crooning to it and stroking its fur. Faintly repulsed, I took a few steps back.

'Have you had any of those spiders yet?' my mother asked Christine.

'Don't tell me. The wall spiders? Aren't they ghastly?'

'Is that what they're called, wall spiders?'

We left the house with a kitten in a small cardboard box and my mother saying to me conspiratorially, 'Your father's going to have a hernia.' I didn't like it when my parents spoke like this about each other to me, it was like a game being played.

'Oh God,' my father groaned when he saw the kitten that night. 'Rose?'

'Yes?' My mother was all bright-eyed and defiant.

'Do we have to have a cat?'

'It will kill scorpions and snakes and those . . . things,' she said firmly and my father couldn't argue with that.

'Where did you get it from?'

'Oh, aren't we the one asking questions today?'

My father sighed and sat down to take off his work shoes.

'I got it from Christine. She has two. She got them from this woman Carol, and then after I admired them she insisted I have one.'

'Mmm.'

'Which was rather nice of her, wasn't it? She even gave me a couple of cans of kitten food as well.'

Our new kitten, which had immediately gone and hidden itself behind the cooler in the kitchen, got my mother reminiscing about England, which she very rarely did. I could never get a firm impression of the country of which she spoke. Apparently it was a small island where it rained every day and I wondered why my mother could possibly want to leave such a wonderful place. But it was also cold, she said, and people died of the cold. Buildings were tall and my grandparents' house, she told me, had two whole storeys to itself. 'Then why don't we go there?' I asked, having no idea of distance.

'We would have to travel all day in a plane,' my mother said and she left it at that.

In those days I couldn't say 'aeroplane' in English and mispronounced it as 'European', which my father loved.

'There goes another noisy European,' he would say pointing at the sky as a plane went by.

When I saw a plane, what I actually wanted to do was to make it crash down so that it would be near enough for me to see it. After a careful study of the book Christine had given me and consultations with my friend Thebe, I drew Jesus into things and asked him to help. 'Please, Jesus, make that plane crash,' I'd pray, squinting up at the clear blue sky as a plane flew overhead. About this time I also started a small book, which later became my Joke Book. It was just a small pad of paper with a flimsy cover my mother had given me, but I pored over it, practising the writing that my mother was teaching me and the numbers my father gave me to play with. I spent hours on this little book, working methodically and refusing to be rushed.

One weekend in November Christine sent Frank over to ask my mother if she wanted to see the place where the pre-school would be. Christine had apparently made friends with the big boys who ran the mine and they had come to some sort of agreement whereby Christine could hire a house for a very low rent. The building was on the outskirts of Jamestown on one of the outer roads which ran around the township. The bush behind the house had already been cleared. It was a high-cost house in a large yard with a sturdy tree.

'It's in a lovely place,' my mother said, looking around admiringly. 'God, it will be nice to be a teacher again.'

There was plenty of room outside for the two trailers which Christine explained she had ordered and which were on their way up from South Africa. Christine told my mother that she wanted her approval before they signed any rent agreement for the house, but it appeared that Christine had already made up her mind. She had come prepared with cleaning equipment, for though she had instructed her maid to clean the house before she inspected it, she obviously thought that only she really knew how to clean.

My mother was a little surprised that she was expected to help Christine to clean, but I was ecstatic because I thought it meant I would get to sweep. Instead, I was given a cloth and some cream and a bowl of hot water and set to wipe the surfaces, as Christine called them. Obediently I went to work. Christine strode around, beginning one job and then abandoning it to start another. Actually, this is a habit which I have noticed affects a lot of expatriates here: they want to be in charge of everything, so they never finish a task because they are already off on to the next thing and they can't bear to give anyone else any responsibility.

'I can just see it,' Christine enthused, standing in the middle of what would have been the living-room, and she twirled around. 'There we will build a counter' – she gestured to the kitchen – 'and the children will be served there at break-time. Here . . .' – she brought her attention back to the living-room – 'here we'll have some more cupboards built for toys to be stored in, I have already asked for donations, and all along this wall we will have a blackboard.'

My mother nodded and gave me the broom to sweep with.

'We could get those desks that lift up,' she suggested.

'Exactly.'

'And we'll need a bell too. God, it's like being a kid again!'

The first real rains came that night. In the afternoon it got hotter and hotter until it reached that point where, as my mother always said, we would either explode or it would rain. When my father came home from work, the sky was a glorious dark grey. My parents stood in the garden and, looking around, pointed out to each other where it was raining.

'It must be *pouring* over there,' my mother said admiringly, gesturing in the distance to the sky behind our garden.

'Shame. It's just spitting over there,' she added.

It seems that the English have as many terms for rain as we do for cattle. If it really rained, then my mother would announce proudly, 'It's pissing down.' Or if it was slight, then she would say to me dismissively, 'It's just a light drizzle.' Then she would sing her song: 'It's raining, it's pouring, the old man is snoring', while my father would reminisce about how when he was a child they used to have a proper rainy season and he and the other children would hitch up their underwear and jump in and out of puddles. Now I think about it, that year was probably the beginning of our six-year drought.

We sat outside and watched our dog witness its first real rain. We had named the dog Champion, and Champion knew something was going on, for it was rushing this way and that. Each time Champion settled itself down with a snort, the kitten came rubbing itself up, trying to suck on the dog's overgrown ears. Champion shrugged the kitten off and went for a quick whiz around the house.

'Shall we put them inside when it really starts raining?' my mother suggested hopefully.

'They are animals, Rose,' my father said sternly.

'So are we,' she replied.

By the time we were eating our food, the wind and lightning had begun. The sky rumbled and dust blew in through the open windows. My mother kept on getting up and going outside to check what was going on while my father tried to talk about the plans for the pre-school. While we had been at Christine's house, he had had a business meeting with Frank.

Then the first big drops began to fall. My mother took the kitten indoors and Champion ran around the house again. As the rain came down, my father turned off all the lights, which he always did when it rained, and we stood together by the open screen door watching. But after only an hour or so the rain suddenly stopped and we were left with a hot night and a gassy smell in the air.

Frank must have had very little to do at work because two days later there were new posters up around Jamestown advertising the soon-to-open pre-school. The posters were in English only this time and they urged parents to apply early to ensure their child a place. 'A new community school,' the posters said. 'Give your child the start he needs in life.' In small letters at the bottom of the poster, it said fees would be decided after 'consultation'.

'This is all moving a bit quickly for me,' my mother confided to my father after she saw the posters.

'Mmm?'

'I mean, how the hell did Christine, or Frank, get all the legal stuff done?'

'Mmm.'

'You can't just set up a school, can you? Just like that?' My mother knew how long such things took to happen in Botswana.

'These Boers have friends in high places,' my father said, but he seemed impressed himself.

'Christine is not a Boer,' my mother said, but added, 'And now she wants me to organize the fund-raising.'

'At least you'll have a job at the end of it,' my father said.

'That's true. She says it'll be a community school. What do you think?'

'We'll have to make sure it is.' My father lay down on the sofa. 'Who let that cat in here?' he asked, opening one eye.

Chapter Twelve

It was late November. There had hardly been any rain at all since that one evening and most everyone in the township was talking about the weather. Rib-thin donkeys wandered through the streets of Jamestown and looked as if they were about to keel over. On the radio the President advised people to pray.

Jamestown had a relatively reliable water supply, though, unlike the nearby villages whose boreholes seemed to be drying up. Ignoring the authorities' appeal to use less water, the expatriates continued to clean their cars at weekends and sprinkle their lush green lawns. Jamestown was a haven of luxury in a desert. The expatriates knew little of the empty hands, the dying cattle and the hungry people.

Throughout November we sweated except on an occasional cloudy day. My mother would get off her bicycle and lift up the hem of her dress to wipe the sweat from her face. My father would come home from work and immediately remove his shirt, and I ran around in my knickers. Butter taken out of the cooler melted immediately and hot water came out of the cold tap.

As the drought continued and the sun beat down in a sky so blue it hurt your eyes to look, animals started wandering in search of water. Stories of visiting animals spread through the township and were passed among lethargic employees at the post office and expatriate women in their air-conditioned houses. Some forty kilometres away a group of buffalos turned up at a tourist lodge on the edge of the pans and stood looking longingly through the fence at the lodge's swimming-pool. My father came back from work to tell us the National Parks team had decided to have a shoot-out, killing all the buffalos and then auctioning the meat at the Kgotla.

'That will be some nice biltong,' my father commented and my mother banged a dish in annoyance.

'Why do they have to *shoot* them?' she asked.

'Perhaps to show that they can,' my father replied. He knew, I suppose, what men with guns like to do.

While my mother wasn't strongly into conservation – she was one of those people who eat meat but refuse to participate in the killing of an animal – she was upset at such a brazen show of force.

Then an elephant turned up a few kilometres from the salt mine, flapping its ears and looking for water. Some of the Boers, who were very righteous when it came to wild animals, urged the mine to herd the elephant to water.

My mother was very excited by the news. 'Just imagine, an elephant!' she said and sat down to write a letter to her mother.

'It's not so unusual,' my father said dismissively, though I was also excited and longing to go and see it. 'This used to be their ranges after all.'

'Want to go see elephant,' I urged.

'"I want to go and see *the* elephant,"' my mother corrected. But my father vetoed the plan, saying that we shouldn't bother it and it could find its own way to water.

'Here comes Her Majesty's messenger,' my father announced one evening as we heard our gate open and caught sight of Frank ambling up the path.

'Frank!' my mother yelled in a fine imitation of Christine, and my father began to shuffle apologetically out of the door. My mother collapsed with an attack of the giggles.

Our puppy, Champion, circled Frank and wagged its tail. Frank bent to pick it up and the puppy slobbered on his face and waved its paws happily in the air. My father shot out of the door because he hated Champion to be picked up and petted. What my father wanted was a guard dog. Expatriates often picked up and petted their dogs and my father wanted to train Champion to bite people. His idea of training meant kicking Champion when it sat on the flowers and starving it so it would grow up nice and mean. He could tell me not to pet the puppy – 'it's not a baby,' he would say – but he couldn't very well tell Frank. When Frank picked Champion up, I waited for my father to tell him the dog was not a child and was rather disappointed when he didn't.

'Ah, Mompati,' we heard Frank say apologetically, 'ah, well, I know we owe you the money for the teaching, but Christine had just paid for a pool.' Frank rolled his eyes with the suggestion of 'You know how women are.'

'Can you possibly wait until next month?'

My father nodded. What else could he do? It wasn't exactly a large amount of money. 'I'll have to charge you interest, though,' he said. And Frank laughed agreeably. Frank had been sent over to collect my mother for a fund-raising Ladies' Night and my mother, having overheard the exchange, told me to put my shoes on and rather ungraciously we left. The closer I grew to Thebe and my other young friends the less I wanted to be dragged along to the Fishes' house, but my mother insisted. Perhaps she thought I would act as a sort of buffer between her and Christine.

We arrived to find Christine inside her mansion with the curtains drawn and the newly installed air-conditioner on as part of her struggle against the heatwave outside. Workers had begun to install the pool but hadn't finished yet. Now that summer was here my mother was swimming at the so-called public pool again, but Christine had not been there again since that time when they first met.

In the living-room there was iced coffee and sherry set out on the table. Christine had a pile of papers on the floor which her kitten was busy rifling through. Two other women were present, perched politely on either end of the leather sofa, and Christine was selling them the idea of the pre-school. As usual she was talking over the sound of the TV. She kept it on all the time even if the only pair of eyes watching belonged to the dog. She once said, plaintively, that it kept her company, but she paid no attention to it at all.

'Ah, ladies,' Christine said, smiling as my mother came in, 'here's Rosie.'

My mother bowed her head and headed for a chair.

'Oh, and Dimpho too.' Christine reached out for me, perhaps to show the other women that she and I were friends. I stiffened.

Christine gave up. 'Carol,' she said, gesturing to the more comfortable-looking of the women, 'whom I think you might know, and, I'm so sorry . . .?'

'June,' the other woman said apologetically. Christine had a way of making people sorry that she had to interrupt herself to find out such a minor detail as their name.

' . . . are here,' Christine continued, 'to help us with some fund-raising ideas.'

The women nodded their heads at my mother, apparently trying to place her in their scheme of things, while taking little glances at me and at the objects scattered around Christine's room.

'I have your kitten,' my mother said to Carol.

'Oh yes, that's right. How is it?'

Christine clapped her hands together quickly as if calling for order and began on business. I sat on the floor with the kitten and pulled its tail. While our kitten was still a skinny little thing, this one was almost twice its size and, as if to emphasize this, it swung its back leg over its head and began to lick its well-fed body lovingly.

'Loads of money,' Christine mouthed to my mother during a break in the kitchen, explaining the presence of June and Carol. I stood by the fridge waiting to be given an ice-cold Coke. Christine asked my mother to lay out the quiche and cakes, which she said she had made herself but which looked so perfect they must have come from a shop. Then we returned to the living-room, bearing the gifts.

'Don't stand on ceremony,' Christine cried and she waved her cigarette at the food.

'Oh, oh,' June said and covered her stomach with her hand. 'Not me, I'm afraid.'

Christine ignored her and handed the plate to Carol, who was looking worriedly at her friend. Carol took a slice of quiche, nibbled a tiny bit and then laid it sadly back on her plate. My mother determinedly helped herself.

They covered, as women do, a huge range of subjects, always returning to the fund-raising plan. In the many adult conversations I had sat in on, I had noticed that men talk on one or two subjects all evening, while women jump around.

'Ladies,' Christine smiled, 'it's so nice that *some* of us want to do something for this community.'

The two other women smiled, pleased with themselves.

'So, if I have it right, Carol, this is our mission now,' Christine continued just as Carol was reaching hesitantly for a piece of cake. 'What can your exercise club do for us?'

'A walk?' Carol suggested, deciding against the cake and leaning back again.

'Fine, fine. Sponsored?' Christine lit a cigarette and took a sip of her drink.

'Yes.' June got interested now and put her glass of iced coffee down. 'We can walk to the mine and back.'

June was one of the expatriate wives who prayed to the god of fitness. Only I wonder if it really was fitness that the women were after, rather than a sense of purpose to their lives. June was from South Africa and three times a week she held a keep-fit session in the hall near the Baobab Club. The women drove to the hall in their families' second cars and then leapt out in a mind-boggling assortment of clothes. Batswana walking past stared open-mouthed at the leotard with a thong that went up June's bottom.

In the summer months it was even more fascinating because June led the women into the swimming-pool, where they did keep-fit in the shallow end. From what I have since seen of aerobics in the States, the Jamestown women were way ahead of their time. The keep-fit women would line up in the shallow end and try hard to ignore the small group of children, including me, who gathered outside the fence to watch. We children were extremely good at watching and the expatriates were extremely good at providing entertainment. 'Don't stare,' my mother was always telling me. 'It's rude to stare.' Early in the mornings I would sometimes see June's women marching through the streets of Jamestown with tight shorts on and little weights attached to their ankles and wrists for all the world as if they were a chain gang.

Because their lives never demanded that they walk, walking became part of the fitness campaign and was done with gusto. June explained to Christine and my mother that she weighed the women several times a month and encouraged or yelled at them according to whichever method she considered most useful in the circumstances. I suspect few of the women actually enjoyed what they were doing and my mother said most of them hated June, but it gave them a routine in their routineless lives, a goal to strive for, a feeling they were not just frittering away their days in Jamestown.

The problem of life in Jamestown, the barrenness and the boredom, the lack of shops and the back-biting, was put on to the problem of weight. There was a notion, I suppose, that if they lost weight their lives in general would improve. It was something that they could control, and I understand now that it was part of their upbringing. And there was a lot of self-control called for, because though the women's maids did all the housework, the women themselves cooked the evening meals for their husbands. With a lot of time on their hands they cooked huge feasts and then had to prevent themselves from doing any of the eating.

Christine gave June a list of pointers for the sponsored walk, and then turned to my mother. Throughout the meeting Christine worked hard to maintain her position at the centre of the group. If she went to the kitchen, she got one of the women to accompany her, like girlfriends going to the toilet together. And if she found any two of the women talking seriously to each other she soon jumped in to break it up.

'Now, Rosie, here . . .' Christine began. 'How can we use her?'

My mother laughed nervously.

'Of course, I don't mean *use* her. She is the boss's wife, after all!'

June, the power of organizing having gone to her head, ignored the question and said to Christine, 'Why don't you join us?'

Christine shook her head brusquely and took up a pen.

'Yes,' Carol said, sensing the opportunity to convert a non-believer. 'You know, it's boredom that makes you eat so much in this place.'

'In Jamestown there's not much else to do,' June laughed supportively.

'Did you hear about the elephant?' my mother said suddenly, changing the course of the conversation, bored with the fitness routine.

There was a long pause and then June and Carol began again. 'You just see the fat falling off you,' June enthused.

Christine looked furious, but June and Carol didn't seem to notice.

'You'll see the difference in a month, I promise you,' June continued.

Christine looked as if she was losing control, so she said deceptively nicely, 'Well, ladies, I used to walk every day back in South Africa. I walked Butch all over the place. We lived in a very *quiet* area, you know. But here in the village there's – you know . . .'

The other women knew. 'I wouldn't let my daughter out on her own here,' Carol said, looking around for confirmation.

'Nor me,' June agreed. 'I tell them, "You play inside the garden and if I *ever* catch you outside alone . . ."'

My mother took a breath and tried to join in. 'I feel very safe here, safer than in England,' and then she laughed, perhaps to temper the fact that she had disagreed with them, for she was a guest and should stay polite.

'Oh, yes,' Christine said immediately, 'but still . . .'

'My Kirsty,' Carol said suddenly and forcefully, 'she tells me there's a black here who hangs around the bush – you know, near the shop – and takes pictures of little white girls.'

'Pictures?' my mother queried. 'What on earth do you mean?'

Carol unexplainably changed tack after a quick glance at June. 'And that bush really is filthy. I don't want to be vulgar, but really, the bl – the locals – you know they just wipe themselves and then leave the paper right there!'

'Well, really, I don't think that's likely,' my mother said and got up rather shakily and went to the toilet. I sensed something was wrong and pretended to be very interested in the pattern on the rug until my mother returned to the room.

When she did come back, a sense of business had been restored and Christine had instructed June to take down notes, which she was obediently doing.

'And ladies,' Christine said, 'do get your husbands to help with the heavy work.'

The women all laughed and there followed a talk on the general uselessness of men, tempered, however, with a degree of reverence because of the women's upbringing and the fact that the men worked at the mine all day long. What they did there was obviously important or else why would they have dragged the wives all this way? And then it was the men who were earning the money, so who were their wives to criticize them?

The wives passed on snippets of information and repeated phrases their husbands often said to them of an evening like, 'Mark my words, that mine's going to close down soon.' But in reality the wives were kept in the dark, as the expression goes. And having been brought up in South Africa, they didn't feel safe in Jamestown and imagined the Batswana swarming around the township biding their time. According to my mother, they talked in hushed tones to each other when a white person was killed down in South Africa and were always calling the bank in Thabeng to see what was happening to the exchange rate and all their money.

As Carol and June were preparing to leave, Carol brought up the subject of the wandering elephant, which my mother had mentioned before. What they knew had been gleaned from their husbands.

'Oh but it's gone now,' Christine said with authority.

'Is it?' Carol asked.

'My husband saw it, you know,' June offered.

'And the lion?' Christine interrupted.

'Lion?' both women said in unison and Carol put her hand gently to her neck.

'You haven't heard?' Christine said innocently, although she seemed to enjoy their reaction.

'When was this?' my mother demanded.

'Well, we only heard about it, but some of the locals saw it out by the new bar.'

'Really?' My mother was interested. 'Who saw it?'

But Christine, having made herself the centre of attention again, now said she didn't know and began to thank the ladies for all their help.

As a result of the meeting, the women had collected a list of fund-raising possibilities. A jumble sale was in the offing, the sponsored walk and a Christmas dinner dance at the Baobab Club. Once Carol and June had gone, saying it was getting late and their husbands would be wondering where they'd got to, Christine and my mother settled down to discuss them and the ideas they had come up with.

'Must have a weight problem, that June,' Christine said by way of starters.

My mother mumbled something.

'Now, Rosie, there's something I want to ask you.' Christine stressed the word 'you' as if my mother should be flattered. Christine picked up her kitten and laid it on her lap, but the kitten complained at being woken up and leapt off again.

'Don't laugh at me,' Christine warned, waving her cigarette in the air, 'but I think we're being bewitched.'

'Oh, yes?' my mother said vaguely. I perked up and moved nearer to her.

'Of course I'm joking,' Christine said, stubbing out her cigarette violently, 'but still. You remember the bone?'

'The bone?'

'You know, the bone Frank found when you and Mompati came for dinner that time?'

My mother nodded.

'We found another one. It must have been placed there while I was away at the vet's. Now, I hear you bury these things in the garden of someone's house – muti they call it down south, so that –'

'I don't think it's bewitchment,' my mother ventured. 'It's just an old dog bone, Christine. Don't worry about it.'

'Well, and I don't know how to say this Rosie' – Christine leant forward conspiratorially – 'but people around here, and I'm not being racist, I have lived in southern Africa for a while you know, and the blacks, the locals, well, there's a famous witch-doctor I hear in Kgadi.'

My mother laughed. Not because she didn't believe in what a traditional doctor could do, but because Christine believed she was a victim of one.

'Why would someone bewitch you?' she asked. ('What does Christine know of bewitchment,' she said later to my father, 'except that it's *dark* and *dangerous* and the realm of the blacks?')

'Exactly, why *would* someone bewitch me?' Christine replied, lighting another cigarette and inhaling dramatically. 'Perhaps that maid I fired? There is a lot of local witchcraft. I have heard of it, you know.'

'Not in Botswana,' my mother said firmly in an effort to squash the topic.

I knew this wasn't true and was dying to interrupt, but my mother clearly didn't want to continue the conversation.

'You never know, though,' Christine continued.

'Oh, don't get carried away, Christine,' my mother said rather sharply.

'Are you saying there's no such thing?'

'No.' My mother seemed at a loss to know how to continue this conversation. 'I'm not saying that. Of course there is traditional medicine, and some of that can involve bewitchment and so forth. And yes, there are ritual murders too.'

Christine blew out some smoke with satisfaction. 'Ritual murders,' she said and picked up her drink.

'And people don't get murdered every day in England?' my mother asked with a raise of her eyebrows.

'Well . . .' Christine began.

'But on the whole,' my mother determinedly continued, 'it's not an exciting thing. It's just that often, when things are going badly, people believe they have been bewitched. You know that woman in the post office, for example? Well, she was blind for a year because someone bewitched her.'

'Really?'

I could see that my mother regretted having said this.

'Have you ever been bewitched?' Christine was breathing heavily now.

'No, of course not.'

My mother, exhausted from the fund-raising meeting, wanted us to go, but Christine accompanied us to the gate and continued talking even after we were standing outside on the road.

'When are you coming to use the washing machine?' she asked eventually.

'Well, if it's not a problem . . .'

'Of course it isn't, Rose. Why don't you come round with the clothes and I'll set it up myself, then you can come and collect them all later.'

My mother looked unsure about someone else handling our dirty clothes and probably suspected it would be the maid, not Christine herself.

'Well, thanks for the offer, Christine, but we really don't need . . .' she began.

'But think of the work it'll save you,' Christine urged. 'We'll just pop them into the machine and that's that.' Christine leant on the gate. 'And the next Ladies' Night, could you possibly just bring a salad this time? I know how wonderful your salads are.'

My mother nodded. She knew how one thing had to be exchanged for another, and took my hand.

Christine leant further over the gate, adding, 'And tell Frank if he's not back in ten minutes I'm locking the door.'

'I think we'll wash them ourselves,' my mother said to me as we headed home in the dark.

We returned to find Frank and my father red-eyed.

'She says you are to go home,' my mother said, sitting down on one of the chairs outside.

Frank looked up guiltily. 'She said that?'

My mother nodded and avoided looking at my father, who was smiling stupidly.

'Oh dear, oh dear,' Frank said worriedly, but he didn't make a move to go. He tapped absent-mindedly on the sand with his foot.

'Well,' my mother said, getting up to go into the house, 'she says she'll lock the door if you're not back in ten minutes.'

'She said that?' Frank got up then and knocked over his beer can and my mother bent down to retrieve it.

My father accompanied him to the gate. Then my mother locked up our house, pretending not to realize that the kitten had run inside. But my father discovered it and put it firmly outside. 'It is a cat and it can look after itself,' he told her.

The following day, despite what she had said, my mother went over to use Christine's washing machine.

It was my father who encouraged her. 'She won't be in this morning. Frank told me,' he said.

'Are you positive?' said my mother, interested.

'Take her for what she's got. You're just using the washing machine, you don't have to talk to her.'

'You really don't understand, do you?' my mother snapped and off she went, as usual dragging me along. 'It's your dirty clothes too, Dimpho,' she told me.

As my father had said, Christine was not around. But the new maid, Mildred, was and she let my mother and me in. They got the machine working and then Mildred led the way back into the main house. Mildred offered coffee, but my mother said she would make it. Then we sat down and watched Mildred do the ironing.

'Mompati is your husband?' Mildred said after a while.

'Yes.'

'I know him.'

'You do? Where are you from?'

'Lephane.' Mildred pronounced the name of the village the way my father did, the way anyone who'd been living in Jamestown for a while did – with longing.

'You must be sad to be so far from your family.' My mother grew thoughtful and played with the circles her coffee cup was making on Christine's table.

Mildred sighed. 'And I am ill.' She lifted her skirt to show us a wound on her leg.

My mother drew back, shocked. 'Have you been to the clinic?'

'No, the madam . . .' Mildred raised her eyebrows – 'the madam is saying I must finish my work first.'

'Oh, well, that's not fair.'

'And, hey,' Mildred continued, as she began ironing one of Frank's shirts, 'she is always telling me what her problems are and I'm thinking that I don't want to know what her problems are. And she is saying, "Mildred, Can you just get me, Mildred, I want you to . . ."' Mildred did an imitation of Christine talking, a sort of high-pitched nasal voice we Batswana make when we want to imitate a white person.

My mother laughed, but then stopped and looked sharply at me because I was giggling.

'This one time,' Mildred said, starting to iron Christine's underwear, 'the madam gave me – how do you call? – left-overs.'

'They gave you the left-overs from their meal?'

'Yes. And I said, "Madam, I am not a dog. If you are not wanting to feed me then you can tell me that." These Boers,' and Mildred sighed again, 'they are just here to oppress us.'

'What did she do?' My mother shifted a bit in her seat and looked uncomfortable, the way she always did when a Motswana started on about what white people were like.

'She gave me some of her food.' Mildred smiled, put down the iron for a moment and then asked, 'Don't you want a maid?'

'No, sorry.' I glanced at my mother behaving so firmly, but she was picking at the sleeves of her dress.

'You have one,' Mildred said.

'No,' my mother hesitated. 'We don't have one, it's just that . . .'

Mildred looked confused. 'It is my friend, she is looking for a job.'

'Sorry,' my mother said again.

We had barely been back home an hour with our clean clothes when Frank appeared to say Christine was in a state and wanted to see my mother.

'I've just come from there.'

'Well, she's in a terrible way. This, um, accident . . .'

'What do you mean?'

'Please, Rose, could you just pop over and keep her from putting her head in the oven?'

'Let's go, Dimpho,' my mother ordered.

'No,' I scowled.

'You are refusing?' my father asked in Setswana. I scowled some more but didn't dare reply and off we went. Frank stayed with my father and they resumed where they had left off the previous evening.

We found Christine in floods of tears. As we came into the living-room, Mildred was heading out. 'The madam is ill,' she said, looking furious. Christine was slumped at the kitchen table, gulping down Coke and cigarettes while at the same time trying to breathe and stop crying.

'Christine! What on earth is the matter?' My mother hovered over her.

'She's left me, Rose.'

'Who?'

'The maid,' Christine wailed. 'That damn ... Oh, Rose, you know me, I pay her well. I bought her a uniform, for God's sake. I showed her how to wash the bath and use the microwave. And then she just ups and leaves. "Madam," she says to me. "I am asking for time off." Time off! I just gave her time off last week when she said her sister had died. Now she says it's her aunt.'

My mother, realizing nothing at all was the matter, said she must be going.

'And she's been stealing from me.'

'Yes, well, we must be off . . .'

'Oh, Rose, don't go. Don't go *now*.'

My mother hesitated.

'It's Frank,' Christine said and she hauled herself up from the chair and headed for the sofa in the living-room.

'What about him?' My mother sounded alarmed and got up to follow. Christine looked terrible, sort of pale and puffy, and I felt a tinge of something, perhaps fear, to see an adult this way. But having got my mother's interest, Christine decided against saying any more and anyway we could hear Butch happily howling outside, which meant Frank had come back.

'Don't say anything,' Christine mouthed to my mother, who, looking utterly bewildered, just nodded and stood up.

Frank entered the living-room, looking at Christine carefully and patting her on the head.

'Don't take on so,' he said comfortingly as Christine sighed and snivelled.

My mother turned to go.

'Oh, Frank!' Christine yelled to her husband, who was accompanying us out of the house, 'Give Rosie that chicken from the freezer.'

'Oh, no, I can't possibly . . .' my mother protested.

'But I insist!' Christine called from the living-room.

'Take it, love,' Frank urged, handing over the cold white package. 'And thank you,' he said pointedly in a quieter tone.

'What was the problem?' my father asked when we got home. 'Frank seemed to think there was a real problem.'

'Did you ask him what the problem was exactly?' My mother had decided to take out her confusion on my father.

'Mmm?'

'No. Well, men wouldn't do that, would they?'

'So what was the problem?' My father wasn't to be put off.

'Don't ask.' My mother bent down to take off her shoes.

My father waited.

'Christine is a loony. I just don't know what's going on in that house. I think . . .' She hesitated. 'I think she was going to tell me something and then . . . well, when we got there, it turns out the *problem*, the *accident*, is that Mildred the maid has left. We passed her as we went in.'

My father laughed. 'About time.'

'I know. Christine was in such a state though, and I mean doesn't she realize what hell she puts her maids through? Mompati, how can we be friends with someone like that? But then, just as I want to hit her, she starts on about Frank, something he's done.'

'Like what?'

'Don't get all defensive.'

'I'm not . . .'

'Oh, I don't know, I just feel there's something not quite right. I mean why does he come *here*? Why was she in such a state?'

'There are two hundred stories in the naked city and this is just one of them,' my father said, quoting a TV show he used to watch in the States.

'Very funny. You can laugh, you're the boss of their pre-school, you do realize that?' And my mother went off to have a shower.

She came back after a few minutes, having washed in what my father called the European fashion, and sat down wet but calmer.

'And the fund-raising?' my father ventured.

'Oh, that seems to be going fine. They are loaded, Christine says. There were two other women there. I told you, right? This could really be a real school, you know, Mompati. We could open a chain! And we don't need that much to do up the classrooms and get the equipment . . . Just books, really, a board, that sort of thing. Actually Christine says she has a friend who . . .' But at this point our puppy Champion started barking. My father went out to see what he wanted and found Listen from next door standing at the fence. My mother began to cook our food and took up her observation post in the kitchen.

That morning Listen had laboriously loaded into a wheelbarrow the stones he had previously piled up outside and carted them to the back of our garden. This he had done with almost as much care as he brushed his teeth in the morning. For some reason, Listen had recently taken to brushing his teeth outside by the fence. He would be out there bright and early brushing as my father set off to work, and then he would appear in the same spot shortly afterwards combing his hair. He had also taken to giving my mother little waves during the day as he leant on the fence.

My father came back inside smiling and shaking his head.

'What now?' my mother said sharply.

'He wants payment.'

'For what exactly?'

'He says he has to pay the man he borrowed the wheelbarrow off.'

My mother laughed. 'So why didn't he use some of the money you gave him last time?'

'Mmm?'

'Did he tell you before that he'd have to *rent* a wheelbarrow?' She was questioning my father closely as often he forgot to tell her things.

'No.'

'Okay. No more, right? This wheelbarrow is the end of our transactions, right?' She gave a blank little smile out of the window to Listen who was waving at her as he leapt back over the fence.

'You can talk,' said my father. Then he thought for a while, 'And he is family and we Africans believe –'

'Oh, not that again!'

'And, anyway, I didn't give him any money.'

My mother laughed and hit my father on the shoulder.

Chapter Thirteen

It was that same evening that Bopadile came round looking very spruced up. 'Whosit!' he cried, letting himself into the house. My parents looked up from the sofa, where my father had been resting and my mother had been reading an old newspaper.

'Holy shit!' my father said, using another of his favourite American expressions. He looked Bopadile up and down.

Bopadile beamed and gave us a little twirl. He wore shiny new boots, dark blue jeans and a big belt with a silver buckle. His shirt was pink silk and he reeked of aftershave.

'Aren't you boiling in that?' my mother asked.

'Oabona is coming,' he explained.

'Oh, good.' My mother perked up. 'How's she getting here?'

'She is coming with the bus.'

'Are you going to meet her, then? How long is she staying?'

My father groaned as my mother asked her usual round of questions. Bopadile told us that Oabona was arriving from Lephane that evening and would be staying for a while. She was still working as a primary school teacher. It was the first week of December and the schools had just broken up for the long hot summer holidays.

Bopadile came back some time later with Oabona, their tiny daughter wrapped on her back. My mother was pleased. She still held firmly to the idea that a family must live together. But as I've said, families in Botswana were often apart, and my father always defended the practice of children being sent to live with other relatives when the circumstances required. In this way they could form attachments to people other than what my mother called their 'real mothers'.

My mother had been brought up to believe that a good mother was one who devoted herself to her children and that to give them to someone else suggested a failing. In this way I had a different upbringing from other children, because I was part of an extended family only when we went back to Lephane. In Jamestown I was always with my mother and father.

I knew Bopadile's girlfriend, Oabona, from when we had lived in Lephane. Even if you're young, you will remember an adult you like, and children can form instant alliances. She didn't fuss over me the way some adults did, but she was kind and friendly. I can still see them in my head the way they arrived that day. Bopadile in his smart clothes, the small girl the spitting image of her father, Oabona in her travelling best. Oabona looked well, if a little tired after the journey, and she greeted my mother warmly.

'Are you still around?' she asked and my mother answered that she was.

'It has been a long time,' Oabona said, slightly accusing.

My mother was used to this sort of attitude and she just laughed, saying, 'And whose fault is that?'

We Batswana love to take the offensive in such matters and are constantly asking people, 'Where do you stay? I haven't seen you around.'

They went inside.

Oabona made herself at home by immediately helping in the kitchen despite the general lack of space. My mother said later that she was surprised they hadn't gone to Bopadile's house first, as Oabona had just arrived from a long journey. But it shows respect to visit your relatives first. And if you really want to show respect when you visit, then you stay the whole day. This habit drove my mother crazy, because where she comes from people visit for a short while and then they leave, perhaps making a specific arrangement to meet again.

The little girl was put on the floor and she sat rather bewildered on a small rug. My mother had not seen Oabona properly since we had left Lephane, so they had a lot to discuss. My father and Bopadile went outside to talk men's talk as everyone now seemed to be in their rightful place.

By keeping very quiet, I found out that Oabona was here for the long summer holidays. Though she was a primary school teacher in Lephane, she wanted a transfer back to her home village. But of course the powers that be, those who appoint and transfer people, didn't care at all about where someone wanted to be. Oabona looked round my parents' house with great interest because it was such a vast improvement on her own. Primary school teachers weren't treated that well then, and they definitely aren't now, and in Lephane she had been sharing a small two-room concrete house with two other teachers, a relative and her daughter. They had an outside toilet shared by some ten people and they cooked mainly outside too. When it rained, Oabona said, the water gathered up all the shit and litter in the yard and formed a pool through which she had to wade every morning to the school buildings.

'Don't you think I am fat?' Oabona asked my mother suddenly, putting down the knife she was holding to display her stomach.

My mother hesitated, not knowing what would be the best response.

'Mm,' she said, laughing a little to show this could be taken either way.

'You don't think so?' Oabona looked disappointed.

My mother realized she had taken the wrong approach and immediately said, 'Yes, you have put on a lot of weight!'

'Yes, I have really expanded,' Oabona said, looking pleased with herself. But then she looked down at her body and shook her head. 'This will all go now that I am working again.'

'Have you been off work?'

'The baby.'

'Oh, of course.'

'And, hey! My mother, she fed me nicely.'

It was the custom then, and still is in most parts, that when you were pregnant you went back to your mother's place and were fattened up and waited on until you were ready to go back into the world. Oabona went back to the potatoes and began explaining all that happened in the past few months. She said she had had a difficult labour and for that reason had named her child Kedule, meaning 'I have come out'.

Oabona was a comforting woman to be around. Her movements were measured and slow, she was quick to scold but mainly did it for her own amusement, and if you were lucky, she would set off on long stories punctuated by lots of mouth noises and hand slaps. She was starting one such story now while my mother was cutting up tomatoes. She described how another teacher at her school had been given a transfer because her boyfriend was someone high in the Ministry. Oabona was furious because she had been asking for a transfer for years. Now that Bopadile had a job, she wanted a transfer to Jamestown but had been unsuccessful.

My mother kept on interrupting Oabona with her usual what, why, when and where questions, which Oabona answered as best she could without ruining the flow.

Before Oabona had quite finished her tale of woe, my mother started telling her about Christine and the pre-school and even promising her a job. Oabona looked a bit disbelieving and scolded Kedule, who was crying on the floor. She gave me a quick smile as I stood in the doorway listening. I loved to look at Oabona. She had, and still does, such a smooth round face, a bit like my mother's before all the sun got to it, and her eyes are what I believe are called almond-shaped with clear black centres. And she had this way of turning down the corners of her mouth, as if to say, 'Do you think I'd believe that?'

My mother shushed Oabona out of the kitchen, feeling guilty that as a guest Oabona was working, and Oabona took up residence outside, calling me so that she could play with my hair.

'I'm going to make you look so powerful,' she always said when she did this and then she would hold me in a vice-like grip while she combed through my hair. My mother 'humphed' a bit because when she combed my hair I always caused a scene, but who could refuse Oabona? Kedule had been placed on the sand outside and she watched the procedure with careful interest.

My mother, the cooking under control, came outside and sat next to Oabona. She began to tell her again about Christine and Frank. 'I really don't know, Oabona,' she said worriedly. 'You can meet her and tell me what you think, but I'm sure that if this school is going to get off the ground you can get yourself a job. After all, they say Mompati is the boss.'

'Is that so?' Oabona gave some noises of encouragement.

'But, on the other hand, she makes me so uncomfortable, you know?' My mother suddenly remembered something. 'She tried to give her maid scraps off the table as if she were a dog.'

'*Ijo!* As if she were a dog,' Oabona echoed. 'She sounds like a buffalo head.'

My mother laughed. 'No, Frank is the buffalo head, and Christine is Her Majesty.'

'Girl hungry,' I chimed in, gesturing to Oabona's daughter who was eating dirt.

'The girl *is* hungry,' my mother corrected.

Bopadile and Oabona stayed to eat and then, after Oabona had helped to wash up, they set off to Bopadile's tiny house. My parents settled down to talk money: Frank had asked that they invest in the school as this would make it easier for them to be put down as the owners. My father was in the process of applying for a small loan. He would be putting in a fraction of what Frank was investing, he explained to my mother, and there was also talk of pay rises at the mine. My mother got excited at the idea of being a teacher again, and the possibility of working with Oabona too.

Oabona and her daughter had arrived just as we were preparing to leave Jamestown. My father had saved up his leave and we were heading to Lephane for the summer holidays. We were all ecstatic. My father would be able to see his mother and check that she was okay and fill her up with supplies. Though it was clear that there hadn't been enough rain, he also wanted to hire a tractor for her so she could start ploughing. One of his most important jobs would be to give a telling-off to any family members who needed telling off. My mother would be surrounded by people who loved her and I would rejoin all my relatives and have fun in Lephane the way it wasn't possible to do in Jamestown. Though my mother clung fast to her tight idea of family, she was only too happy to see me go off to the cattlepost which I often did during our holidays in Lephane.

The cattlepost is where people keep their domestic animals, their cows and goats. When school closed most children headed off to the cattlepost where they were given various jobs to do. On the whole, only the boys were sent out with the cattle, though it depended on the household.

So our cattlepost was where we kept our family's cattle, in an area of land half a day's journey from Lephane. We lived simply there, often sleeping outside, and not washing for days. In the mornings we drank fresh milk and at night we sat around the fire and told stories. But though I always enjoyed the change of scenery, I was afraid of the cattle. I blamed this fear of cattle on my mother, for whoever heard of a Motswana being afraid of cows? And people laughed at me for my fear.

People at the cattlepost near Lephane also said I danced funny and I blamed this on my mother too. In fact anything that made me not fit in I blamed on my mother. At the cattlepost I much preferred catching chickens or sweeping the huts to anything else. My father had taught me how to catch chickens almost before I could walk and the adults would split their sides laughing as they watched me running round the huts. I would eventually catch the chicken, while my mother, if she was there, would look on worriedly. And then I would present it to my grandmother. 'There is no one who knows how to cook a chicken like your grandmother,' my father would then say approvingly.

Nobody liked Christmas in Jamestown. For the expatriates there was nowhere to buy Christmas presents or decorations, no billboards or television telling them how many shopping days to go until the Big One. There were very few friends to visit and the older children came up from their private schools in South Africa and moaned. Christine reminisced about Christmas decorations in shops in England and piped carols and Christmas trees and snow. I had heard that snow was meant to be beautiful because it coated the land in white. But my mother told me it was so cold you could die in it.

Christmas in Botswana is a time for family, a time for picnics and parties, a time when adults buy children new clothes. Because Jamestown was an artificial place and no one had relatives or roots there, those who could left for Christmas, making arduous cross-country journeys back to their families.

So in the second week of December my father woke us before it was light. The evening before we had heard the first of the flamingoes flying over, crying into the long hot night. Then began the long process of getting ready for a road trip. In the back of the car we loaded battered suitcases of blankets, just in case it rained and the nights were cool. My father strapped down a big plastic container of water, for no trip should ever be taken without water. We also had the spare wheel, the jack, and a drum of petrol. All of this was built around a sort of nest of more blankets, where I would be able to lie down and sleep. Some of the journey would be on sand roads and then we moved slowly, my nest cushioning me from the bumps and blows.

The previous night my grandmother had made sandwiches for the trip and we had filled the cooler with ice to store the food and soft drinks. Although my father would have preferred do the whole long trip in one go, my mother liked to take breaks on the way and that was what the sandwiches were for. We had asked Listen next door to feed the animals, so food for them had to be put out as well.

As the sun came up, we got into the car and off we set. 'Bye-bye, Jamestown,' my mother said cheerily as we headed away from the township and on to the tar road heading north. We passed one or two ostriches tip-toeing across the road in the early-morning light and later a giraffe, which turned its head slowly as we passed. Then we didn't see any more animals except for donkeys and goats and cows until we stopped for our first break. My mother chose a spot under two tall palm trees in an area near the village of Poloko, where she now lives. We piled out of the car and she opened the cooler and got our sandwiches out. My father infuriated her by opening the sandwich and eating the filling first and the bread afterwards.

We arrived in Lephane late at night and, though we couldn't see much, the very smell of the air was different from that of Jamestown. Unlike Jamestown, Lephane was a real village. There were very few concrete houses. Instead everyone had their compounds and when it rained the round, brown houses of the village blended in with the rest of the land. We drove along the main road that cut through Lephane. Women walked slowly by in the hot night, wearing wrappers and scarves around their heads. Men walked by holding hands and talking together. Outside one of the bars electric lights had been strung up and people stood around enjoying themselves and roasting meat. I sat upright in the back of the car, nose to the wind, sniffing the sweet smell of hundreds of small fires.

We turned off the main road and wove our way around houses until we arrived at my grandmother's. People came out from their yards and called and waved at us and a group of small children ran behind the car shouting. We entered my grandmother's compound to find her sitting by the fire and we went forward to greet her. 'Ah, the people of Jamestown,' my grandmother laughed, and she scolded the small children for making so much noise. For the next two weeks we stayed in Lephane and things were just as they had been before.

Many villagers went to their cattleposts for Christmas and slaughtered goats and cows. Back in Lephane the bars stayed open extended hours and the churches were full. The police descended in their small white vans with barred back windows and set up holiday road blocks. The Zionist men in their prison-like uniform stomped their feet in the early hours of the holiday week. People got drunk at picnics and spoke loud, elongated English, competing in the fanciness of their sentences. While in a country like England people might be complaining that Christmas was becoming commercialized, in Lephane Christmas couldn't yet be sold because hardly anyone had the money to buy it. But the missionaries had done a good job, and the people of Lephane cherished the day because of little Jesus.

That year we had rain in Lephane on Christmas Day, which should have been a good sign. Early in the morning my age mates and I hitched up our underwear and played in the puddles. Soon afterwards the frogs came out and sang. Wispy flying creatures shot out of the earth and whirled around in the sky. 'Compliments of the season,' people who knew some English said to each other as they shook hands. My mother loved this expression. 'Compliments of the season,' people would say to each other as late as February. On Christmas Day I wore my new dress, played in the puddles and stuffed my face with meat. Who could have asked for anything more?

Chapter Fourteen

We returned refreshed from our Christmas that year. But within an hour of reaching Jamestown my parents started bickering. All Christmas they had hardly mentioned the mine, the Fishes or the pre-school, but as we reached the turn-off to the township they started snapping at each other about apparently unconnected things. My father was driving too fast, my mother said. My mother was paranoid, my father said. I huddled down in my nest in the back of the truck and wished they would shut the interconnecting window so I wouldn't have to hear them.

We returned to Jamestown to face a new problem. While we had been away, Beauty, our neighbour, had been fired from the mine for using abusive language. No one knew the whole story, but it seemed she had told a white boss that he should go back to his own country. Within forty-eight hours a trial had been held at the mine and Beauty found guilty of insubordination. Oabona, who had been in Jamestown the whole holiday period, told my parents the story. A few days after the trial at the mine, Beauty had been cleared out. Sure enough her house was deserted, my friend Thebe gone and there was a big empty space next door to us. Listen, however, had not left with the rest of the family, instead he had moved uninvited into our tiny servant's quarters.

No sooner did our car pull up than out shuffled Listen, hurrying along the pathway to open the gate for us. 'Dumelang,' Listen said, rattling open the gate. 'Compliments of the season!'

'Dumela,' my father half-heartedly replied.

'Have we come to the right house?' my mother asked.

My father drove the car in and Listen closed the gate behind us. After asking us about our holidays and how the family were, Listen got to the point. 'I have been protecting your property while you were away,' he announced. 'And again, I have been feeding and watering your dog and cat.'

My mother looked daggers at my father. But Listen, it seemed, was off on some errand somewhere and after saying 'farewell!' he hurried away.

'How did he get the key?' my mother hissed. 'Did you leave the place unlocked?'

My father just groaned. My mother briskly unpacked the car and then went and peered around the servant's quarters. The toilet was open and had been cleared up. Through the window of the main room my mother pointed out a roll of foam and Listen's possessions, which were neatly piled in one corner. Glinting in the evening sun was an expensive-looking tape deck. My father later discovered that all the keys of the servants' quarters on our street were the same.

Christine and her ladies had managed to raise some money for the school. Before the Boers went off to South Africa for Christmas and the Batswana to their homes or cattleposts, they had held a jumble sale, a sponsored walk and a dinner dance. With the expatriates earning so much money and having very little to spend it on in Jamestown, funds were easily raised, and the mine also donated money as part of their pretence of helping the 'community'. My father had put in an undisclosed amount and he was named as owner and chairman of the board of trustees. Strangely enough, he didn't have to do anything else, as Christine had taken care of everything. She placed an advert in a national paper for a headteacher and promised my parents that she would set up a school council and a parents/teachers association.

In mid-January Jamestown Tots, as the school was to be known, opened its doors for the first time. On the same day schools across the country reopened for the beginning of the new academic year. Christine rushed around like an over-wound mechanical toy. The sort of toy that seems harmless and childish enough until you look at it closely and see how creepy it really is. At six in the morning a haggard-looking Frank appeared at our gate, while Christine remained in the car revving the engine and beeping for my mother to come to work. By praying to Jesus most of the night before, I was well and truly ill, far too ill, I thought, to go to school. But my father woke me up with the sun and insisted I got ready.

'And don't even think about wearing your party dress,' my mother called sleepily from the bedroom.

If Jesus had done everything I asked of him, I might have stayed a believer to this day. I was not happy with the idea of being under Christine's thumb all day, and I was sulking because my friend Thebe had gone.

It was a sweltering summer morning at the school and there was only one tree to provide shade. It was so hot that when you put your foot down crickets flew up into the air and landed on your arm. It was also the time of year when mophane worms began crawling along the tar road which led into Jamestown, and people were gathering along the roadside to harvest them.

Two beige trailers had arrived from South Africa over Christmas, and Christine let it be known that for the time being one would be hers and the other would serve as the staffroom. In her trailer Christine already had a carpet and on the wall there was a gilt-framed teacher's certificate, which she pointed out to my mother and me.

My mother glanced at it and asked, 'Is it yours?'

Christine, distracted by something outside, said, 'Mm?'

'C. Brown,' my mother read from the certificate.

Christine turned round. 'Maiden name,' she said on her way out.

I trailed after Christine and my mother eventually followed.

Christine asked us to gather for assembly, though some of the younger ones continued to mess around in the sand. Meanwhile Oabona had arrived, having found someone to look after her daughter during the day. When my mother put her name forward, Christine gave Oabona a job on the spot. 'Your reference is enough for me,' she said to my mother. Now the two of them were sitting in the 'staffroom' waiting. Christine sent one of the white kids to go and fetch them and obediently they came out. Oabona, who could never get up on time, was still fussing with the buttons on her dress and grumbling that she'd had nothing to eat for breakfast. But overall she was happy to have a job. This morning she was resplendent in a dress the colour of new grass.

Christine now lined us up in three rows and, looking frantic but pleased with herself, delivered a makeshift address. She told the mothers and maids to remain at a respectful distance under the tree, but as the mothers were paying a substantial amount of money for the privilege of sending their children to Jamestown Tots, they wanted to get as good a view as they could and stayed where they were. They listened now as Christine, in her self-appointed role as headteacher, told us that our parents were expected to provide our uniforms, which could be bought from the school. They were also to pay for books, paper and everything else we used in the school.

Some of the Batswana mothers began shifting in protest. 'Ijo!' said one and she asked her neighbour where the extra money was to come from. But on the whole I think most of them believed that if something was expensive it was bound to be good. As most of the white women had sent their maids, there were only a few expatriates present, and they were now busy chatting happily to each other in a small group. Some were limbering up for their keep-fit class.

Christine took charge of things. At 12 o'clock when school closed, my mother and Oabona were asked to unpack the books and set up a library and I was instructed to help them. Christine told us in passing that she'd ask for another donation from the mine so the school could buy a TV and video. My mother looked amazed. She had in mind some simple reading, writing and colouring.

My mother and Oabona soon discovered that the books Christine had got for the school had one theme – God. Oabona pulled out a highly expensive-looking series of hard-cover books and began flicking through them. She passed one over to my mother.

'Oh God, not missionaries!' my mother exclaimed. 'Mompati will have a hernia.' Oabona raised her eyebrows in the direction of Christine, who was now heading up the trailer steps. My mother went on to another box of books, beautifully illustrated English readers.

'Aren't they lovely?' Christine said, coming up and breathing heavily over my mother's shoulder.

'Expensive?' my mother asked.

Christine declined to answer. 'Just make sure you don't let any of them take them home,' she said and then she breezed off back outside.

'But I thought she just said they have to pay for them?' my mother complained to Oabona. Now that she could talk to Oabona, my mother found it easier to complain about Christine, though not yet to her face.

'Careful, Dimpho,' my mother said as she caught sight of me trying to unpack a set of big shiny dictionaries.

The next day everything was set up. Christine had transformed an empty high-cost house into a real school. The trailers were clean and had new locks on their doors, and some men from the mine were busy fitting an air-conditioner into Christine's one. The class-rooms were spotless and covered with bright pictures. There were about eight wooden desks and a fully stocked bookshelf in each converted bedroom. Under the tree outside Christine had had a blackboard set up and I think she fancied herself teaching in the open air, probably picturing herself in a white dress and a straw hat surrounded by obedient and grateful little brown faces. Near the tree there was a brightly painted climbing-frame and, funnily enough considering where we were, a sandpit.

I was assigned to a class in what would have been the front bedroom and I chose a desk at the back in the corner. While the white children banged around the place asking loudly where the teacher was, we Batswana sat carefully in our seats and looked around reverently. We were the children of parents with money, of course, so we all knew some English, and English was the reason most of us had been sent to the school. Batswana at the mine wanted their children to get on in life and if sending them to a pre-school meant doing without other things, then they were willing to make the sacrifice. The scholarships Christine had promised had not yet materialized.

My mother entered the room and asked us each to get out our English readers. 'Now,' she said after introducing herself, 'lesson one is the national anthem, but I think it would be nicer if we sang Botswana's national anthem rather than the South African one that is here.' And she smiled brightly at us.

We Batswana, immaculate in our school best, rose to the occasion and sang our hearts out. Then my mother invited the other children to sing their national anthems too.

Christine flew in at one point and handed my mother a pile of sheets. 'Religious instruction and a list of concerns,' she said, and breezed out again. My mother, frowning, put the papers to one side of her small desk and continued with what she was saying.

My mother worked hard at the school for that first month and I did too – to prove I could, I suppose. We children got along fine, considering – and with so few of us in the class we all advanced well. It was nice to have something to do in the day now my friend Thebe had gone, and I coloured in my readers happily enough. Oabona was in charge of the youngest children, my mother the middle ones like me, and Christine the older ones. Christine held a little election and a white English boy in our class was elected supervisor. I was elected monitor. We were given little badges with our names and titles on, and we were given jobs like supervising the rooms being cleaned up at the end of the day.

To find out how well we could write my mother gave us a simple question sheet to fill in. She took the sheets home with her and showed them to my father. One of them worried her. A small white boy had written, 'My favourite animal is a Piet, I like it because it is so disgusting. The animal I am afraid of is a Piet, I am afraid of it because it hurts me.'

'What do you think?' my mother asked.

'Sounds scary.' My father came up to look at the sheet.

'What do you think a Piet is?' She handed the sheet over.

'A father?'

'Would he call his father Piet?'

'I don't know. Let's see the others.' He began to read them out. '"My favourite animal is a vampire, I like it because it is scary and it kills people"'. My father laughed. 'What a great education these Boers give their children.' He read another sheet out. '"When I am alone I like to imagine"'.

'Isn't that sweet?' my mother said, smiling.

'"My nastiest thought is to kill people,"' my father continued, frowning.

'Now, are you ready for this?' my mother said, laughing. She got out the list of concerns Christine had given her that first morning. 'Apparently Her Majesty asked the parents to forward any concerns about their kids. Guess who had the most concerns to forward?'

'Our friendly Boers?'

My mother started running through the list. 'Erna has an allergy to bee stings, though it says here she has not been stung. David has hay fever, as do most of them. This one is allergic to milk, and . . . Oh, here's another. This one is allergic to flea bites and cannot eat peanut butter because he gets stomach cramps. What do they think we're going to be feeding them? And this one has bloody noses, which it says here can be stopped quickly with gentle pressure. Good job they told me that or I wouldn't have known what to have done . . . And here's a couple who suffer from heat stroke . . . Dear God.'

'Good job this is not America,' my father said grimly, 'or they would sue you if something went wrong.'

It was in February, after a few hard-working weeks, that my mother had her first real confrontation with Christine. As they worked in the same place all day long, they had not been seeing each other socially. And Ladies' Night had ground to a halt so my mother managed to successfully distance herself from Christine outside working hours. But one day during our class a small child brought a message for her. Apologising to the class, my mother followed the child out. The rest I heard at home that evening.

'I was summoned by Her Majesty,' she told my father as he took off his shoes.

'Mm?'

'You heard! Do you know what that woman said to me?' My mother's voice rose slightly. She was trying to laugh it off, but she was clearly angry and upset. 'Her Majesty said to me, "Rosie" – I wish to fuck she'd stop calling me Rosie. She said, "Rosie . . ."' She waved her head impatiently at my father when he gestured to her not to say 'fuck' in front of me. 'Her Majesty said, "Rosie, I hear you took it upon yourself to teach the Botswanian anthem." Remember, I told you about the South African one, Mompati?'

'Yes.' My father had taken off his shoes and was listening attentively now.

'I mean she actually calls me into her fucking – oh, does it matter? – her damn trailer and *tells me off*!'

'So what did you do?'

'Oh, nothing, I just backed down. I mean . . .' My mother paused and then immediately contradicted herself. 'I stuck to my guns and said, "Well, after all we *are* in Botswana," and so on, but once she'd told me off she became all nice, you know the way she can when she wants to.'

'When she wants something?'

'Exactly.'

'So, what did she want?'

'Nothing. At least she didn't say.' Then she added grimly and with a little flourish, 'For now.'

'Maybe this job wasn't such a good idea?' my father ventured.

'Nonsense,' my mother said briskly. 'As long as she keeps out of my hair it's fine, the actual teaching is great. And I need a job.' She smiled to finish the conversation off on a firm and cheerful note.

'Oh, oh, here comes Listen,' my father said and he pretended to duck under the table. Listen, however, was off on one of his mysterious missions and he hurried past the window not even stopping to give his usual little wave. Listen, the Self-Appointed Servant, my mother had taken to calling him. But Listen kept himself to himself in our servant's quarters and nothing had been said about him moving out. Neither my mother nor my father could quite bring themselves to do so, though my father had refused point-blank to give him any money. He was a distant relative, so it was hard to kick him out of a room where no one was staying anyway.

Listen did do odd jobs around the place and he seemed to have become best friends with Bopadile, who had a mysterious number of days off, and they spent a lot of time together. Bopadile had begun spinning fantasies about how the Batswana should arm themselves, kill all the Boers, take over the mine and then set up guerrilla bases in the bush.

School went on for another month with little mishap. A distant relative from Lephane came to stay with us briefly on his way down to the capital in the south. He brought some watermelons with him. My mother and father had very specific ways of eating watermelons. My mother would insist on slicing them up, whereas my father would cut them in half, using his fingers to scoop out all the flesh. I had loved the watermelon season back in Lephane, for we would all go to my grandmother's fields and harvest her crop, usually plentiful despite the lack of rain. We would work our way from one end of the field to the other, picking up green, white, yellow speckled watermelons often as large as my head.

Ater the business of the national anthem, Christine more or less left my mother alone to teach and my mother and Oabona threw themselves into their work. As the teacher's daughter I kept a low profile and tried not to pull too many faces in class. 'You're improving,' my mother would say when we got home.

With my mother out half the day at work, domestically there were many arguments. She resented working both inside and outside the house. She came home from school and got into rages over dishes in the sink and sand on the floor. She began over something small, perhaps a stubbed toe, or a cup slipped from her hand, and she would swear under her breath. Then she would swear out loud and my father, feeling intimidated, would walk outside. In the end my mother made a rota of housework, but my father was so used to having a woman looking after his life in one way or another that it simply didn't occur to him that certain things needed cleaning half the time. When he did these jobs he did them well, better than my mother, and he enjoyed them. But they were rarely his idea. If he had been the one at home, however, I'm sure everything would have been shipshape, to use my mother's expression.

Things didn't stay quiet at school for long. One day, as my mother was teaching, she paused in what she was saying to listen to the noise coming from next door. In Christine's classroom a girl was screaming. My mother was about to rush next door, but then Christine's voice cut in louder than the girl's, and there was silence. We carried on with our lesson. Some of us giggled. The new batch of prayer sheets from Christine lay upside down on our desks and we were busy drawing on the clean side, but we were all alert to the silence next door. When the supervisor rang the bell, we streamed outside to find out what had been going on. That afternoon my mother told my father what had happened before he had even time to take off his shoes.

'I think Christine is hitting them.'

'Yes?' My father had had a long day and was only half listening.

'Today . . .' My mother looked round to see where I was before she continued. 'Dimpho, take this note round to house number 75, give it to the mother of Kgomotso. You know her?'

I nodded. Kgomotso was a girl in Christine's class.

'It's about the parents' association. Go on now.'

I obediently took the note, but hesitated in the doorway to hear what my mother was going to say next.

'Today she hit one of the girls, I think. I couldn't find her afterwards to see what had happened.'

Now my father, being a Motswana, wasn't so much bothered by the hitting, but he was wary of Christine. 'Was it a black kid?' he asked.

'I don't know – Dimpho, are you still here?'

I ran off with the note.

It was an early summer evening, warm and bright outside. I hurried off, passing Christine's house on the way and walking on the other side of the road to avoid Butch's drooling face up against the fence. I passed three boys from school. One greeted me with, 'Hello,' and then they passed, deep in conversational competition but walking slowly like they didn't want to get home.

'They did have machine-guns then,' one of the boys said, kicking a stone along the pavement.

'In World War Two?' the second boy asked incredulously.

The third boy was walking with a stick held menacingly in front of him. 'That was in olden times,' he said and made to hit a tree.

I wondered what they were discussing. At breaktime all the white boys played together, always with guns, shooting and killing. And they always played with toys their parents had bought for them from shops. There was something aggressive and yet pathetic about the way they played. I knew that what they wanted was for someone like me to try and join in so they could close ranks and refuse to allow me to participate. I was in a dream until I heard Christine calling me and I hesitated, wondering if I could pretend I hadn't heard.

'Dimpho. Hey, over here!' She was at the fence and waving frantically, so I went over, dragging my heels on the tar road that had become sticky in the summer sun.

'Ah, Dimpho.' She smiled down at me and said in the voice she reserved for children, 'Come here, I want you to take something to that mother of yours.' She laughed as if my mother had done something naughty but had been forgiven. 'Butch!' she yelled, and she collared the dog and ushered me up the driveway. It was the first time I had been at Christine's alone and I felt a dreadful sense of foreboding.

Christine abandoned me in the living-room and I stood silently looking round. She took some time to reappear and just as I began to think she had forgotten me, her voice called me down the corridor. I entered the doorway from where she had called and breathed in a smell of perfume and sour milk.

It was half dark inside the room. Christine was sitting on a bed writing on a pad of paper and there was something wrapped up in tin foil next to her. But it was how she looked that stopped me short. She had let her hair down, and instead of the usual tidy bun there was a straight, lanky mass hanging down her head and face and even below her shoulders. I had never seen such long, straight hair, my mother's being short and curly, and I was shocked. When Christine looked up, I stepped backwards without thinking, she looked so different, her face tired and flushed with this doll hair pouring down her sides. One move and the strands went all over the place, and because her hair was usually tied up, it seemed sort of secretive to see it this way.

'What's wrong?' she said sharply.

I mumbled that it was nothing, but I was still staring uneasily at her hair.

'Well take this, then,' she said and I reached out my hand to take Christine's folded letter and the tin-foil package, which was warm from whatever food Christine had packed inside.

I left the house shakily, feeling I had seen something private, something I wasn't meant to see. Christine was really beginning to make me nervous. There was something a little too charged about her, something wild. Perhaps, in retrospect, it was because she was often drunk and as a child I could sense this air of unpredictability.

Outside it was slightly cooler and, reassured by a gentle breeze, I continued on my errand and then took Christine's letter and package home to my mother. She took the letter, interested in any new development, and read it to herself. The food she put to one side saying, 'I wish she'd stop sending us this stuff, we're not a charity, you know.' Then she sighed, handed the letter to my father, put on her shoes and wiped her hands on a tea towel. 'And you can come too,' she told me, though as far as I knew I had done nothing wrong. Perhaps she just wanted the company.

By the time we got to Christine's, it was nearly dark and the street lights were on outside the high-cost houses. As Butch never bothered her, my mother opened the gate confidently and went into the house with me trailing behind. Frank's car was not there and the only light from a house usually ablaze with lights was coming from the bedroom. My mother called loudly and when there was no reply we went in. We found Christine in her bedroom. Now my mother, who wanted to know about the screaming that day at school, wasn't about to be lured into confidences and for once she stood her ground.

'I'm in here,' Christine called in a stage whisper from down the corridor.

'Well, we'll just wait in the living-room until you're ready,' my mother replied.

'I feel terrible,' Christine said but eventually she came out, clutching a silken robe and holding her head in one hand.

'Oh, yes?' my mother said, smiling in a tight fashion.

'You heard about today?' Christine sat down on the sofa.

'You mean the girl?' My mother was obviously relieved that Christine had brought the subject up herself – in fact, I think the wind was rather taken out of her sails.

'Oh, I shouldn't have hit her, I know, but Lord, she was behaving badly.'

'It was . . .?'

'Ka . . . Ka . . . Oh, I can never remember her name . . . That tall dark one.'

'Kgomotso?' my mother offered.

'That's the one. Well, she tore up one of the girls' books and then denied it. I told her off, punished her with lines and she insulted me.'

My mother raised her eyebrows, surprised that a Motswana child should even consider insulting an elder. In those days this was relatively uncommon.

'You know how it is when you've had a bad day?' Christine appealed, rubbing her temples frantically.

'And then Frank.'

My mother looked alert – something had felt wrong ever since we had entered.

'What about Frank?'

'Well, as you can see he's not here,' Christine said bitterly, sweeping one arm around the room.

'He's at work?'

'If only we knew,' Christine said sarcastically.

My mother didn't look like she was sure how to take this. I hung my head, embarrassed and longing to leave.

'Is there something wrong?'

Christine opened her mouth and two big tears rolled down her cheek. 'He's done this before of course. I thought that being here it would be different.' She lit a cigarette and her hands were shaking.

'He may seem all lovely – oh, I know his act. In South Africa he had an affair, you know.'

My mother, looking appalled, said she didn't.

'Well, I just thought as everyone else knew, you might have done too.'

My mother looked confused.

'Oh, yes. When I was pregnant last time, that's when he started having his little affair with a woman at the company.'

'I thought you had been teaching?'

'Yes, but this was before that.'

My mother sat down at last.

'So, good old Frank was having an affair with a secretary, would you believe?' Christine's eyes brimmed. Then she shook herself and got up and went to the kitchen. She returned with a full glass and one for my mother. She seemed to have forgotten I was there and my mother appeared rooted to the sofa.

'And they had a child.'

'You're kidding!' my mother said and then bit her lip.

'No I am not *kidding*. They had a child.'

'My God,' my mother said, obviously shocked. You never really know about people, she told my father later, you never really know what anyone has been through in their lives.

'And then he moved in with her,' Christine continued.

'While you were pregnant?'

'Exactly.'

'My God.'

'Dimpho,' Christine said to me. 'Take that picture down . . . No, the one next to it.' I handed over one of the photographs on top of the huge TV. 'You see?'

My mother peered closely at the photo. 'You're pregnant.'

'Yes. And I lost that child. And that woman named her child Mpho, meaning 'gift' of course,' and she laughed. 'So, you see . . .'

There was silence for a moment. My mother, who, though a

born questioner, never pried into something she considered personal, was at a loss as to what to say next. Then we all stiffened as car headlights swung up the driveway and Butch started barking.

'Shall I go?' my mother said. 'I have a lot to do for tomorrow,' she added lamely. 'But if you want me to –'

'Yes, yes.' Christine wiped her face dry. 'Thank you so much, Rose,' and she looked quite pitiful, as if any attempt at a smile would end in more tears.

We hurried out. Frank, who said a cheery 'Good evening,' stood looking puzzled as my mother pushed past him without a word and out the gate. I ran to catch up with her.

'You'll never guess what . . .' my mother said breathlessly as we hurried into our house. 'Dimpho, isn't it time for bed?' I pulled a face and remained in the doorway. 'Oh, you difficult child,' she said, but she smiled as she pushed me gently towards my room. She was eager to talk with my father.

Talking about other people, gossip as it is called, was a way for her to read the world around her and she enjoyed it. I lay in bed that night and listened to the up and down tones of my parents talking until I drifted off to sleep.

'No wonder she's like that,' I heard my mother say.

'Terrible,' I heard my father mutter.

It was about this time, March, when Jamestown Tots had been running for a couple of months and the first term was almost over, that my father tried to get more involved with the school. As in name he was the owner, he thought he should check the place over. So one afternoon he took time off from the mine and went to the school. Getting time off was, in itself, a long, frustrating process. If you were a white person, then you were high up and just gave yourself time off. But a Motswana had to ask their boss and fill in a form and get the form signed and submit the form and then wait for the outcome.

My father spent about an hour at the school and then came

home and told us all about it. He said he had arrived at Jamestown Tots to find Christine very cold and unfriendly. He had knocked politely at the open door of her trailer and she had gestured impatiently that she was busy on the phone.

'So did you just stand there or what?' my mother asked.

'No, I went in and she treated me like a stranger. "Do have a seat," she said. "What can I do for you?"'

My mother laughed.

'So I told her I had come to see how things were going. "Well, Mompati, that really wasn't necessary," she said to me. Then she shouted for that white boy and said, "Take this gentleman round."'

'As if you were an official visitor?'

'To get me out of her hair, more like.'

'But how can she,' my mother wailed, 'after all her problems I've listened to? Right, that's it, Frank or no Frank, I'm not taking any more.'

And it was soon afterwards that my father became ill. That weekend he complained of a headache, and as he was never ill, or at least never complained of being ill, my mother was worried. I was sent to play outside. My father retired to the bedroom and the curtains were drawn. He lay in his sleeping position like a soldier. I spent the time filling in my joke book very neatly with jokes the white children had taught me at school.

Chapter Fifteen

It was early April and almost a year since the Fishes had arrived in Jamestown. The weather reminded us for a week or so that winter would come eventually. And then, the reminder over, it was summer again. On the main road which connected Jamestown with Lephane and the capital, tourists in their giant open-topped trucks were heading up to the Okavango Delta for their holidays of greenery and water. The trucks lurched from side to side on the sections of the road that had yet to be tarred and the tourists laughed in delight.

In mid-April Christine held an end-of-term assembly, at which she made us all sing a song to Jesus and urged us to work harder. She had delusions of grandeur and seemed to have forgotten how young we all were. Then she took a long break and went down in the mine's private plane to South Africa to get books and other supplies, or so she said. Since her revelation about Frank, Christine hadn't sent any messages inviting my mother to come round. Perhaps it was because she didn't want to be reminded of what she had told us, or so my mother suggested.

One time Frank came round, but my parents hid inside the house and sent me to say they were out. I worried about whether Jesus was listening and what he would do about me telling a lie — the book Christine had given me said that he was everywhere and saw everything. My father said he even avoided Frank at work, which was easy enough. The mine had finally begun a management training programme, which my father became preoccupied with. It was this that marked the end of his illness. The headaches which had forced him into his soldier position in the darkened bedroom disappeared and he said he felt like a new man. He began whistling when he went to work and estimating the pay rise he would receive when he became a manager.

My mother was very pleased when she got her first term's pay cheque and she had propped it up on the table so we could all see it. Out of her money she bought me a pair of shoes for winter. She also bought some new sheets, a cheap dress for herself and a set of kitchen pans.

Even though the school holidays had come, my mother and Oabona continued to work hard preparing for the new term in two weeks' time. But they had, as my mother put it, a bone to pick with Christine, because Oabona had received her first pay cheque after my mother and was getting paid less though she did the same job.

Oabona had come round to our house in a fury waving her cheque in the air as she marched up the path. She kicked Champion out of the way because it was under her heels and she sat down outside.

'You see?' Oabona declared.

My mother took the cheque and studied it.

'Frank was the one who gave it to me,' Oabona explained. 'He gave it to Bopadile at the mine.'

'Well, what a surprise,' my mother said sadly, looking at the cheque.

'That woman!' Oabona began.

But my mother distracted her. 'Oabona,' she said as she settled herself outside hoping for a breeze, 'do you know what Christine told me about her husband?'

Oabona shook her head and motioned that I should get her some water.

'It seems,' my mother lowered her voice, 'that Frank has a habit of playing around with other women . . .'

Oabona made a loud noise of disgust. 'Is it so?'

'Yes it is so.' My mother smiled at the phrase. 'And, while Christine was pregnant with her last child, which she lost, Frank, Mr I-am-so-nice-guy, moved in with a South African woman and had a child with her.'

'Ao! shame,' Oabona said sympathetically.

They were silent for a while thinking about things, the pay cheque forgotten.

'Come here and let me make you look powerful,' Oabona crooned to me and obediently I went over.

One day my father came back from work upset. The father of Kgomotso, the girl who had earlier been beaten, had mentioned that his daughter had been hit in front of the whole class with a wooden spoon. The punishment was apparently for asking too many questions and not, as Christine had told my mother, for destroying property and insulting her. And once Kgomotso's father spoke up, others came forward with similar tales. My mother tortured herself over why she hadn't known what was going on. She still worried about the boy who had written that he was afraid of a Piet, but who had now been transferred elsewhere. In mid-May school reopened and, with Christine still away, my mother organized some new school elections and Kgomotso was elected overall supervisor.

Christine returned to Jamestown full of herself for having organized new supplies and a set of uniforms on her trip south. One morning Christine summoned my mother to her office in the trailer. She was having a heater fitted for the winter and seemed embarrassed about it. 'Mompati, you should just see her office,' my mother began her tale. 'Obviously I was wondering what I had been called out of class for. Anyway, she says I should forget about what happened in March, seems Frank was in fact working overtime that evening she told me about his affair. God, I feel a bit bad about pushing past him that evening, I can tell you! She says she made *rather* a mistake.'

My father looked relieved. 'I didn't think he was that bad.'

'I know, I know. But you can't really blame her for thinking the worse when Frank has done this kind of thing before, can you?'

'What happened, then?'

'Well, Christine moved on quickly to school business.'

'Did you ask her about all the complaints about the beatings?'

'Shit, I completely forgot.'

My father raised his eyebrows and looked disbelieving.

Just then Frank appeared at the gate and my parents went outside to meet him. 'Ah, Mompati . . .' Frank hesitated and my mother, taking the hint, went back inside and took up her post in the kitchen to watch them from the window. Frank had his head bowed and was talking urgently, opening the palms of his hands and then closing them again.

He left eventually and my father came back inside.

'So what's the drama this time?' said my mother. 'It's like Clapham Junction in this place.'

'What is Clapham Junction?' I asked.

'Where trains go.'

'What is a train?'

'Later, Dimpho.'

'Frank's in a real state. In fact,' said my father, and he considered for a moment, 'he seems terrified.'

'Oh?'

'Christine left him in charge of the house, as she always does, and she left him a set amount of money for bills, which she told him to pay. But he can't account for where all the money went.'

'Probably went down his throat,' my mother said unsympathetically.

'Mm, anyway, he wanted me to juggle the figures for him.'

'Did he ask for money?'

'Mmm?'

'You heard.' My mother banged a pot into the sink.

'Yes, as a matter of fact. Just to tide him over, he said.'

'Oh, for god's sake. He gets paid ten times the amount you do.'

'Don't I know it. Anyway, I said we didn't have any.'

'And Jesus! He still hasn't paid you for teaching Her Majesty's children last year.'

'I know.' My father sounded miserable.

'Who is the idiot?' my mother began. 'The one who borrows or the one who lends?'

'I didn't give him any, Rose. And he says the school is making a profit.'

'Hmm.' My mother sounded sceptical. 'Managed to build a swimming-pool, though, didn't they? So you didn't give him any?'

'As I said.'

'Well, good for you. Dimpho, go and feed the animals.'

That evening Oabona and Bopadile came round, and Oabona made me powerful by combing and plaiting my hair. My hair had grown quite long, and I was insistent that I didn't want it cut. There was a white girl in my class and her hair was long and shiny and I hoped if mine grew it would grow like that, rather than the stringy sort of hair that Christine had. The men – my father, Bopadile and Listen – sat outside and drank beer. This made Oabona annoyed and she plaited my head tightly, jerking my head around.

Bopadile complained about the Boers at the mine and imitated each of them in turn. He discussed which one he would shoot first and how the mine would be run once his guerrilla army took over. 'Oh, for god's sake,' my mother said finally as Bopadile leapt around the garden with an imaginary gun.

The next day Frank appeared again, this time with a message inviting my parents over later on for a 'talk'. They set off determinedly with me trailing behind. I had wanted to go and play with my small friends – now Thebe was gone I was the indisputable leader – but my mother said it was late and she didn't want me 'imposing' on anybody's mother, so off we all went.

Frank met us at the gate. He hung back and mouthed something urgently to my father. As my father was trying to puzzle out the message, Christine strode outside in a golden dress and ushered us pointedly into the house.

'Mompati,' she said, smiling brightly as we entered the living-room, 'Frank did give you the money for teaching the kids, didn't he?'

My father, obviously aware of Frank hovering in the doorway, said, 'Mmm.' My mother looked at him sharply. I sighed, it was going to be another one of those evenings. Frank's presence was pervading the room from the doorway, where he still stood. Look-ing flushed, because she dreaded confrontations, my mother said, 'Well, actually he didn't.'

'As I thought. Frank!' Christine yelled, though he was standing only metres away. 'You've been caught out this time.'

Frank came into the room and stood by the sofa. 'Write them a cheque,' Christine ordered and Frank took his cheque book out of his pocket.

Christine set off down one of the corridors and returned with a brightly wrapped packet. 'For you!' she said to my mother.

My father was standing and holding Frank's cheque up to the light as if checking for a forgery.

'Oh, Christine, you *shouldn't* have!' my mother said, sitting down abruptly. My mother loved being given presents, though she always said, 'Oh, you *shouldn't* have!' Being given a present, she thought, unbalanced things. It meant you were beholden to the person that gave it to you, something Christine must have been well aware of. It was always when my mother seemed to be most disillusioned with her that Christine either produced a present or offered a piece of intimate information from her rather stressful life. But how could my mother not accept a present? She looked as if we shouldn't have come over, and then she looked at my father as if it were his fault.

My father, whom Frank had given a beer and a wink to, stared vacantly at the TV which was blaring away in the corner of the room and which only Snowy was paying any serious attention to.

Its muscly tail was erect as it appeared to closely follow a cartoon on the screen.

My mother opened the package and exclaimed loudly. 'Oh, wow, look at this, Mompati.'

She took out a small wooden statue and I knew from the way in which she held it up that she found it grotesque and didn't know what to say.

'Wow,' my father echoed, also at a loss.

Christine grabbed the statue and started to explain it to us. 'It's a fertility statue.' She held it up and twirled it around. 'The Zulus use them. And, they also say they have other . . . um . . . darker powers,' and she gave a shrill little laugh.

'Darker powers, eh?' My father frowned and wiggled his finger in and out of his ear. But before he could counter this story, Christine pointed out a new picture on the wall.

'Isn't it marvellous?' she crooned, 'and you must come and see the one in the bedroom . . . And guess what?' Christine headed off down the corridor expecting my mother to follow. 'Our son is coming next week and so we have the perfect person for senior supervisor at last!'

'Supervisor?' my mother queried. 'I thought your son was still at school?'

But Christine was heading off at a fast pace to the bedroom. Feeling bold, I followed.

'Here it is,' Christine said, putting on the light and standing back to watch the ecstasy she clearly expected to appear on my mother's face.

My mother and I found ourselves looking at a gigantic painting of a black woman. The colours were garish and the woman seemed to have snakes woven into her hair. My mother peered a bit closer and read the title which was written in capital letters beneath the painting: AFRICA.

'Well,' my mother said rather uselessly. 'That must have cost a bit.'

Christine giggled. 'Frank insisted.'

My mother coughed, either at the fact that Frank had insisted or because she didn't believe he had.

We walked back into the living-room and then Christine headed to the kitchen. 'Frank!' she yelled and he went off to see what she wanted.

'I thought we were here for a meeting?' my father complained.

'It's horrible,' my mother hissed, pointing at the statue and then gesturing down the corridor to the bedroom.

'What the hell is this 'my son' business?' my father asked rather loudly.

Because my parents were not as pliant as they usually were the Fishes seemed to be bending over backwards to accommodate them. Frank, under orders from Christine, set some chairs outside on the patio, and my father went to take over the fire as much from habit as anything else.

'Your son . . .' my father began to Frank, who was handing out more beers. I was given a Coke, which I cradled in my hand, enjoying the cold. My mother shifted on her seat. '. . . Your son will be supervisor?'

Frank nodded.

'But he's not at the school. Is this part of a foreign aid package or what?'

Christine came out and sat down, interrupting smoothly. 'Mompati, as you know, we need someone who can keep the kids in order when Rosie and I —'

'And Oabona,' my mother added, her mouth full of peanuts.

Christine waved away a fly. 'We two, three, can't be everywhere at once, obviously. The children have a break, they have a drink, we need someone to supervise.'

'But you already have a supervisor,' my father said and he drained his beer.

Christine raised her eyebrows and shot a look at Frank.

'Kgomotso,' my father continued. 'The child you hit.'

My mother looked worried in the pause that followed, then she got up and said she had to go to the loo. My father chuckled like Father Christmas and poked at the meat on the braai.

'Yes, well.' Christine pulled herself together. 'I don't think a Batswanian is the best person to get on their high horse and complain about corporal punishment.' Then she laughed to show they were all still friends.

My father didn't say anything, but began peeling chunks of meat from the plate Frank had just handed him and laying them lovingly on the fire next to those that were already cooking. They sizzled. My mother came back from the toilet, taking sideways glances as she sniffed the air like a springbok about to come into the open.

'Your husband here,' Christine giggled to my mother, 'seems to be taking me to task.' My father silently pushed at the meat with his fingers. Frank went off to get some wine now that the food was almost ready.

'Anyway' – Christine sounded businesslike – 'I was thinking we'd have a meeting about the school and so forth, and elect a proper board of trustees, people from the community.'

'I think that would be a very good idea,' said my father, still standing. 'Legally, I believe, we must have a PTA at least. I also think' – he pushed the meat again and blew on the coals, he obviously hadn't forgotten the way he'd been treated when he had gone to visit the school – 'there was a mistake in the pay cheques.'

'Oh, no,' Christine said aghast.

'Oh, yes,' my father said. 'Oabona, as you probably know, didn't get as much as Rose.'

'Oh, my God!' Christine shot up, almost wringing her hands. 'That's terrible. What must she think of us?'

'It was a bit embarrassing,' my mother said and chewed some more peanuts.

'I can imagine. Frank! You must do something about that first thing tomorrow – I mean Monday morning.'

After the meal Christine hurried my mother and me into the

kitchen. My mother began piling the plates into the sink and then she turned the tap on.

'Leave it, leave it!' Christine said.

'Well, I thought I'd just rinse them.'

'Rosie, the maid can do that.'

'Oh, yes,' my mother laughed slightly hysterically, 'I forgot.'

'Is Mompati angry with me?' Christine wheedled, her back turned as she looked for a fresh bottle of wine in the fridge.

'You could say so, yes. It is a community school and he does feel, we both feel, that if it doesn't help the community it was intended to benefit, then things are going awry.'

'Absolutely,' Christine said firmly and led the way back to the patio.

'Dimpho, leave those bloody magnets alone,' my mother snapped.

'I'm tired,' I complained.

'Aren't we all?' she retorted, dragging me out of the kitchen by my elbow.

On Monday morning Christine announced at assembly that Jamestown Tots would be holding exams. 'You may still be small,' she told us, 'but exams are a way of life, so you may as well get used to them, and at this pre-school we believe in exams.' My mother and Oabona looked at each other in surprise. I stood there on the sand wondering what exactly exams were. Christine kept my mother and Oabona back at school after the day was over and asked them to staple question sheets together while she worked on a poster announcing a meeting to elect a board of trustees. I sat on the floor asking, on and off, to be allowed to go home.

'Christine, this must have taken you ages to do,' my mother said half admiringly as she flipped through the pages of multiple choice questions.

'Oh, well, yes, it did as a matter of fact.' She put her head to one side modestly and then hurried back to her trailer.

'Time to go,' my mother said eventually. Oabona was still immersed in the exam questions. 'I'm just going to see Christine for a second. Dimpho leave that alone. In fact you can come with me.'

We walked up the three mini steps of the trailer. Christine looked up briefly, a cigarette halfway to her mouth. 'Shut the door, Dimpho,' she said.

'Um, sorry to bother you,' my mother said unconvincingly, 'but I can't find the answer sheets, and I was thinking, well, I was rather surprised to hear they are having exams. It is only a pre-school.'

Christine appeared to consider this for a moment. 'Let's try this my way first, Rosie, okay?'

My mother tried another tack.

'These scholarships . . .' Christine shifted some papers around on her desk in a manner to suggest she had better things to do with her time.

'Have they begun? Because if it really is a community school . . .'

'Oh!' Christine said brightly, 'that's *exactly* what I wanted to tell you about. Silly me. We have another donation, so we can go ahead.'

'That's good,' my mother said, waiting for more. But the phone rang. Christine picked it up and we left.

That night Frank came round. He said he wanted to ask my father's advice. My father set a chair for him outside. In the past he would then have told me to fetch a drink from the cooler, but today he didn't.

'It is so peaceful here,' Frank said, looking around. Our dog Champion was settled on the sand and the cat was happily sucking in its ears. Frank laughed to see the cat and dog together, but my father told him rather dismissively that it was nothing unusual.

'What I wanted to ask you was . . .' Frank looked around as if expecting someone to be eavesdropping in the bougainvillaea bushes. 'About this motorbike. I've always wanted a good motor-bike,' he said rather wistfully as if it were something he had always been denied.

'Which motorbike is this?' My father didn't sound very interested. He lent over to pull two grape-sized ticks off Champion's back. The dogs in Jamestown, or at least those that lived outside, were almost continually plagued with these ticks. Sometimes my father and I would spend half a morning picking them off Champion and then killing them. My mother said her system was too delicate to watch.

Frank waited while my father ground a couple of juicy ticks with a stone and then stared at the spurt of blood that seeped on to the sand at the foot of his chair.

'Well it's your brother's,' Frank said.

'Bopadile has a motorbike?' My father looked surprised.

'Yes. Didn't you know?' Frank looked a bit puzzled and pulled at the creases in his trousers.

'No. Why?'

'Well, he wants to sell it. I thought, you know, you could tell me about it. Bargain down the price for me.' Frank laughed, but my father just leant forward, drew back Champion's ears and pulled off a couple more ticks. Champion yelped and shot off. Frank ummed and ahhed for a while, describing the motorbike and adding that if Christine found out she would put her foot down. My father looked back at him blankly, wondering what he was supposed to do. My mother came out to water the plants and, having overheard the conversation from the open kitchen window, she smiled to think of Frank on a motorbike.

The next day my mother, unsure of the answers to the exam and realizing that a lot of the questions were about God, tried in vain to pin down Christine, who was in overdrive and rushing around. After school she joined me and Oabona in the staff trailer. Oabona was sitting on the floor carefully looking over the uniforms Christine had bought in South Africa. Though the school was in its second term, none had yet been issued. We Batswana went to school still wearing our best clothes, while the white children were beginning to look scruffier and scruffier.

'How much is Her Majesty asking for these?' Oabona asked and my mother told her what she had already paid for my uniform.

'Well, these are made in Zimbabwe,' Oabona said. 'I know they cost some few pula.' She held up a red scratchy dress with a white collar.

'Jesus!' My mother sat down. 'You tell her.'

'Oh, no,' Oabona laughed, 'you tell her. I don't meet with Majesties and Buffalo Heads.'

My mother sighed, swore and then got to her feet. 'Bring that with you, Dimpho,' she said, pointing to the uniform I was inspecting. She knocked briskly on the door to Christine's trailer and entered. Christine was talking on the phone with her back to us.

'Yes, that will do nicely,' she said in her official voice. 'Of course, Mrs Van Herden ...' She dragged on her cigarette. 'We'll send down a batch at the end of each term. Yes, as I said, I can promise they'll be in good condition.'

My mother took a step backwards as Christine put down the phone and swivelled round to face her.

'Oh, Rosie!' She laughed rather nervously.

'What's being resold?'

'Nothing, nothing really. Just the books. You know – if we have some spare and everything, I thought we could resell them. I meant to mention it to you. I have a friend in Gabs,' she said, using the expatriate slang for our capital, Gaborone. 'Was there something else you wanted?'

'Yes, actually.' My mother took a deep breath. 'Christine ...'

Christine stubbed out her cigarette, leant forward over her desk and smiled brightly.

'The uniforms – don't you think they are overpriced?' My mother took the one I was holding and lifted it up.

'Really?' Christine frowned. 'They cost us quite a bit to buy, you know, from a firm in Jo'burg, and they are rather well made, and after all we are a business and we don't want to run at a loss . . . I could let you and Mompati have one at a discount, of course . . .'

'I've paid for Dimpho's already, remember, and the point is that you can buy these uniforms from Zimbabwe for a third of the price.'

'Really?' Christine patted her bun in surprise. 'Thank you for telling me. I'll have to look into that,' she said as if she were speaking to a stranger.

My mother led the way back to Oabona in the staff trailer and relayed the exchange. Oabona flung down the uniform she was holding on the floor. 'That's why Her Majesty is refusing.'

'Mmm?'

'To allow the children to take the books home. She is selling them. And as for these, phu!' Oabona made a loud slapping noise as she swept one hand against the other. 'And I know why she cannot give you an answer sheet. It is because she does not know the answers! And you know why that is?'

My mother wearily shook her head.

'It is because she has stolen the questions.'

'From where?'

Oabona shrugged. 'I have seen these questions before.'

'I wonder,' said my mother. 'I wonder if Christine is a teacher at all? Have you *seen* that qualification in her trailer?'

'Oh, we Batswana are not allowed into her trailer,' said Oabona and she sucked her teeth in disgust.

My father's illness started up again about this time. It was early June, the beginning of winter. In the mornings he looked haggard as if, he said, he had been ridden to Lephane and back by a witch. My mother said it was stress and asked many questions as my father slowly got ready for work.

'What hurts exactly, Mompati?'

'Here.' He touched his head. 'And down here.' He stroked the small of his back.

'If it doesn't clear up by the end of the week, you're going to the clinic,' my mother said firmly and she gave him a kiss.

'Rose!' my father cautioned. 'We're in public!' He nodded to the open window, where outside people could be seen on their way to catch the bus to the mine.

So in the mornings my father set off for work, but often by the early afternoon he was home again, retiring to the bedroom, where he took up his soldier position and lay with his eyes closed.

Christine had arranged a school meeting for that Friday, but my father was so ill he couldn't attend. My mother was worried. His pains seemed hard to pin down. He suffered most during the night, when he felt as if something were strangling him. He gave up smoking cigarettes, thinking they were causing the problem, and indeed he was okay again for a while.

But the pains soon returned, this time in different parts of the body. Unable to go to work, he lay in the bedroom darkened against the winter sun outside. I tiptoed around the house, bringing him things my mother decided he needed. Frank brought over a large container of soup from Christine. He entertained us with stories of his escapades on the motorbike which he had finally bought off Bopadile and was storing at somebody else's house as Christine did not approve.

My father, once Frank had gone, refused to eat the soup.

'I am not eating anything that woman makes,' he declared firmly.

'Oh, Mompati, don't be ridiculous!' But my mother didn't force him and eventually she gave the soup to our dog, but even Champion refused to eat it. The cat came along to sniff it but was distracted by a lizard. So the soup remained in the sun, where it gave off a pungent smell until the crows came down during the night and ate it all up.

Oabona came to see how my father was and she agreed with my mother that he should go to the clinic.

'They will just give me aspirins,' my father wailed.

'And perhaps an injection,' said Oabona.

My mother laughed in agreement. She knew that the Jamestown clinic was understaffed and underfunded and pacified Batswana by giving them injections, but she said that as the doctors were there to treat you, my father should use their services.

Of course the expatriates went to the white doctor at the mine and he referred them to specialists in South Africa. Often, in the early days of Jamestown, when a white wife was bored and wanted to amuse herself with some shopping, she faked illness on the understanding that the mine's doctor would refer her to someone down in South Africa. So the wife would be flown down on the company plane and put up at a hotel at the company's expense. She would see the specialist for half an hour perhaps and then she would go out and shop. It was Christine who had told my mother about this, not to illustrate the corruption of the mine but because she was bitter that she had arrived too late to get in on the scam. The mine managers had begun to discourage the practice as the company wasn't making any money. But that didn't stop them giving themselves fancy company cars – even if there was hardly any tar road to drive them on.

Seeing my father so constantly ill, Oabona suggested he should go to the church.

My mother snorted. 'I'm surprised at you, Oabona. They'll charge money and gabble something at you and you'll be back to square one.'

'No.' Oabona was firm. 'When I had trouble, when I was pregnant for ten months . . .'

My mother opened her mouth in surprise.

'. . . I tried everything. And so finally I went to the church people. They told me to drink something, urinate in a certain place, and, they said, this baby, she will be born on the following Monday. And she was born on that following Monday.'

'Did they charge you?' My mother was intrigued.

'No.'

'Well . . .' My mother thought about it. 'That's good. But let's try the clinic first, okay, Mompati?' She didn't suggest the white doctor at the mine because we all knew how my father would be treated there.

'He's not getting to work, and he missed a school meeting because of this,' my mother said to Oabona later as they stood together in the kitchen.

'Perhaps somebody is bewitching,' Oabona laughed, but not because she was amused.

My mother considered this carefully. 'But why?' she puzzled.

'Some people, I can say they are jealous,' Oabona said, speaking as one who knows. 'Come here and let me make you look powerful,' she said to me.

We couldn't be sure if my father was being bewitched because no one ever is. It is simply one possibility when something goes wrong and you have tried other ways of curing it. If all else fails, if the illness is mysterious and sudden, there's a good chance that you are being bewitched.

Often a person is bewitched for revenge, but it can also be for envy. After all, my parents had a house, a car, a job and a business. So it was quite possible that someone was jealous of them.

The next day my father came back from the clinic saying he felt better, but he was clearly upset. He put the brown paper packet of aspirin the nurses had given him on top of our cooler after swallowing two of them.

'There was a delightful woman there,' he began.

My mother and I looked up to listen. 'A white woman?' my mother asked, catching his tone.

'Indeed. How did you guess?' My father grunted as he slipped off his shoes.

'What was a white woman doing in the clinic?'

'That mine doctor is away.'

'Gone shopping, has he?'

My father laughed. 'So, this woman, she stood in the clinic like this' – he stood up to imitate her – 'and she yelled, "I want a white doctor. Do you hear me? I am white," and she pointed to her arm like this.' My father pinched the skin on his hand.

'Ha!' My mother screamed. 'This place is driving me crazy.'

At the end of the week my father went on a two-day management training course somewhere down south. He left behind the aspirins saying they didn't work. When he returned – ill once again – it was then that he seriously suggested that he was being bewitched, although he was torn between this explanation and one of his favourite expressions, which was, 'There's a logical explanation for everything.'

'What's logical about being bewitched, Mr Africa?' my mother said, in an attempt to lighten things up. 'I would have thought it's just the opposite. You are beginning to sound like Her Majesty. Why would someone bewitch you, Mompati?'

'Well' – my father got up and paced around the small room – 'you don't know about these things.'

Unlike my mother, he knew that sometimes these things just happened. Lots of people knew of cases of bewitchment, if that's the right term. It is something that can pass, but if the cause is jealousy you may be left broken and a shadow of your former self. You may lose your possessions, your health, even your sanity. What you have to do is identify who is responsible and then you can deal with it. Very often it is a relative, a fact that upset my mother a great deal. When someone was ill, what she wanted was a name for the illness. She couldn't believe that no one knew what was wrong with my father, and though she had been told of cases of bewitchment, I don't think she really believed them.

Chapter Sixteen

By late June it was truly cold. The weather stopped playing with us and by July the mornings and nights had become bitter. 'Christmas is coming,' said my mother as she did every year, so used was she to linking cold nights and shortening days with Christmas and a notion that the year was about to end. Every morning she rubbed cream over me until I shone.

The bush around Jamestown was dry and bare, the empty trees revealing well-worn paths not usually visible in the summer months. My parents had their annual argument about whether they could afford to buy an electric heater. My father said no, and won, which resulted in endless trips outside Jamestown looking for fire-wood and then evenings huddled before a giant, slow-burning fire that scorched your front and left your back exposed, chilled and tense.

At the mine one of the workers was crushed by a heavy machine. The man lay bleeding for three hours waiting for the mine's white doctor to come from a cocktail party he was attending in Jamestown. Just before the man died he told his friends, who were gathered hopelessly around him, 'Even if that doctor comes, I will not let him treat me.' My father was called out as a witness. He came back home early, told us what had happened, and then shut himself away in the bedroom.

People began not just complaining about the mine among themselves, but to management and even, it was rumoured, to the government. The union maintained a low profile, but it was beginning to be pushed to do something. As an attempt to placate people, the mine donated money to build a place for the Batswana to worship.

Christine issued an ultimatum in assembly: those without regulation jumpers would have them confiscated. The following week she told five Batswana children to step forward from where they were standing at assembly and removed their non-uniform jumpers. A constant stream of kids waited outside her trailer to be called in and told off. They came out jumperless and shivering. 'If your parents can afford the fees,' Christine said, 'they can afford proper dress.' She seemed to take it as a personal affront. My mother was incensed and Oabona stopped talking to Christine.

My father came home from the mine one day, saying there were rumours that Jamestown Tots was in trouble. The primary school that the company had set up for the children of its expatriate employees was apparently making inquiries after Christine had made noises about future expansion. But some Batswana parents had already made complaints to the Ministry of Education about the syllabus we were studying, which had become unashamedly religious. Other Batswana complained that their children had been waiting for a place at Jamestown Tots ever since the school had opened. Christine had a poster made and taped it up in the staff-room trailer:

When once the master of the house is risen up, and hath shut the door . . . there shall be weeping and gnashing of teeth.

Luke 13:25,28

My mother gnashed her teeth and took it down.

Kgomotso's father, who was now leading the complaints of the Batswana, was, Christine said, a troublemaker. Frank relayed this piece of information to my parents when he came round one evening to complain about Bopadile.

'Your brother . . .' Frank began.

'What is the problem?'

'Well, it's the motorbike, of course.' Frank sounded annoyed for once. 'It's not working.'

My father suppressed a smile. 'It is an old machine, Frank.'

'That's not the point.' Frank sounded, for a moment, like Christine. 'The point is, I bought it on the understanding that it was in good condition. So when it broke down, I gave it to him to fix. That had been the arrangement. However, now that he has apparently fixed it, he's offering to return it to me' – Frank gave a bitter laugh – 'but at a cost. In other words, he wants to sell it to me twice.'

My father looked uncomfortable at being called to account for his brother's activities. Shortly afterwards he got up to walk Frank to the gate, a habit he found hard to break. 'So you refused?'

Frank looked puzzled.

'You refused to pay him for repairing it?'

Frank nodded. 'I don't have the money,' he said. Frank turned as he heard the kitchen window bang and then he left.

Moments later we heard the triumphant roar of Bopadile on the motorbike. He drew to a halt in front of our gate and took off his helmet with a flourish. 'Whosit!' he said to me as he strode up the path.

'Frank was just here,' my mother told him when he came into the kitchen to see what was cooking.

'That Buffalo Head!' Bopadile didn't look at all concerned. 'Where's Mompati?'

'At the back,' my mother said, 'and how's the bike?'

'Sharp!' Bopadile beamed.

When later Bopadile left, we heard him roaring all the way home several streets away.

'That'll teach him,' my father said of Frank.

'Hmm?' My mother was laying out our food.

'Well, maybe we should take Bopadile's approach to life.'

'And do what exactly?'

'Hey, these people are in *our* country and they are treating *us* like shit.'

'Yes, yes.' My mother had heard all this before.

'You know, we Batswana are not racist, but perhaps it's time we were.'

Christine, who had taken to leaving little notes for my mother in her box in the staffroom trailer rather than talking to her face to face, left a note the next day asking her what she intended to do about that thief, Bopadile.

Perhaps it was this note which sparked off the confrontation. Whatever it was, the next day my father took another afternoon off work and visited the school. Christine received him in her trailer, which was like a well-heated cauldron compared to the winter chill outside.

'I told her we needed to have a meeting,' my father explained to us that evening. 'I told her there are complaints we don't have a board of trustees, that people are asking questions at the mine. I told her –'

'What did Her Majesty say?' my mother asked.

'She said, "Well, Mompati"' – my father put on a high-pitched nasal voice to imitate Christine – ' "We did hold a meeting but because you as the *most* important person didn't make it . . ."'

'But you were ill,' my mother protested.

'I know. But she said they couldn't elect any committees without me. "We are working on a very tight budget," she told me.'

'Ha!'

'I told her she seemed cosy enough.'

'Good for you,' said my mother.

'So Her Majesty asked me, "Do you know how many hours I put in here? Do you realize what would happen if I withdrew now? The school would collapse."'

'Don't tell me she thumped her Bible as well,' my mother cut in.

'Almost. So then she asked me if I knew how much it cost to run an "operation" like this one. So I told her I did, and reminded her that I am actually an accountant. I said perhaps she could give me the financial statements and I could see where she had gone wrong.'

'Good for you!'

'Then she told me she "resented" my tone. So I told her I expected to see the school records over this weekend. Then she said the financial problems are because we *Batswanians* haven't paid our fees and that no wonder nothing succeeds in this country.'

'She said that?'

'So I asked for a list of those who haven't paid. I told her this is a community school and we don't mean the community of the white people. I told her this school is now being run like the mine and I for one was going to stop her. They think, you know, that we Africans are passive, that is what their history has told them. They think that they colonized us and we just sat back and wept.'

My mother nodded. 'So then . . .'

My father paused to drink some water. 'Then she asked if I was accusing her of *racialism* . . .'

'Did she rock up and down in her swivel chair?'

'I replied that if she was so defensive, then something must be true in what I was saying.'

'Oh, I bet she didn't like that.'

'No. In fact she yelled at me to get out of her office.'

'No!'

'She said she was sick and tired of me. So I walked out.'

After my mother congratulated my father some more, we built a fire and sat around outside roasting meat. In the distance we heard the roar of Bopadile on his motorbike. My father was more thoughtful than he had been earlier.

'I can't believe I put all that money into it, I must be mad.'

My mother tried to comfort him. After all, hadn't she been the one who had defended Christine half the time? 'We weren't to know, Mompati. She changed, she wasn't like this before. It's not our fault.' But she seemed to recall the clues that had told her to be wary of the Fishes right from the start.

My father became ill again. Looking back, it now seems likely that his ill-health was caused by what he had to put up with both at the mine and the pre-school, but back then we thought it was just a mysterious illness. This time his headaches were too painful to allow him to sleep or to work. He finally went to the white doctor at the mine and was sent to see a specialist in Thabeng, as the company was reluctant to send a Motswana all the way down to South Africa in their private plane. My father said he didn't want to go to South Africa, anyway. It would be like jumping out of the frying-pan and into the fire.

The specialist in the town couldn't find anything wrong. My father was given some injections and three packets of white pills which looked like aspirin. He returned to Jamestown none the wiser, but quite a bit poorer.

My father decided to consult what is known as a traditional doctor. First he went to a local one, who said he had been bewitched and with enough money and time they could tell who by. The doctor threw the bones and gave my father something to drink, I have no idea what as it was all very hush-hush. My mother was totally confused by the proceedings. In England there is no real equivalent for the doctors we have here, or at least that's what she said. Here witchcraft is like life: you are always vulnerable to it. When your life is going well, when you have cattle and money and perhaps a small business, then beware, because there is the possibility that someone's jealousy will take it all away from you. My father was not doing that well, but, it was suggested, perhaps this was because he was being bewitched.

Once again my father seemed to recover. He praised the Tswana doctor and said at least the man knew what he was talking about. But my mother thought that you could only be bewitched if you let yourself believe you could be. She said this often to Oabona, who partially agreed.

'It is lucky,' Oabona said, 'that white people don't know how to do these things.'

My father gave up alcohol, saying that though he felt better he couldn't sleep at night and perhaps this was the problem. He was still trying to find a logical explanation and, although he insisted that he had recovered, there was a defeatism in his attitude these days.

When my mother cut his hair one evening, he instructed me to go around and pick up every single strand so he could burn it himself, in case someone got hold of the hair and used it against him.

Christine, encased in her trailer at the school, was keeping a low profile. She sent round several sheets of numbers to my father which showed that the school was making a profit. But that didn't answer the question of where the profit was going. Kgomotso's father withdrew his daughter and sent her down to Gaborone for her studies. Christine sent her son Peter, who had been installed as some sort of supervisor, away for a holiday after there were tales he had beaten three girls for scraping their chairs too loudly. The English boy who had previously been supervisor was appointed to temporarily fill Peter's place.

My father became sick again. Overnight, or so it seemed, he had grown extremely thin. There was a series of deep, fine lines around his eyes, and he permanently looked as if he had just woken up from a nightmare. He took yet more time off work and travelled to Zimbabwe to see a famous traditional doctor there. He had little faith now, but couldn't think what else to do. My mother said that if he didn't believe in traditional doctors, then they wouldn't be able to cure him. In Zimbabwe my father went to a European 'specialist' as well. He couldn't concentrate enough to drive, so he took Listen with him as chauffeur. The doctors in Zimbabwe did various things and my father returned saying he felt much better. Oabona began once again urging my mother to get my father to the church.

At Jamestown Tots my mother spent her time chasing after Christine. All pretence of friendship had been dropped. She began to question me closely on what I knew.

'Dimpho, have you seen anyone being beaten?'

I nodded.

'By Christine?'

I nodded.

'Oh, you're just like your father. Give me some information!'

I began wondering whether God really could be watching everything all the time.

'Well, I'm just glad you're almost old enough to start primary school,' my mother said and gave me a cloth to dry the dishes with.

My father became ill again – it seemed to come and go in great waves. He wasn't sleeping at night, his ribs were showing and his legs gave him a lot of pain. He travelled north to see another doctor who came back with him to the house and did what I suppose you could call a protection ritual. We all waited outside, while the doctor went through the rooms sprinkling powder. Then he drew my mother inside and said she was being bewitched too and that it was necessary to make some small incisions in her flesh. My mother, willing to do anything to help my father and also quite terrified by the man, agreed. The doctor made her lift her arms up into the air and with a razor he made three neat cuts on her armpits. Then he did the same to my father. And then he went and de-bewitched the car. 'Someone is trying to injure you,' he told my father firmly as they discussed payment.

The very next day Listen, while driving my father to work in the car, had an accident with a donkey. Listen insisted it was because a woman must have touched the four big Coke bottles of water the church had given him to place at the four corners of his bed to ward off whatever was cursing our family. My mother rubbished this. 'Why is it okay if a *man* moves those bottles?' she complained to my father.

'Is that what he said?'

'You know it is, Mompati.'

'Because women are more powerful?' my father offered.

'Are we, really?' my mother said and rubbed at her armpits. 'This business of filling bottles with water,' she began again. 'What a load of old superstition.'

My father laughed. 'And your people, of course, are not superstitious?'

'Okay, okay,' my mother shrugged. She had a whole array of superstitions herself, like not letting a black cat cross her path, not walking under a ladder, knocking on wood, and saying 'Bless you' when somebody sneezed. The worst of these, in my opinion, was when a mirror broke. That earned you seven *years'* bad luck.

Meanwhile Christine had been spreading stories about my father, that he was too ill to run a school and that this was why the school was doing so badly. One day in early August my mother was fired. In the morning there was a note in her box in the staffroom saying that Christine regretted having to 'let my mother go'. My mother pulled me from the playground and we stormed off to Christine's trailer.

'You could have knocked, Rosie,' Christine said as we marched in.

'So I am being let go, is it?' My mother laughed. 'I thought Mompati was the boss of this school!'

'Rosie,' Christine said patiently, 'this doesn't have to be permanent. We just don't have the funds to keep on employing you.'

'Then I wonder what you are going to do. You people are all the same . . .'

'"*You* people"?' Christine laughed.

'I thought you were different,' my mother said shakily. 'Stupid me.' And we marched out of the trailer leaving the door wide open.

We immediately went round to Oabona's house. Oabona had given up going to Jamestown Tots a few days earlier. She was sick of Christine and was going to apply for a teaching job at a government school again. We found her outside her small house preparing some vegetables. Her small daughter was sitting on a blanket in the sun. Oabona looked up and smiled.

'What do you say, Rose-we?' she asked, using the affectionate form of address.

'No talk,' my mother said in her shorthand way, 'I've been let go.'

'Let go?'

'I have been fired.'

'Ijo!'

'Yup.'

My mother sat down and Oabona sent me inside to fetch some water. They sat silently for a while thinking things over until finally Oabona said, 'We will go to the meeting.'

'What meeting?'

'The one Her Majesty has called.'

'I didn't know she had called a meeting,' My mother sounded furious. 'But then it seems I don't know anything much these days.'

Oabona looked sympathetic. 'It is next week.'

'A parents' meeting?'

'Yes. I think that is so.'

'Perfect. You'll come with me?'

Oabona nodded that she would. 'We should take them to the Kgotla and get them thrashed,' she added, getting up. My mother laughed because she thought this was unlikely. Who had ever heard of white people being thrashed at a Kgotla?

My mother and Oabona waited until the day of the meeting and then went uninvited. It was being held at the hall near the Baobab Club. When we arrived, we found several cars already parked outside. Inside the hall, chairs had been set out in rows and a group of parents were sitting staring ahead at a table where Christine sat in judgement. There was the usual pile of papers in front of her and a big jug of water and two glasses.

Christine was in mid-speech when we walked in and she frowned in our direction. Oabona led us to the front row and we sat down. Oabona sucked her tongue loudly and began settling herself comfortably on a small plastic chair. She had left Kedule at home for the morning.

Christine paused while more people entered the hall. Being Jamestown, people sat in groups according to colour. After some time Christine said that those who wanted to speak could and my mother got up, her fingers trembling. She and Oabona, as arranged, turned to face the people in the hall and Oabona translated my mother's words into Setswana. This took some time because a phrase in English sometimes needs a whole story in Setswana.

My mother said she wanted to apologize because she had been involved in a project that wasn't what she had thought it would be. She said my father was ill because of Christine. I was proud of my mother and I took her hand as we walked home.

My father's illness immobilized him for another week. At the mine he was warned about missing so much work, and without the usual overtime he couldn't keep up with the payments on the loan for the car or the loan he had got to invest in the school. Things looked bleak and we had no more money to spend on any more doctors.

One Saturday morning the police arrived and asked to search Listen's room. Only my mother and I were home. The police came swaggering up the pathway, taking their time the way men in uniform can afford to do. They greeted my mother and she greeted them back. Then she waited for them to get to the point, knowing that if she rushed them they would only get annoyed.

'We are asking to search this side,' one of the policemen said, gesturing to the servant's quarters where Listen stayed.

My mother indicated that they were welcome. They spent some time, the five of them, all grown men in shiny boots, tight belts and blue uniform, circling the servant's quarters, while my mother looked for the spare key. She stood in the doorway while I watched with my mouth tight shut as the police began their search. Seeing us standing there, they closed the door and continued in private.

Eventually they came out with a long gun and big smiles. My

mother, who had no idea what was going on, was taken to the police station for questioning, under the assumption that Listen was her servant. Everyone knew she was married to a Motswana, so there was something odd about her to begin with, and the police could treat her the way they couldn't treat someone with a white husband.

Later when my father returned and my mother was allowed to come home, she passed on the tale. 'An AK-47!', she said. 'My God, it's like a bad adventure film. What on earth was he going to do with it? Set up a guerrilla movement with Bopadile?'

'Does it matter?' my father asked. 'Isn't it bad enough that he had one and he kept it *here*?'

'But I wonder where he got it from . . .' My mother was still questioning all sides.

'Perhaps they planted it?' my father said suddenly.

'You were in America too long,' my mother laughed, 'but then again it's perfectly possible. Shit. They shut the door. I didn't see what went on.'

'Hmm.'

'What now, Sherlock?'

My father stroked his chin. 'Being as we are Batswana, we will probably not hear anything for a while.'

'What will happen to him?'

'Listen?'

'Yes.'

'Like I said, there will be some discussion.'

'But this is *serious*.' My mother looked annoyed. 'And as for us, I think we should get out of here. Who do you suppose alerted the police in the first place?'

That night there was a freak winter storm which my mother insisted was a good sign.

Chapter Seventeen

In August schools across the country closed for the winter holidays. But by the beginning of the new term it seemed that, despite my mother's and Oabona's absence, and the fact that most of the Batswana children had been taken out, Jamestown Tots would go on. Christine got two white women, Carol and June, to come in and help. Which meant, my mother said, that now there was no one qualified at the school.

My father, whose training programme had ground to a halt, gave in his notice at the mine because he said he would never get anywhere. I was about six years old and therefore big enough to attend primary school. My parents constantly discussed where they would move to. Lephane was out of the question, because my father didn't want to go back to his old job and there was little work there anyway for someone like him at that time. We would live in Gaborone with a relative, he finally said, and he would apply for a job in a government department again. So it seemed we had to continue moving south, further and further away from where we all wanted to be.

As I was no longer at Jamestown Tots, I stayed at home. In the mornings Oabona came round and drank tea with my mother. They held more long discussions about what to do, always going over old ground. As for the school, there was nothing to do until the ministry sent someone up to investigate, and who knew how long that would take? My mother and Oabona cleaned their houses until there was nothing left to clean. Our servant's quarters stood quiet and empty. Listen had left one morning without saying a word. It wasn't clear if the police had finished their investigations as they never came round again.

My mother began clearing out our house ready to move. Champion lay miserably outside sensing that something was going on. The cat developed ways of getting into our one wardrobe, where it would climb on to the second shelf and make itself cosy even though summer was beginning outside. My mother hoped it would kill the pink spiders due to arrive any day now, but it didn't show any hunting inclinations at all. Oabona entertained my mother with witchcraft stories and tried on all her clothes. Kedule crawled around on the floor supposedly under my supervision.

'This one time,' Oabona began, smoothing down one of my mother's dresses, 'it was in the village where I was born. Hey, we had a lot of cattle at that time . . .'

My mother laughed. You can't tell a good story without mentioning some cattle.

'And someone was bewitching us. So, we discovered that it was our neighbour . . .'

My mother looked up from where she was packing boxes on the floor.

'And you know what she had done, this neighbour? Well, she had been riding my brother all night long . . .'

'She was a witch?' my mother asked.

Oabona nodded. She was being interrupted too much, but she enjoyed having an attentive audience. 'So, we had an area. What do you call . . .?' She gestured round the edge of the room. 'A yard. And in the morning there was the witch caught right there on the spot!' Oabona showed us how the witch had been standing, one foot suspended in the air.

'And it was your neighbour?' my mother asked.

'Yes. And she was wearing only a half-slip.'

I giggled.

'A black half-slip.' Oabona liked to give certain details.

'So what did they do?' My mother began on another box.

'Well, they arrested her and took her to the police. But she escaped.'

'So did they go to her house and get her again?' my mother prodded.

'No.'

'But she was your neighbour, they knew where she lived.'

'Yes, but I don't know. She made the police forget about her.'

'Oh.' My mother sounded confused, she wanted a proper ending to the story.

'What will you do, Oabona? Stay here?'

Oabona tutted a bit and shrugged her shoulders. 'Bopadile does have a job. Perhaps we can stay in Jamestown and save money.'

My mother snorted to show what she thought of this plan.

'I don't like this place,' Oabona said, offering to tape down one of the boxes. 'I can say that I hate this place,' and she bit off some tape with her teeth.

My father was given a leaving party at the mine. One evening in September he came home and picked up my mother and me to go to the party. We drove to the mine in the warm early evening light and parked the car under the shade cloth usually reserved for the white managers. It was understood that if you were someone relatively high up, if you worked inside the offices rather than outside on the salt pans, then you were given a leaving party when you left. But my father said later he wished he had never gone.

Round the back of the offices a makeshift bar and a small braai stand had been set up. My father, mother and I stood in a cluster of Batswana near the bar. Around the edge, looking very sure of themselves, stood the Boer men. Every single one was wearing khaki. Some wore shorts, and above their long white socks bulged tanned hairy knees. They all had big stomachs, every single one. None of them had brought their wives, so they stood together and talked men talk and crushed beer cans in their hands. Every now and again one of them would come over to my father and slap him on the shoulder or the back and then walk off again. My mother had a glazed expression on her face and she held her wine glass tightly. A couple of the Batswana got as many free drinks as they could and began acting loud to show that this was their place and they didn't have to bow down to the foreigners.

After a while my father's boss called for attention and everyone gathered round – that is, they gathered round in their separate groups. Frank had not had the decency to show up. The boss said how much everyone had appreciated my father's hard work. One of the Batswana women, a secretary who was a little tiddly, snorted loudly and asked her neighbour why in which case they hadn't properly trained or promoted him. The boss said that my father's health wasn't too good and he had decided to move to Gaborone to be with the rest of his family. 'What?' my mother asked, looking confused.

The boss said that because my father had decided to leave at such short notice, they hadn't had time to buy him a leaving present. Then he pulled a rather crumpled envelope out of his shirt pocket. My father looked furious. As he went forward, some of the Boers clapped lightly, expecting a speech, but he took the envelope and, without saying anything, marched back to where we were all standing. Then the Boers looked at their watches and left. The Batswana hung around a bit longer, grabbing the free food and drink and trying to make up for the humiliation. My mother hardly said a word.

One bright, clear Sunday morning my father took me to collect firewood. Although the weather was warmer and it wasn't necessary to build a fire any more, I suppose he wanted something to do. We were driving along the tar road that led out of Jamestown and through the bush. He was silent as usual and I busied myself looking out the window, for I was in the front seat for once. The Mophane bushes were half brown and half green and it was hard to tell if they were growing or dying. A stream of slow-moving cows crossed before us, followed by an old man. Birds flew up in shimmery groups forming and reforming, and their wings sparkled in the early morning light.

As we continued along the empty road, we saw a policeman up ahead who was waving for us to stop. I wondered what he was doing on this deserted road so early in the morning. Getting nearer, it looked like he was hitching a lift. My father slowed down, because you can hardly refuse a lift to a police officer. The man had a dreamy look on his face and afterwards I remembered being puzzled about why his uniform was so creased and dusty.

Instead of getting in, the policeman gestured over to the other side of the road, where a car had pulled over. He beckoned us to cross the road with him, saying that there were people in need of help.

Glancing at the vehicle which was parked at a slant, we saw the front had been neatly cut away, as if a knife had been taken to a child's toy. A woman, who had been standing by the vehicle, came up to us with a frighteningly blank expression on her face. My father greeted her. It seemed he knew her from the mine. Distracted, she greeted him back. Another woman was lying on the ground some distance away, and then even further away I saw Frank. Suddenly I recognized that the car was his.

My father would have held me back, I'm sure, but it still hadn't hit us what had happened because the policeman and the woman seemed so calm. I noticed for the first time that the policeman had a brilliant red cut on his face and then I turned to look at Frank on the ground. I looked at him, wondering why he was so still, and I moved closer to stare. I looked at his face, and though my mind took in that something was wrong I turned away and looked again. There was something ugly about his face that I couldn't pin down and I had to keep on looking. Half his face was smashed in and I suppose the inside of his head had been forced out. I didn't realize this until later when I heard my father talking to my mother in hushed tones. I kept on expecting Frank to get up, or for someone to go and wipe off the blood, but everyone was keeping well clear of him.

The policeman went over to the woman lying on the ground. She must have been a passenger in the car. He carefully rolled her over until all that was visible was her slightly hunched back, as if she had curled up on the sand to have an afternoon nap. The other woman, the one with the blank face, was carefully picking up bits and pieces that must have rolled out of her bag, or her friend's bag. Is she dead? I wondered, looking at the rolled-over body. And at last I realized – that was what was wrong with Frank, he was dead. But still I stole glances back at him, his head rested up against a small stone and his brains frozen in a clump on his face.

It seemed we all came to at the same time. My father wrapped his arm around me and pushed me back to our car. The policeman crumpled down on to the sand as if all the energy it had taken to stop us had suddenly left him. The surviving woman equally suddenly headed off into the bush letting up a long, eerie moan. She crashed through the undergrowth uncaring, and I kept on thinking, But there are wildebeest around there. I had an unknown fear of wildebeest then, even though they are peaceful creatures and easily scared off.

My father called out to the wandering woman, but she just headed further and further into the bush howling. The policeman got up and shouted the woman's name, walking slowly after her as if wading through mud. It was like we were all suspended in time.

The policeman brought the wandering woman back and sat down again. She leant on our car for a moment and then, as if sleep-walking, stumbled back into the bush, letting out a low moan as if looking for her friend, who was now dead on the roadside. Or as if calling to any gods to bring her friend back. Another car pulled up, but the people, tourists, didn't get out, they just stared.

My father covered Frank with his jacket and tried to get the wandering woman into our car. I found myself sitting down on the sand. The adults walked around me and the tourists looked out of the windows of their car and stared. Why are they just looking? I thought. My father and the policeman got the wandering woman into our car, but she kept on getting out again.

'It's a problem,' the policeman said flatly.

My father agreed.

They discussed what to do with Frank and the woman passenger, both dead on the ground. The policeman kept on ordering my father to put them in his car and my father kept on saying it was best not to move them, as if there were a chance they were still alive. The policeman lit a cigarette and said, 'If you are refusing to help . . .'

'I am not,' my father said.

The policeman sat down on the sand.

The tourists now drove off and, as they passed by, I saw four white faces staring at me. I looked away. Eventually, with the policeman and the wandering woman in our car, we drove home, so slowly that it was as if we were not moving. My father's hands trembled at the wheel.

That was the final thing that happened before we left Jamestown. I hear now that Christine, who threw a fit at a minor event like an absent maid or her children arriving, coped with Frank's death well. I suppose in many ways she was quite a resilient person. It was the police who notified her. The dead woman was Frank's secretary, but this subject was left well alone. The woman's family took her away from Jamestown, seeing as there was no burial place in the township in those days. The funeral was held in a nearby village and people came from far away.

Christine flew away on the mine's plane with the body of her husband and we never saw her again. My mother wrung her hands as if there was something she could have done. She kept on asking what had *caused* the accident, though it was obvious that Frank had been coming back drunk from a late night with his woman friend.

The policeman had been hitching a ride. So Christine had been right all along.

That week ended with Independence Day, September the 30th, and my mother insisted we all attend the township celebrations. For a few weeks beforehand people had been muttering angrily that expatriates had no interest in our Independence Day. Although Jamestown Tots had been asked by the Setswana primary school to participate, Christine had said that as far as she was concerned the day was a holiday and they would be going south. With Frank's death, of course, the school closed.

Early in the morning my parents and I, still dazed after the car accident, set off to watch the running races around the township. Then we sat outside the council offices, where a big wooden stage had been set up the day before and a large green awning protected the crowd from the heat. The mine had donated the awning and some meat and drinks as if to say, 'There, that should shut those damn Batswana up.'

Considering that Independence Day was usually seen as an opportunity to laze around and get drunk, there was a good turn-out of some seven hundred people, who sat patiently waiting for the singing and speeches. Everyone wore their best clothes. Two white people showed up and took some photos of the traditional dancing and then left.

The chief of Jamestown, resplendent in a dark suit and pink bow-tie, led the Crime Prevention Choir in a song about corruption. 'Chief!' the woman next to us cried ecstatically as he led the dancing and women deep in the crowd let out long ululations. We sat at the back with Oabona, who had turned up late. To the right of the stage sat the Important People. You could tell they were important because they all had chairs and were being served with soft drinks. Sitting in the middle was the only woman, who wore a yellow, satiny cloak. I stared at her with interest and asked who she was.

'Miss Independence,' Oabona told me.

Behind the Important People sat their wives, who were given a measure of acknowledgement because of whom they were married to. Miss Independence, who had been elected the night before, sat looking hot and out of place.

The chief executive of Jamestown, the head of the town council, stood up to the microphone and made his welcoming speech. With a council now in place it was only proper that he tell the people of Jamestown what was planned for their new town. But as he spoke in English, a lot of people couldn't understand. The managing director of the mine was supposed to be there too, but he had sent someone in his place and gone off on holiday to South Africa.

'This is an opportunity to update you on the development programmes we have been striving to achieve,' said the chief executive formally. 'The level of development stands thus: the construction of staff houses, the purchasing of vehicles, the extension of street lighting . . .'

There were some murmurs from the audience, most of whom had low-cost houses, no vehicles and, of course, no street lighting.

'By the end of next year it is hoped all these projects will be completed. By then Jamestown will be a bigger and better place, offering all sorts of amenities characteristic of a proper town.'

Someone in the audience clapped and heads turned to see who it was.

'But our problem is that we don't have the funds. We are pushing for funds from the government in the same way one uses a cattle prodder.'

For a Motswana the chief executive kept the speech short, but already the sun was creeping through the awning and the Important People fanned themselves with their programmes.

'If you think the government has done nothing for you,' continued the chief executive, 'and you might be justified in thinking this, you should think anew and ask yourself what have I done for my country . . .'

He paused and drank the water he was offered. Then he wiped the sweat from his brow. 'Celebrate and enjoy yourselves in remembrance of the significance of this day,' he told the crowd and he left the stage and returned to his seat.

The young children sat in a group on the sand in front of the stage and chatted to each other. I saw some friends and went over to join them, wishing Thebe had been there to share the day, for there would be a lot of eating later on.

The guest speaker, some member of parliament who most of us had never seen before, told us that when Botswana had been a protectorate we had had absolutely nothing, with the implication that now we had. I glanced back to where my parents were sitting: my father was wiggling his finger in and out of his ear and my mother leant over to say something to him.

'We had nothing,' the guest speaker continued, repeating himself as politicians love to do. 'There was no electricity, no telephones, no university, no towns, nothing, not even mines. Now we have roads leading this way and that way. We had to go abroad even for work and for education, and people thought we were crazy to want to run this country ourselves . . .'

A couple of the Important People smiled.

'. . . No blood was spilt in the transition to independence,' the guest speaker boomed out.

Miss Independence shifted, sweating in her golden cloak.

'. . . The land was given to a democratic leader, may he rest in peace, and the transition was blessed.' The guest speaker paused and then started again. 'In the beginning there was no cheating going on.'

He looked around at the crowd, who sat patiently listening. The Important People covered their heads with their programmes to shield themselves from the sun. I told the girl next to me to give me one of the sweets she was eating.

'. . . We've done better than most countries who were given independence and went into war and instability,' continued the guest speaker. 'We had rulers who were real men and who were answerable to the people, and we are trying our best to be a nation of togetherness. This is what the government wanted to do, it wanted to ensure social justice for all and basic human rights. It wanted developments that moved us forward and it wanted to push to make sure Batswana were actually the ones running these things. Though some people have tried to exploit our national principles for their own gain, the evils that elsewhere have resulted in human suffering have failed to conquer our belief in stability and peace.'

'Amen,' somebody said as if it were a church meeting.

More choirs took the stage and in the distance I saw a group of girls from the Setswana primary school marching towards the council area. They wore blue shirts and white skirts and each held a little stick. 'Drum majorettes,' they sang in carefully rehearsed English as they neared the stage, 'are marching girls. I am one of them, and so are you.' I watched enviously as their teacher crowded them on to the stage.

There were more speeches, but to the right of the stage a commotion began. An old woman who had been walking on a pathway next to the stage area stopped in surprise at seeing the celebration. You could tell by her features that she must have been one of the people who had been in the area before the mine and the township were built. She was hunched, her clothes were old and she walked with a stick. She moved unsteadily towards the Important People and demanded a seat. The Important People glanced around annoyed at this break in decorum and then turned their attention back to the church group that was winding its way on to the stage to sing.

The old woman then wove her way, staggering slightly, towards the stage. She seemed to know the song the choir was singing and she joined in, waving her arms. The Important People smiled at each other, adjusted their ties and raised their eyebrows. 'Oh, these people from the bush,' they seemed to be saying to each other.

'They will embarrass us with their backward bush ways.' The chief executive told someone to go and get rid of her.

Another school group got on to the stage and the chief went up and put some paper money on the floor in front of them. The old woman made a lunge for the notes fluttering in the slight breeze, but someone held her back.

'Let the eating and drinking be unlimited,' the final speaker said after he had passed on the President's Independence Day message to the nation. The President's message warned against complacency and mentioned a lot of bottlenecks and things that were in the pipeline.

The old woman sat down suddenly on the sand. Then she leant over and threw up.

'Hey! These bush people,' one of the Important People muttered in English to distance himself and off he went to enjoy the unlimited food and drink.

Shortly after Independence Day, we left Jamestown and moved to Gaborone. Our car was loaded up with boxes and Champion was tied to the spare wheel so it wouldn't jump out. Champion strained at the lead, nose to the wind and front feet twitching whenever a bird flew up above us or a goat crossed the road. The cat had decided to leave for the bush a few days before. Or perhaps it had been taken by one of the giant black and white crows.

'Bye-bye, Jamestown,' my mother called as we turned on to the road heading south. My parents didn't talk about Christine or Frank in front of me any more, but they must have been thinking about them as we left the township. I wondered where God fitted into everything. He must have been angry, I thought. What had he seen that he had decided to punish? But I kept these thoughts to myself. If someone could be dead just like that, then what guarantees were there that any of us would be here tomorrow? I had begun to get nervous whenever either of my parents left me alone.

Our first stop was Thabeng and I was amazed. Everywhere there were cars, nose to tail like cattle, and big buildings. We stopped at a take-away and bought chicken and soft drinks and continued on our way. I slept for the next few hours and woke to find it dark and that we had arrived at our relative's house in Gaborone.

My mother almost immediately got a job at an English medium school – that is, a private school full of the children of expatriates. It was easier for her to get a job there and of course the pay was much better than at a government school and we needed all the money we could get. Her job also provided us with a house and me with a free education. My father eventually got a job with the government department of water utilities.

We lived in a cluster of streets just outside the main shopping area of the city, although Gaborone wasn't declared a city until some years later. Where we lived was like a bigger version of Jamestown, except there was no bush behind our house. To me Gaborone was a metropolis, though my mother told me that compared to London it was nothing, the implication being, my father responded that London was something.

Behind our house, trucks rumbled past coughing smoke into the air by day and by night. My mother and I drove to school because it was so far away and we passed through traffic and piles of rubbish at every turn. In the years that we lived in Gaborone the population doubled. Though construction was slowed down by the drought, the building never stopped. Roads were widened and within a few weeks they were congested again.

The houses where we stayed were white with red roofs and set in fenced yards where nothing would grow. Or perhaps people were so unsure about whether they would stay that they didn't bother to plant anything. And who had time to plant anything when they were out working all day to pay the rent on the house they saw only at night? When they got back home, they let themselves in and shut themselves up. During the day they left their small children with strangers, young women who came round looking for jobs. I didn't even know who actually lived on our street and as the streets looked all the same I was afraid I would lose myself if I strayed too far away.

No children played on the roads and people passed each other as if they were enemies. If you greeted someone, my mother complained, they looked at you sharply, wondering what you wanted from them. I was constantly afraid. The boy who lived next door filled me in with stories of robbers. In the afternoon when school was out he would stand at our connecting gate and watch for suspicious people. If a young, badly dressed man was walking by he would say, 'See the robber.'

'How do you know?' I would challenge him, afraid.

He laughed. He was a city boy and he knew these things, his laugh said.

At night I would urge my parents to check that all the doors and windows were securely locked. We had burglar bars on each window and two sets of locks on the front door. My father pointed out that if there was a fire we would never be able to unlock ourselves and get out of the house quickly enough, but my mother continued to lock us up.

A couple of years after we arrived, those South African Boers did their night-time bombing raid looking for 'terrorists' and killed, as they always did, innocent people.

The school I attended was like a bigger version of Jamestown Tots, only we had proper lessons. The head teacher was a white woman, as were most of the other teachers there. They were kind to us, however, me and the few Batswana children who were rich enough to attend, and our classes were small and we had new books and pens. My mother didn't like the school though, and she applied for a job in a government senior secondary school as soon as she could.

When I was about thirteen, I went to a community junior secondary school and I was in for a shock. With my English medium background I stuck out 'like a sore thumb', as my mother would say. I was used to small classrooms, and not being beaten up all the time. I was used to tuck shops selling imported chocolate bars and hot dogs, not soft porridge. I was used to asking my teachers questions, not just writing down what they said. I once challenged a teacher over a mathematical equation and was never forgiven. Many of the teachers thought I should be taken down a peg or two, so I was often struck across the head with a stick for being disrespectful.

I was also shocked by the students' behaviour. The older ones were rude to the teachers, swore, drank and smoked. It seems strange now that I was so shocked by this, but I was. A couple of years later I went to senior secondary school and by that time I had settled down again. I had several close friends and I did effortlessly well at school. I even won a maths and science fair one year and my father took my trophy with pride and put it on top of our TV – oh, yes, we had a TV by then.

But though I did well, I decided not to apply to our university. I don't know why exactly. Unlike my father before me, I didn't have to get myself educated in order to get my parents out of poverty. But one day, sitting in the shade outside our house drinking tea, I read an advertisement in the newspaper for scholarships to study in the States and I applied. The rest, as they say, is history.

When we first arrived in Gaborone, my father was in and out of hospital for a while. At home he lay in bed or sat quietly outside and seemed to be recovering. He couldn't forgive himself, though, for what had happened in Jamestown and he felt that by leaving the mine he had given in. People questioned us, interested, about Jamestown, and my parents warned them not to go there. 'Let me tell you about the US of A' was replaced by 'Let me tell you about Jamestown.'

BOOK THREE

Chapter Eighteen

More than a decade later and I still remember Frank's death clearly. Perhaps because it was the first death I saw, or perhaps because it was tied up with so many other things. Unlike a lot of people in our part of the world, I had not witnessed a violent life. I had seen no wars, for example, though wars there were on our borders and I am ashamed to say I knew very little about them.

Jamestown Tots was one of the first educational disasters of its kind. And the mine, the salt mine that everyone had been so proud of, led to one of Botswana's first public inquiries. The inquiry confirmed that racism was rampant and that many of the Boers were unqualified. The company had never made a profit and the list of creditors was long. As a result the mine was temporarily closed down and Jamestown almost became a ghost town. There have, of course, been several such schools and business disasters since then and you wonder when we are going to learn from our mistakes. Every day, or so it seems, the government brings in outsiders to tell us how to run things. And now, with independence in South Africa, the Boers are too paranoid to want to go home.

Though the mine is still closed, many of the Boers have just moved to somewhere else in Botswana – they know when they're on to a good thing. They know, as my mother frequently said, how to feather their nests when the opportunity arises. Today a lot of the early buildings in Jamestown are deserted. Most of the mine workers have gone and the golf course at the Baobab Club is a permanent scar on the landscape.

But the club itself is a busy hotel and it puts up people travelling on holidays to the north and government workers in their exhausted, over-driven government vehicles attending conferences and seminars and so forth. There is a two-storey building where the first council offices used to be, but in the winter Batswana still stand outside to bask in the sun. There's little for the council workers to do however, and people say they are waiting for the mine to reopen.

A few flamingos stop off at the pans around Jamestown, but most try to breed further afield. There's a squatter camp on the way into the town, though the council are forever trying to burn it down. The Kgotla is quiet these days. The chief still calls public meetings, but the government police have taken over responsibility for most of the court cases. There's even a prison cell in Jamestown.

I went to Jamestown once on the way home to Lephane, which was a bit unnerving because so much had changed. Going back somewhere you lived as a child shows you how selective your memory can be. I drove myself there and it was a pleasant journey, driving alone for hours on the tar road listening to the radio, passing villages where nothing has changed for the last fifteen years.

For a moment, as I neared the Jamestown turn-off, I had second thoughts, but then I told myself, what the hell, it's my country and I can go where I like. It used to take some twenty minutes to get to the township from the main road, but now that the place has expanded it takes only ten. It was nice to drive along a green avenue and see that the trees the council workers had planted all those years ago had survived, but it felt very odd having nowhere to stay. I drove this way and that, not sure where to stop.

Seeing the place through adult eyes, I found it not quite as terrible as I had remembered. It seemed peaceful somehow. Where the shop in the trailer used to be, there was now a whole complex of shops, though I couldn't think who had the money to go and buy things there.

I stopped in front of our old house. I could hardly see it as the hedges were so dense. All the houses on our old street now had trees and bushes sheltering them from the sun and from the eyes of people walking by on the road. I thought about rattling the gate, but then I wondered what I would say. Hello, I used to live here fifteen years ago? I thought back to the games Thebe and I used to play in our yards, and when I heard a motorbike in the distance I half expected to see Bopadile roaring past.

As someone came out, I read the number over the front door, and realized with a shock that I had been looking at the wrong house all along. A woman greeted me and I greeted her back. Then I drove round the corner and past the Fishes' old house. I saw two Batswana children playing by the gate. I called to them but they just stared.

I stopped off eventually at the Baobab Club, which, though it had actually expanded, seemed smaller and less grand than I remembered. It was a pleasant surprise to find that all the management were Batswana and the bar and restaurant were packed with *locals* having an afternoon out. But I suppose we are a new generation and in some ways more sure of ourselves. I had a very nice time there and it was reassuring to be with my own people again. I spoke for a long time with the food manager, a woman who, like me, is young and going places, as they say.

I questioned her closely on the inquiry over the mine, because when it happened I was so far away. There had been a lot of testifying going on, she said. People had come forward and spoken their minds, and for once the government ministers had listened. The union had taken to the streets of Jamestown with placards and the expatriates had barricaded themselves into their houses.

I spoke to other workers at the club, some of whom remembered my father fondly. They said he had been a very kind somebody and they were glad to hear his health had improved.

Although my father had always been so anti the United States, I went there to study, just like him. One of the chosen few, you could say. And like him I came home as fast as I could. I took my course in business studies, taking classes in management, accounting, public relations and so forth. I did this with the aim of going into tourism. Why did I choose to go into tourism, you might ask. Well, the answer is obvious. Tourism is our new industry, and if there aren't people like me in charge of things, you can imagine what might happen. I left Botswana in the year of our general election, 1994, when the newspapers were full of the 'shocking' election results because the opposition had got themselves quite a number of seats for once.

When I went to America it was my first time, of course, to be on a plane. I got a combi to Sir Seretse Khama Airport, free of charge because I have a friend who works in a hotel in Gaborone, and I sat crammed in with two Englishmen. They had big rucksacks bulging at the seams and I listened on and off to their sarcastic bantering. One of them had a pink sunburned face and rat-tailed hair and he said, gesturing round the streets of the city, 'The population of Manchester is bigger than this whole country.'

'Am I interested?' his scruffy friend asked.

'Yeah, you look it,' rat-tail replied.

Then they talked about how hot it was.

'Open the window,' said the scruffy one.

'Yeah. That'll really help,' said the rat-tailed man.

We were held up in a traffic jam and I decided to be bold and ask them if they were teachers.

The men laughed. 'Are you a teacher?' rat-tail asked his friend.

'No. Are you?'

'No, but I've done quite a lot of teaching over here!'

I returned to staring out of the window.

In the airport I watched other Batswana who were going abroad to study as they posed stiffly for photographs to be taken by relatives and even some reporters from the newspapers. I got on to the plane and entered this long, thin living-room full of bolted-down chairs. I sat next to a man who had been teaching pilots in Botswana. He told me he had to teach them how to use a knife and fork first. This was the first thing he said to me and I had to sit next to him for thirteen hours until we reached the UK and changed planes. He showed me his duty-free magazine and asked me what perfume I liked best. I said I didn't like perfume. 'Oh,' he said, 'I was gonna get you this one,' and he pointed at a picture of a bottle.

I opened my magazine at the duty-free section, and I read about perfumes that were tender yet opulent, profoundly floral but with a hint of sensuality, and one in particular which expressed the spirit and soul of a woman. This bottle was in the shape of a woman, if a woman could have no head, arms or legs, but a tight waist and pointy breasts.

My neighbour was reading a story in the magazine about Princess Diana and the British royal family and began to talk about her to me. He had established by this time that I was a Motswana and apologized for his earlier remark about knives and forks. 'Just kidding, love,' he said.

'She couldn't take the strain,' he told me confidentially, gesturing to the article he was reading, 'could she? She just wasn't up to the job.'

I nodded, not knowing what on earth he was talking about.

The plane doors were closed and our pilot greeted us. We were shown a video on flight safety, on what we should do if the plane crashed. I hoped there was no child like me down on the ground pointing at the 'European' and praying to Jesus it would fall out of the sky so she could have a look at it. The flight-safety video instructed us to lean forward and bow our heads. This seemed simplistic in the extreme. I paid close attention to the exit doors and the way to turn the handles on each one. The video told us that when the plane landed on water, some yellow, inflatable chutes would drop down from the sides and we would swoosh down to safety.

'Have they really *tested* these things?' I said to myself, tightening my seatbelt.

'Oh, yes,' my neighbour said, although I had not been talking to him. 'This is the safest way to travel.'

Across the aisle was an American woman on her way home enthusing to a stranger about her holiday in my country. 'Oh,' she was yelling, 'it was great!'

Americans are so easily pleased.

'We went to Chobe and Savuti and we got chased by a lion! Yeah, we saw *everything*!' The stranger seemed impressed, but as we were about to coast along the runway the American woman was asked politely to sit down and strap herself in.

It had never occurred to me that a plane would take off nose first and I was terrified as I felt myself pulled backwards, the things above me rattled and I heard with alarm the ping-ping of lights going on and off.

Shortly afterwards, when we had become horizontal, the rituals began. I thought we would just sit in the plane and look out of the window until the journey was done, but no – those plane people had a lot planned for us. First a woman came down the aisle with a trolley of drinks, the sort of trolley they have in a hospital. My neighbour, the pilot teacher, asked for two small bottles of whisky and a Coke. I couldn't make my mind up, the choice was so vast. The woman got impatient and suggested a white wine. But it tasted funny, like palm wine, only sour and bad-smelling. My neighbour drank his whisky and settled down, putting his arms on both arm rests the way men love to do. He decided to take me as a represent- ative of my country and asked me why the women of Botswana let themselves go to fat. I just fumbled with my fold-out tray.

'I won a lot of money in the casino in Gabs, you know,' he told me.

'Oh, yes?' I said, like my mother does when she's not very interested.

'I was staying in the Sun Hotel, you know ...' He paused as if waiting for me to be impressed. 'And all the hookers were after me! So I hid the cash in my room and put two chairs in front of the door to keep them out!' He looked pleased with himself. It was the first time I had heard the word 'hooker' and it took me a moment to work out he was talking about women.

'It's a hard job for a man,' my neighbour said later as we watched the male flight attendant hand out more drinks and small packets of stringy old biltong.

'For anyone,' I said, although I had determined not to talk to him any more and was desperately looking round for an empty seat elsewhere.

'Yes,' my neighbour nodded, 'but for a *man*, you know, having to serve all day long.'

Shut up, shut up, I said in my head. I contemplated going to the toilet and having myself sucked down the chute, which I had been warned could happen to you on an aeroplane. Or European, as I used to call them.

Why can't I just shut him up? I thought again as my neighbour began telling me how much he had missed England during his year in Botswana.

I spent much time on that flight staring at the backs of people's heads. They were nearly all white people and had such soft, thin-looking skin. Do they all look like this? I wondered. It was the first time I had been surrounded by so many, at least since my days at the English medium primary school. And their hair, blown slightly by the air-conditioning, revealed white, white scalps beneath as if it were just layered on top and could be blown off at any time. They were quite a range of colours though, something I hadn't really noticed before, from white to pink to red to pale brown. And such varieties of hair colour, too. I had read many books, especially by Americans, describing the colour of black people, and it's always as if we are something good to eat: this person was *chocolate*-brown, a book might say, and another the colour of *fudge* or *treacle* or *coffee*.

After the second drinks trolley we were given trays of food and a little menu to choose from. All round me people bent over their trays as if praying. My neighbour used a knife and fork, though the portions were very small, and stuck out his elbows as he ate, which made it hard for me to get comfortable. Then the plane people put on a film for us, and my neighbour, to my embarrassment, had to show me how to use my headphones. All the way through the film he made little comments, loudly so that I could hear through my headphones. 'Oh, this looks *interesting* . . .' he would say pointedly as a woman came on to the screen with hardly any clothes on. Eventually I closed my eyes and pretended to sleep.

Chapter Nineteen

I spent my first week in the States in Washington, DC. There I attended a baffling orientation course where the CIA tried subtly and not so subtly to recruit the African students on scholarships. Next I flew to a small city in Massachusetts, not far from Boston, where I enrolled at Rush College. I was the only person from Botswana doing my course and I had to find my way alone.

The city which surrounded Rush College was old. I quickly learnt that the Americans loved old things, but not old people. Shops boasted the year they had been established, while billboards warned against old age and promised ways to stay looking young. The city had old stone and concrete buildings and streets, old shops and stores, old industries no longer in use. Everything was concrete except for far out of the city, where the roads were narrower and boarded with green. The time of year I arrived, autumn, I saw orange pumpkins sitting big and glowing on white, wooden porches.

I found things larger than life, as I had been told I would. The trees in the avenues were huge, as were the groceries in people's fridges, as were the fridges themselves. But perhaps the first thing that struck me about the States was the smell. No clear, slightly dusty sunlight here, but a mustiness and a feeling that the sky was lower to the ground. And then there was the crowdedness. In the two years I was there I never saw the famed open spaces I had read about in books.

I began by living on campus but it was so restrictive and bewildering that I moved to a house in the city. Initially in the dorms I tried to fit in. I listened with puzzlement to the other young women who talked constantly about their bodies and about movies, and who all had stuffed animals on their beds. But I became tired of people asking me ignorant questions about Africa. 'Hey, it's *hot* there, isn't it?' they would say. And they liked to pat my hair. 'Wow, your hair is so *cool*.' I fell into romanticizing my home in the way some African Americans encouraged me to, and I lied to white Americans who asked me stupid questions. Yes, I said, in Africa there were lions everywhere. And I never mentioned the things I had never seen before, like wallpaper.

But though the students at Rush College didn't know where I came from, they sure wanted to go there. 'Oh, Africa,' they'd drool, 'I'm gonna go there some day. Give me your address!' Those who wanted to join the Peace Corps always asked to see photographs and I ended up giving most of mine away. The photographs I had were mainly of family and schoolfriends, and a few of Lephane which people found cool.

'What do you, like, make these out of?' they'd ask wide-eyed, pointing at my grandmother's hut.

'Mud and cow shit,' I replied.

'Do you live in one of these?' they'd smile encouragingly.

The people on my course seemed bright and friendly, but this was deceptive. They talked to me and asked questions, sometimes very intimate ones, but then they backed off.

There were a handful of other Africans at the college. I suppose we were part of some 'helping the third world' scheme. We didn't get on, though everyone else expected us to be best friends. In the first week I met two African men, but they expected me to take a back seat to their own disorientation. I remember a party where one of them spent his time enjoying the limelight of white female attention, and the other remained sullen. I watched as a white man came up to my sullen compatriot, said, 'Hey, Buddy,' and did some complicated handshake the African man didn't understand. People

238

at that college divided Africans into those who were 'okay' and those who weren't. So they'd say, 'This is Suleman, he's okay.'

The course was easy and I had about four classes a day held in big windowless lecture halls. The rest of the time I was free. Though the classes were simple, the surroundings and equipment were expensive and I took pleasure in that. No one really thought I could cope with anything, so I just coasted along. Overall in that first year my experience was one of depression and aggression. I lost my sense of direction because I couldn't remember where north and south were.

Most of the Rush College students came from rich families and had very little contact with the people of the city. In the first week I attended an orientation course given by the campus police chief. He warned us foreigners against walking alone at night. He told us to stick to the campus and misled us into thinking that then we would be safe. 'It's not a bad world,' he told us, 'it's just that there're some bad people out there.'

The Rush College campus was an oasis of money. In the centre was an area called a quad, a small piece of grass surrounding a pole, and a square of concrete mysteriously known as Freedom Square. At first I felt exhilarated to be in a new place and there was an energy in the autumn wind that rustled the trees in front of the large ivy-covered brick buildings. These were the sort of buildings I'd seen in films, where rich white students hurry up and down wide steps clutching files and books under their arms.

The students kept to their tiny dorm rooms except briefly in summer. They studied and partied without a care in the world, or so it seemed to me. They wore new clothes and drove low, fast cars and had hang-ups and therapists. A few of the foreign students, mostly the sons and daughters of ambassadors and such like, rented whole apartments outside the college, stuck together, and avoided anything termed political.

In the short summer months the young white men would lie on the grass in the sun and play with frisbees. They would hang out of their dorm windows and yell, 'Yeah, buddy,' at each other. There were lots of Yeah Buddies at the college and they reminded me of young Boers – white and rich and confident about themselves. They walked into local diners and greeted each other with, 'Yeah, buddy!' They hollered down from rooftops, where they sunned themselves like bloated chameleons in the summer. 'Yeah, buddy!' There was no equivalent word for women, so in this way I was left alone.

The people just on the other side of the walls outside the campus, with whom the students never mixed, hurried in and out of their houses, afraid of the street or afraid of the police. In warm weather young men hung out on Main Street outside the Spanish American Supermarket and the cheap music and clothing stores. Sometimes the police cruised by and arrested them for crossing the road at the wrong time. Occasionally, on a Saturday evening, the rich white college students went to listen to Blues at dives on Main Street and to slum it for the night.

I wandered up and down Main Street often that first summer, reassured because people didn't stare at me all the time and because they had a way of lounging on the street talking like people sometimes do at home. But very soon the men began to harass me, calling me by my private parts, and I realized the lounging was a sign of poverty and not people just out enjoying the fresh air.

When I moved into a house in the city, I had two 'room mates' as they call them, though we didn't share a room. They said I was cute. They liked my accent, they said, and they would just love to come to South Africa and see all the wild animals. I kept on telling them that Botswana was not in South Africa, but they kept on forgetting. I guess they were kind people, though very touchy about having their country criticized and they were forever telling me to 'chill out'.

The houses in my neighbourhood rose up from the pavements with pointed tops and wooden slats, and on every floor the windows were lined with curtains. At first I had a constant need to sit outside, and I sat on our porch, from where I could see straight into the houses across the road belonging to people I would never know.

I was tempted to greet them as I passed them sitting – like me – on their steps looking out at the world. But then I realized you didn't greet someone – you either jumped right in or you ignored them. People in the States walked quickly to where they were going, and they always seemed to be going somewhere. In no time at all I began to walk quickly, too.

In the sticky summer months sometimes I went to a local lake with my room mates, its shore packed with Americans braaing the same way the Boers used to do in Jamestown, only this time with noisy radios and baseball games. They couldn't just be in a place, they had to do something else while they were there in order to enjoy themselves.

I soon got used to living indoors. There were lots of fat squirrels and fat cats where I lived, but the dogs, like me, lived inside. In the winter there were thunderstorms that threw me literally away from the window of the house, but no one seemed particularly happy to see rain. I wondered at people – that we can do so many things and yet we still can't make rain. I was furious that there was no way to take this rain back with me to my own country, which needed it so badly.

My mother wrote to me once a month with news from home. She explained her and my father's plan to move to Poloko and start a chicken farm. 'A chicken farm!' I said out loud as I read the letter.

People in my neighbourhood spent their time driving up and down in wrecked cars with loud music pounding out of the open windows and no smiles on their faces. The women walked around weighed down with shopping and they looked hard somehow, so I was afraid to approach them. The buildings were grimy and not shiny the way I had seen in films. At night I heard police sirens and arguments. This wasn't what I had been led to believe America was like. There were no drums or chickens or donkeys. In the city there was a big white courthouse with a concrete sign about Justice on the outside. I missed seeing young boys and old men holding hands. I missed the sky, which here was never more than a watered-down view above the tops of buildings.

On buses people avoided sitting next to me and in shops they watched me convinced I was a thief. So disorientated was I that one night I managed to fall up a set of stairs. During the long winter I ached, my bones from the cold and my mind from lack of sun. I slept huddled up, trying to get warm and woke to find my joints stiff with cold. No wonder people lived an inside, concrete sort of life.

There were places in my neighbourhood where everyone knew you were not supposed to walk. But if you lived in one of those places, then what were you to do? Soon after I arrived, a woman was found murdered in a polluted pond in the city park. No one could tell me anything about it, simply that she was a woman and she'd been murdered. There was a myth of danger in the city, myth because it was a story shared and believed in, not because it wasn't true.

I felt almost guilty for being so unhappy at first and I had a nagging sensation that there was something wrong with me. I felt responsible to those back home because I was where so many people only dreamt of going. A place, according to the movies, where people who looked just like Africans spoke only English, a place of massive buildings and car chases and nightclubs and music.

For many weeks I hung back and just watched. Then one night as I was sitting alone at home, I asked myself what my Uncle Bopadile would make of this situation and I decided he would do his best to have fun. So from then on I shut my ears when I heard someone saying something I didn't like. And when someone invited me to a party or on a road trip I would say, 'Yeah, why not?'

But still, I romanticized my country which no one had even seemed to have heard about, and I couldn't wait to leave. I convinced myself of how much better things were at home. Back home women weren't paraded or billboards, and had only just started being afraid of walking out alone at night.

I wondered at our innocence or generosity that we should choose a flag for ourselves that has the colours that are said to represent black people and white people and the blue of rain, when we are so badly treated abroad by those same people whom we represent on our flag. I completed my course, received my certificate and left. In the last week I went shopping and bought things for people back home – blue jeans and good-quality jumpers.

On my way home I spent some time in England. My ticket allowed me to break up my flight, so on impulse I decided to 'go for it', as the Americans would say. I pretended I was searching for my roots. In the week I was there I stayed with my grandmother in London because I didn't know anyone else. It was a difficult time, we didn't know what to say to each other. Mainly we sat in her small, carpeted room drinking tea and watching TV. Her favourite programmes were snooker and the Sunday service. I sat in a beaten old leather chair, sent to sleep by the sound of snooker balls being clicked across a brilliantly green table and preachers droning on. But she was surprised at my English being so good, and this finally reassured her enough to show me to some of her friends, whom she referred to as her 'cronies'.

She didn't say much about my mother, except for muttering that she had 'let herself go' and she never mentioned my father. But she showed me a box of letters – rather proudly, I thought – and some photographs. One of the rare times she acknowledged where I came from was when we were watching the news and she said, 'He wears nice suits, your leader,' as Nelson Mandela came on to the screen.

My grandmother's refusal to acknowledge my father was the root of the whole problem. She would take me round her small yard and point out the few pathetic flowers, telling me they were having a mild winter and filling me in on what she wanted to grow. 'Yes,' I would say. 'My mother loves gardening, and so does my *father*.' Or one time, when she showed me a photograph my mother had sent her years and years ago of the school in Lephane, I said, 'Yes, my *father* took that picture.' But she never rose to the bait.

She would talk about the past, though – that is, her past. She talked about how, when her husband was still alive, they had lived in the country somewhere and they had lived very well. I presumed this was the two-storey house my mother had told me about. I was dying to see a picture of my grandfather, that 'right bastard' as my mother had always called him, but I was sorely disappointed when one was finally dug up: he was just a skinny white man sitting astride a bicycle with a cigarette dangling unconvincingly out of his mouth.

The room I slept in was half dark: it had a sort of white curtain that couldn't be moved to one side but hung permanently down. I went to bed early as my grandmother did, and lay listening to the rain outside.

Occasionally my grandmother would offer me titbits of my mother's past life. She said she had been very 'promising' when she was a girl and they had hoped she would have a career. But she had a career, I said. She was a teacher. My grandmother chose this moment to leave the room. I couldn't get over the fact that she thought my mother's move to Botswana a step *down* in the social scale. As if she had lost her civilized upbringing and 'gone native'.

One day I said to her, as we were watching a wildlife programme on TV, 'You should come to Botswana, you know.'

'*Me?*' she said incredulously, and then hurriedly gave reasons for why she couldn't, like bad health and lack of money. She rarely left the house, except to go to the corner shop to buy a newspaper or some sugar and tea. I noticed she liked a certain kind of biscuit, so one day I bought several packets for her, but she wasn't pleased. Nothing I did seemed to please her. After the people I had met in the States, the English were so reserved and half the time I didn't know what they were thinking about. I couldn't imagine my mother living there at all.

'We were very close, you know, your mother and I,' my grandmother said another time as we sipped our tea to the sound of the clicking snooker balls on TV and the gentle rain outside. I perked up, thinking more was to come but it didn't. I wasn't sure whether it was rude or not to ask. My mother's not dead, you know, I wanted to say. I wondered whether my grandmother had fallen out with her daughter and couldn't now make her peace.

'I brought her up to be polite and tidy,' my grandmother said. Then she grew thoughtful and added, 'I wish he hadn't slapped her so much.'

'Who?'

'Your mother's father, of course.'

'But I thought . . .' I began. I thought people in England didn't hit their children.

'Well' – my grandmother rearranged herself on her chair, her fingers playing lightly over the TV controller – 'she played up to him, always asking questions, embarrassing him in public. I remember once she had borrowed something from a neighbour and then she lost it. That was a bad time.'

Then she turned up the sound on the TV.

'Would you like to do some shopping for your people?' she asked me another time. She drew a map for me so I could get to some big shops. She even pressed a ten-pound note into my hand. This embarrassed me, because back home it is the young people who give their elders money. I can't count the times I watched my father hand over cash to all the old people in the family. So for an elder to give *me* money was very strange.

I was amused by the rituals of English life, rituals I had heard about long ago from my mother – the way when you walk into somebody's house, they immediately say, 'Tea?' A couple of times when I said, 'No, thanks,' I was dismayed to see this response stopped my grandmother in her tracks. She just stood there, one hand suspended over the kettle, until I changed my mind and said, 'Yes, please.' Going into shops was a scream, as my mother would say. I would ask for 'half a pound of this, *please*'. They would hand it to me and I would say, 'Thank you.' Then I would pay and they would say, 'Thank you'. Then they would give me the change and I would say, 'Thank you.' This touching and rather pointless exchange could take all day.

One late winter afternoon we went for a walk in a nearby park. As we climbed up a slight hill in the middle, I took my grandmother's arm and had a sort of good 'we are relatives' feeling. At the top we looked out over old London town. The sun was setting and its last rays, straggling through the misty white cloud over the tops of office blocks, made a beautiful sight. But when I said how beautiful it was, my grandmother got very annoyed, as if I was mocking her in some way.

One day a letter from my mother arrived for me. When I woke in the morning to find it sitting on the hall carpet by the front door, I realized how much my mother's letters must have meant to my grandmother during all those years.

I picked it up and padded off on the carpeted floor to the small front room to read it. Outside I heard a small van go by delivering milk, the bottles clinked in a musical way. I turned on the gas fire and sat down on the floor to read.

My mother enclosed without comment a letter she had received from Christine Fish. I was shocked that Christine had tracked us down. She asked whether I was in England yet and whether I would like to come and have tea one day. There was an address and a phone number. I threw the letter away as I suspect my mother hoped I would, but it wasn't easy to do. I was tempted to contact Christine because I was so lonely in this vast city, and I wanted to see what she was like through adult eyes, but I resisted.

Only much later in the day as I put on a borrowed raincoat and went to the corner shop did I realize with a jolt the implications of Christine's letter. How did Christine know I was in England? Obviously because my mother must have told her. My God, I thought, don't tell me they have remained in contact all these years. All these years! Was my mother mad? There was something hopeless and also slightly endearing about the fact they had kept in touch. But it was creepy too and I stuffed that letter far down in the bin outside as I set off to the shops.

Towards the end of my short stay in England, I met two old friends of my mother's. She had given me their phone numbers in her letter and she said it would be nice – she probably meant *polite* – if I 'looked them up'. Suffocating in my grandmother's house where each day felt like a week, I was only too eager for any distraction.

My mother's friends, friends from her school days, took me out to a pub and asked me questions all night long. I was aware once again that I was to be representative for my country and this time for my mother too. My mother had almost moved back to England at one point, they said, after she had lost her job at a pre-school. Well, I knew nothing about this, so I couldn't tell them much.

'So, she lives on a chicken farm now?' one of the women asked me.

'Yes,' I replied, a trifle defensive. 'It's a very big chicken farm.' And we all laughed. They were keen to hear about wild animals and couldn't believe what I told them.

'But Rose always *hated* that sort of thing,' one of the women said.

'She couldn't even go on camping trips without making a fuss!' the other said.

As the evening ended and I got ready to leave the pub, they said to me rather sadly, 'Do tell her how we are.'

And how are you? I wanted to ask, for it seemed to me neither of them was very content in life.

I found most people in England polite but reserved. They came to life only when I asked for directions. I was slightly surprised not to find the place full of people like Frank and Christine Fish. The people who had left and come over to our side of the world seemed very different.

It was cold when I was there, but then I understand it is cold most of the time. The sky fought a losing battle to be seen, a thin grey cloud permanently hovering over us. Never have people seemed so much like ants as they did in England.

When I finally did return home, I found many of my memories false. My people seemed at first rude and uncooperative after all the smiling servers I had seen in America. I spent about a month at my father's house in Gaborone, from where he runs a small account-ancy business. Now Gaborone is one of the fastest-growing cities in Africa. It's funny how the men go around wearing European suits and other such clothes, how they listen to American music and eat foreign food. But they still expect women to remain the keepers of culture, and protest if they straighten their hair or wear non-African clothes. My father told me that while I was away a group of men had taken a dislike to a mini skirt a woman was wearing. She was just peacefully waiting at a bus stop when they went up and ripped off her clothes.

After a month I set off for Lephane to take up my post as manager of a tourist lodge. Lephane had truly *developed* in my relat-ively short absence. But it was home, and I found myself forever walking into a shop or an office and seeing a relative or someone I was at school with down in the south. I stayed with my grand-mother and we spent quiet days in her compound drinking tea. Like my father, she never questioned me, unless I volunteered some information myself.

Then I started working at the lodge, though let's dispense with feminine modesty and say that I am the boss. I have my own house just behind the main building. We have about ten roundavel rooms which can sleep two or three people in each, a small swimming-pool and a thatched bar area. Because we are by the river we have large trees all around the lodge, fed by the river water.

Those with power in Lephane are busy carving things up. Soon, it's clear, you won't be able to get a plot of land to farm on any more. Here come the vultures, as my mother would say. There is now an area in Lephane where the white people stay. It has short stretches of tarred road and street signs and even a set of traffic lights, but it all ends rather abruptly in sand. Lephane is not the peaceful village it used to be. There have been murders and other crimes in recent months. People act surprised when they hear about these things and some believe they can turn the clock back to what it was like before. Innocents, I suppose, like my parents had been.

Bopadile is back in Lephane, I saw him just the other day, and there are rumours that he is involved in diamond smuggling. He and Oabona got married and they have four children. Oabona is still a primary school teacher. Listen also turned up in Lephane and somehow or other managed to ingratiate himself on to the land board. Christine's son, Peter, by the way, is now an educational advisor in Namibia, and her daughter, Lizzie, runs some type of aid agency.

My father is no longer ill. Those doctors never found out what exactly had been ailing him, which supports the idea that he was being bewitched, and that is what many of our relatives and friends still say. He talks sometimes about white witchcraft and wiggles his finger in and out of his ear. He has many friends down in Gaborone and a young relative to cook for him. He says as soon as he gets himself together and closes his accountancy business, he's going into politics.

My parents' chicken farm is doing well these days and my mother divides her time between that and trips to Gaborone to be with my father. My father is about to move up to Poloko for good. They will expand the farm and perhaps open a small shop as well. My father was pleased that I came home from America and sometimes he asks me questions, but mostly he waits until I tell him something. My mother and he, whether in my mind or in reality, have become individuals now.

These days, after years of thinking I was turning into my father, I find I am turning into my mother. When I came home after so long away and visited her on the chicken farm, I was shocked to find her behaving just like me – the way she cuts up an onion, for example, or works herself into a rage. But of course in many other ways she's very different from how she used to be in Jamestown. She finds it hard to understand why I am in the tourist business and warns me against yuppy flu, while I don't understand why she refuses to have electricity installed in her house and keeps all these mangy dogs. I am in fact perfect for the tourist industry because I know what tourists like. I have learnt to switch a smile on and off at demand and this gets me quite far when it comes to dealing with outsiders. What I want to do is to set up a safari lodge just for Batswana, so we can be tourists in our own country. I have already started teaching some courses in management and business studies at a small centre which has just opened in Lephane. I may be only in my twenties and very young for the role I play, but I think people are getting used to the idea that I know what I'm talking about. People tend to listen to you when they hear you have been to America. The land board has been playing around with my application for land, as I knew they would, so the process could take some years. However, that doesn't put me off and I am quite determined.

My old friend Thebe is in Lephane too. I was walking past a take-away restaurant about a month after I returned and saw a familiar figure in the window licking her lips over fried chicken. I knew without question it was Thebe. So I rushed inside and made myself known. She works at one of the banks here in Lephane, so when I need a loan I know who I can go to.

We in the tourist industry try hard to keep up the myth that people who come here will be at one with nature. Until recently we said nothing about the people who were cleared away like so many weeds to make way for the animal parks. But we can no longer ignore this truth and when I set up my own safari lodge for Bat-swana it is something that will have to be confronted.

Not long ago a friend of mine who works at a lodge in the far north told me a story about her camp. A lion entered one night and took hold of a young child who was playing outside by her parents' tent. The tourists, my friend tells me, rushed to get their cameras so they could record the scene.

On the plane I took to come back home from England, I met a South African woman. She was a little drunk and she talked to me a lot. She told me she had a British boss, by this she meant white, and she said to me, 'He's a give and take, would you say those people are give and take?'

I was unsure because of the words she had chosen what she meant and I was about to say, no, I don't think they give and take when she added, 'He gives me something and then he takes it away again!'

Then, of course, I agreed.

Author's Note

All the places portrayed in Botswana are fictional, except for
Gaborone.

READ MORE IN PENGUIN

In every corner of the world, on every subject under the sun, Penguin represents quality and variety – the very best in publishing today.

For complete information about books available from Penguin – including Puffins, Penguin Classics and Arkana – and how to order them, write to us at the appropriate address below. Please note that for copyright reasons the selection of books varies from country to country.

In the United Kingdom: Please write to *Dept. EP, Penguin Books Ltd, Bath Road, Harmondsworth, West Drayton, Middlesex UB7 ODA*

In the United States: Please write to *Consumer Sales, Penguin USA, P.O. Box 999, Dept. 17109, Bergenfield, New Jersey 07621-0120.* VISA and MasterCard holders call 1-800-253-6476 to order Penguin titles

In Canada: Please write to *Penguin Books Canada Ltd, 10 Alcorn Avenue, Suite 300, Toronto, Ontario M4V 3B2*

In Australia: Please write to *Penguin Books Australia Ltd, P.O. Box 257, Ringwood, Victoria 3134*

In New Zealand: Please write to *Penguin Books (NZ) Ltd, Private Bag 102902, North Shore Mail Centre, Auckland 10*

In India: Please write to *Penguin Books India Pvt Ltd, 706 Eros Apartments, 56 Nehru Place, New Delhi 110 019*

In the Netherlands: Please write to *Penguin Books Netherlands bv, Postbus 3507, NL-1001 AH Amsterdam*

In Germany: Please write to *Penguin Books Deutschland GmbH, Metzlerstrasse 26, 60594 Frankfurt am Main*

In Spain: Please write to *Penguin Books S. A., Bravo Murillo 19, 1° B, 28015 Madrid*

In Italy: Please write to *Penguin Italia s.r.l., Via Felice Casati 20, I–20124 Milano*

In France: Please write to *Penguin France S. A., 17 rue Lejeune, F–31000 Toulouse*

In Japan: Please write to *Penguin Books Japan, Ishikiribashi Building, 2–5–4, Suido, Bunkyo-ku, Tokyo 112*

In Greece: Please write to *Penguin Hellas Ltd, Dimocritou 3, GR–106 71 Athens*

In South Africa: Please write to *Longman Penguin Southern Africa (Pty) Ltd, Private Bag X08, Bertsham 2013*

READ MORE IN PENGUIN

A CHOICE OF FICTION

Asta's Book Barbara Vine

In 1905, Asta and her husband Rasmus came to East London from Denmark with their two little boys. Over seventy years later, Asta's diaries are published ... 'Barbara Vine has once again done her readers proud ... for a good, absorbing, well-told story, you could hardly better the unveiling of Asta's secret' – *Sunday Times*

Peerless Flats Esther Freud

Lisa has high hopes for her first year in London. She is sixteen and ambitious to become more like her sister Ruby. For Ruby has cropped hair, a past, and a rockabilly boyfriend whose father is in prison. 'Freud sounds out as a clear, attractive voice in the literary hubbub' – *Observer*

One of the Family Monica Dickens

At 72, Chepstow Villas lives the Morley family; Leonard, the Assistant Manager of Whiteley's, his gentle wife Gwen, 'new woman' daughter Madge and son Dicky. Into their comfortable Edwardian world comes a sinister threat of murder and a charismatic stranger who will change their lives forever. 'It is the contrasts that Dickens depicts so rivetingly ... she captures vividly the gradual blurring of social divisions during the last days of the Empire' – *Daily Mail*

Varying Degrees of Hopelessness Lucy Ellman

'Funny and furious ... what the author is interested in is the hopelessness of life. Her merry little novel is a vehicle for disgust. Lucy Ellman is clever, and very angry' – *The Times*. 'An irresistible cocktail of satire, slapstick and tenderness' – *Cosmopolitan*

The Killjoy Anne Fine

Nobody has ever treated Ian Laidlay in a natural way. Presented with his hideous facial scars, everyone he meets falls back on distant courtesy to hide pity or disgust or shock. But then someone laughs ... 'A wonderful and original piece of work ... a horror story which rings absolutely true' – Alan Sillitoe

READ MORE IN PENGUIN

A CHOICE OF FICTION

The Battle for Christabel Margaret Forster

Rowena wants a baby. What she doesn't want is the baby's father. Yet five years after the birth of Christabel, Rowena is dead, tragically killed in a climbing accident. The battle for Christabel has begun ... 'Poignant, impeccably written ... especially heart-rending because it is so believable' – *Company*

Cleopatra's Sister Penelope Lively

'A fluent, funny, ultimately moving romance in which lovers share centre stage with Lively's persuasive meditations on history and fate . . . a book of great charm with a real intellectual resonance at its core' –*The New York Times Book Review*

A Family Romance Anita Brookner

Paul and Henrietta Manning and their solitary, academic daughter Jane have nothing in common with Dolly, widow of Henrietta's brother. But when all Dolly and Jane have left is each other, they discover that history and family create closer ties than friendship ever could. 'This small history unfolds slowly, with delicious wit or bitter pathos, and finally with a marvellous, lingering human resonance' – *Sunday Express*

A Rather English Marriage Angela Lambert

Roy, a retired milkman, and Reggie, a former RAF Squadron-Leader, are widowed on the same day. To assuage their grief, the vicar arranges for Roy to move in with Reggie as his unpaid manservant. To their surprise, they form a strange alliance, based on obedience, need and the strangeness of single life.

The Girl Who Trod on a Loaf Kathryn Davis

'Davis writes of a love between equals that still has tragic modulations. This is the real thing, caught in a language that hovers enticingly between the laconic and the poetic ... this is a novel with secrets, one that repays work, and its prose is exquisitely rhythmic and open-ended' – *Independent*

READ MORE IN PENGUIN

A CHOICE OF FICTION

The Collected Stories William Trevor

Whether they portray the vagaries of love, the bitter pain of loss and regret or the tragic impact of violence upon ordinary lives, these superb stories reveal the insight, subtle humour and unrivalled artistry that make William Trevor the contemporary master of the form.

The Complete Enderby Anthony Burgess

Comprising *Inside Mr Enderby*, *Enderby Outside*, *The Clockwork Testament* and *Enderby's Dark Lady,* these dazzling comic entertainments are a celebration of Burgess's irrepressible creation. 'Ferociously funny and wildly, verbally inventive' – *The Times*

Sugar Cane Paul Bailey

'Bailey has captured two remarkable voices, of a woman who comes to love a young man with maternal solicitude, and of the boy himself, an outcast within his own family ... A powerful, painful and evocative novel ... written with such feeling that it makes the reader laugh and weep' – *Spectator*

Dr Haggard's Disease Patrick McGrath

'The reader is compellingly drawn into Dr Haggard's life as it begins to unfold through episodic flashbacks ... This is the story of a love affair that goes terribly wrong ... It is a beautiful story, impressively told, with a restraint and a grasp of technicality that command belief, and a lyricism that gives the description of the love affair the sort of epic quality rarely found these days' – *The Times*

A Place I've Never Been David Leavitt

'Wise, witty and cunningly fuelled by narrative ... another high calibre collection by an unnervingly mature young writer' – *Sunday Times* 'Leavitt can make a world at a stroke and people it with convincing characters ... humane, touching and beautifully written' – *Observer*

READ MORE IN PENGUIN

A CHOICE OF FICTION

The Lying Days   Nadine Gordimer

Raised in the conservative mining town of Atherton, South Africa, Helen Shaw, seventeen, longs to escape from the sterile environment that has shaped her parents' rigid attitudes and threatens to corrode her own fragile values. At last, finding the courage and maturity to stand alone, she leaves behind the 'lying days' of her youth.

The Eye in the Door   Pat Barker

'Barker weaves fact and fiction to spellbinding effect, conjuring up the vastness of the First World War through its chilling impact on the minds of the men who endured it ... a startlingly original work of fiction ... it extends the boundaries not only of the anti-war novel, but of fiction generally' – *Sunday Telegraph*

Strange Pilgrims   Gabriel García Márquez

The twelve stories in this collection by the Nobel prizewinner chronicle the surreal, haunting 'journeys' of Latin Americans in Europe. 'Márquez's genius is for the physical. Characters urinate, devour songbird stew; old people remember their youthful lovemaking ... It is this spirit of generous desire that fills his work' – *The Times*

Millroy the Magician   Paul Theroux

A magician of baffling talents, a vegetarian and a health fanatic with a mission to change the food habits of America, Millroy has the power to heal, and to hypnotize. 'Fresh and unexpected ... this very accomplished, confident book is among his best' – *Guardian*

The House of Doctor Dee   Peter Ackroyd

When Matthew Palmer inherits an old house in Clerkenwell he feels himself to have become a part of its past. Compelled to probe its mysteries, he discovers to his horror and curiosity that the previous owner was a practitioner of black magic. 'A good old-fashioned spine-chiller of a ghost story ... which will also be taken as a serious modern novel' – *The Times*

READ MORE IN PENGUIN

A CHOICE OF FICTION

Crazy in Alabama Mark Childress

Way down South – in Industry, Alabama – 1965 was the year the orphan Peejoe discovered it wasn't sage to treat black people the same way you treated whites. Perhaps it was around the same time his Aunt Lucille arrived with her husband's head in a Tupperware box – he never could be sure ... 'A truly wild, uplifting book' – *Time Out*

Memories of the Ford Administration John Updike

'Vintage Updike and a cracking good novel ... Updike is always a polished performer. No other writer has explored the muddle of modern America with such honesty, clarity and plain good humour' – *Sunday Express*

The Children of Men P. D. James

'As taut, terrifying and ultimately convincing as anything in the dystopian genre. It is at once a piercing satire on our cosseted, faithless and trivially self-indulgent society and a most tender love story' – *Daily Mail*

The Only Problem Muriel Spark

Harvey Gotham had abandoned his beautiful wife Effie on the *autostrada* in Italy. Now, nearly a year later, ensconced in France where he is writing a monograph on the Book of Job, his solitude is interrupted by Effie's sister. Suddenly Harvey finds himself longing for the unpredictable pleasure's of Effie's company. But she has other ideas. 'One of this century's finest creators of the comic-metaphysical entertainment' – *The New York Times*

Collected Stories Beryl Bainbridge

Women in fox furs, not-quite-travelling salesmen, the twilight zone of genteel hotels and lodging houses – this is quintessential Bainbridge territory. This volume also contains the novella *Filthy Lucre*, written when the author was thirteen.

READ MORE IN PENGUIN

A CHOICE OF FICTION

The Devil's Juggler Murray Smith

A lone corpse in New York's Grand Central Station; an SAS soldier missing on active service during the Gulf War; and hideous unseen carnage in a South American cemetery – the deaths demand vengeance. 'A damn good read ... tense, topical and brutally authentic' – Frederick Forsyth

Triple Cross Tony Cape

When the Defence Minister's secretary is killed in a horrific car accident, and a top-secret nuclear document is found in her posession, questions get asked in the highest circles. Fast-rising MI5 agent Derek Smailes leads the investigation – but others are playing a much more dangerous game – a fight to the death for survival, with Britain's intelligence empire the prize.

Gone South Robert McCammon

Dan Lambert's experiences in Vietnam have left him no stranger to psychological wounds or death. Years later, they have also left him divorced, broke, unemployed – and on the run. For Dan, to his shock and his shame, has become a murderer ...

Till the Fat Lady Sings Sean Hardie

A man goes missing in Central America. His son drops everything to find him. But Joe Wilde soon discovers more than he bargained for ... 'While Hardie keeps very close to his efficient thriller plot, lurking behind it is a tough moral fable ... when the full pattern of guilt and betrayal is revealed, the ripe sense of evil ... comes within hailing distance of Graham Greene' – *Observer*

Scoundrel Bernard Cornwell

Boston-Irish Paul Shanahan, part-time marine surveyor, IRA arms dealer and suspected CIA agent is a full-time scoundrel. But so is everyone else in the lethal world of terrorism, where even the offer of five million dollars in gold can't be trusted ...

READ MORE IN PENGUIN

A CHOICE OF FICTION

Body of Glass   Marge Piercy

'Outstanding . . . I have not read a more disturbing or moving novel about artificial intelligence since Mary Shelley's *Frankenstein* . . . It elevates its author to the pantheon of *haute* SF alongside Doris Lessing and Ursula Le Guin' – *Financial Times*

The Madness of a Seduced Woman   Susan Fromberg Schaeffer

In her search for all-consuming, perfect love, Agnes Dempster, a beautiful young woman in turn-of-the-century Vermont, becomes infatuated with a man who, frightened by her intensity, betrays her. 'I can't remember a single other character in fiction with whom I have ever identified more . . . A great many women have tried to write *the* feminist novel. *This* is the novel they've been trying to write' – Margaret Forster

Now You Know   Michael Frayn

'A constantly witty writer . . . Frayn's book can best be compared to a pin: it is small, shiny, sharp. Its impact will, one hopes, prick people into examining or re-examining one of the most teasing moral problems of our times' – *Spectator*

Brazzaville Beach   William Boyd

'Hope Clearwater lives on an African beach reassessing the complicated, violent and tragic events which have occurred in her life. How much has she been responsible? How could she have forseen the dangers? . . . Boyd is a brilliant storyteller . . . a most serious book which stretches, tantalizes and delights' – *Financial Times*

Emily's Shoes   Dermot Bolger

'A novel of enormous ambition, an attempt to create a folk history for those whose dark sexuality has banished them into the underworld of their own country . . . a serious and provocative work of fiction' – *Sunday Times*

READ MORE IN PENGUIN

A CHOICE OF FICTION

Blue Heaven Joe Keenan

Set in the New York of the rich, the idle and the phoney, *Blue Heaven* tells the story of Gilbert and Moira – the strangest couple ever to marry for other people's money. 'One of the funniest writers alive' – David Leavitt

A Matter of Life and Sex Oscar Moore

From the first stirrings of his adolescent libido to his eventual death from Aids, Oscar Moore's hero confronts his destiny with raw candour, shocking self-awareness, and frightening fatalism.

Carol Patricia Highsmith

Therese first glimpses Carol in the New York department store where she is working temporarily as a sales assistant. Standing there at the counter, Therese suddenly feels wholly innocent – wholly unprepared for that first rippling shock of love. 'A document of persecuted love ... perfect' – *Independent*

Ready to Catch Him Should He Fall Neil Bartlett

'Ceremonial, sumptuous, perverse, this novel is a compendium of a century of gay experience as well as the latest dispatch from London's thriving queer scene ... *Ready to Catch Him Should He Fall* is both journalism and fairy tale and the best gay book of the year' – Edmund White

Such Times Christopher Coe

Intensely moving, yet unsentimental, *Such Times* is an examination of the intricacies of the heart, and a passionate eulogy to a time of lost joys. '*Such Times* is about Aids, and what it does to its victims – although victim is hardly the right word for Coe's fighting spirits ... It is also about the danger of loving too much. Aids isn't the only way that love kills' – *Sunday Times*

READ MORE IN PENGUIN

A CHOICE OF FICTION

A Border Station Shane Connaughton

The story of a young boy's growth to maturity; the love-hate relationship with his father, a frustrated Garda sergeant in the virtually crime-free village of Butlershill, and the adoration of his tender, doting mother are the focuses of his daily life, highlighted in a series of poignant – at times terrifying – but always acutely absorbing discoveries.

A Home at the End of the World Michael Cunningham

'A superb and major novel, ambitious in its scope, its historical largeness, and at the same time intensely, almost painfully intimate. The story of Jonathan, Clare, Bobby and Alice is also the story of the seventies and eighties in America' – David Leavitt

I am the Clay Chaim Potok

'Excellent . . . Potok is a poet and a visionary who writes with breath-taking ease about the limits of human experience, of death, of the superstitious and spirit worlds of the peasants and of courage born from suffering'– *The Times*

Something to Remember Me By Saul Bellow

Dedicated to Bellow's children and grandchildren, *Something to Remember Me By* tells the wonderfully tender and funny story of a young man's sexual initiation and sexual guilt, one bleak Chicago winter's day in 1933. That story, narrated like a memoir, is collected here with Bellow's acclaimed novellas, *The Bellarosa Connection* and *A Theft*.

The Cockatoos Patrick White

'To read Patrick White . . . is to touch a source of power, to move through areas made new and fresh, to see men and women with a sharpened gaze' – *Daily Telegraph*. These six short novels and stories achieve the majesty and passion of Patrick White's great novels, probing beneath the surface of events to explore the mysteries of human nature.

READ MORE IN PENGUIN

A CHOICE OF FICTION

Sacred Hunger Barry Unsworth

'Unsworth's theme is human rivalry; his subject is the slave trade of the mid-eighteenth century ... *Sacred Hunger* is a tremendous performance. Not the least of its achievements is the sense of blood, guts and hurricanes existing side by side with an imaginatively realized interior life' – *Sunday Times*

The Vicar of Sorrows A. N. Wilson

'Hard to resist ... scoring at least three unequivocal triumphs – as a bleakly funny portrait of male mid-life breakdown, as a serious piece of anti-theology and as a satire on Anglicanism' – *Daily Telegraph*

Mayday Jonathan Lynn

'A very funny, insightful and intelligent book and a taut thriller which will keep you turning the pages right to the surprising end' – Eric Idle. '*Mayday* is not a cry for help – it is a yelp for joy. Lynn's movie moguls, mysteries and mishaps leap straight off the page' – Maureen Lipman

Cal Bernard Mac Laverty

Springing out of the fear and violence of Ulster, Cal is a haunting love story in a land where tenderness and innocence can only flicker briefly in the dark. 'A gripping political thriller and a formidable fictional triumph' – *Observer*

Bridie and Finn Harry Cauley

Bridie and Finn are like chalk and cheese. She's motherless and loquacious. He's the quiet type, with a crooked leg from birth. And they become the best of friends. True to the unpredictable twists and turns of life, *Bridie and Finn* creates a hugely memorable mosaic of human relationships.

READ MORE IN PENGUIN

A CHOICE OF FICTION

A Place of Greater Safety   Hilary Mantel

'Mantel's grasp both of detail and the complex sweep of events is quite remarkable ... Little is known of the personal lives of most revolutionary leaders before 1789, and after they became famous, they lived constantly in the public eye. Yet Mantel has managed to get inside them by feeling her way through their writings, families and, quite brilliantly, their women' – *The Times Literary Supplement*

The Green Knight   Iris Murdoch

Professor Lucas Graffe, defending himself with his umbrella against a nocturnal assailant, unintentionally kills him ... 'It explores darkness as well as light, the route from sadness through self-knowledge into joy, and how loss and emptiness, if truthfully traversed, can be transformed into fullness and fertility ... A Romance in the fullest and most positive sense' – *Independent*

Safe in the Kitchen   Aisling Foster

'Aisling Foster's sparkling first novel ... demontrates, in fact, that whatever political history or the craving for jewels may do to them, women are survivors' – Penelope Lively. 'A thrilling story ... the mixture of greed and desire, secret treasure and forbidden fruit is enough to make your brain go pop' – *Guardian*

Bright Lights, Big City   Jay McInerney

Portraying a week in the life of a young journalist on a *New Yorker*-style magazine, Jay McInerney's debut novel explores hangover days and night life in the apartment blocks and clublands of '80s Manhattan. 'Deadly funny' – Raymond Carver

Janice Gentle Gets Sexy   Mavis Cheek

Plump, virginal Janice Gentle writes her bestselling rose-tinted romances with one goal in view: to make enough money to find her long-lost beloved Dermot. 'Just about irresistible' – *Observer*